Imperfect
MONSTER

A DARK ROMANCE

JENNIFER BENE

ISBN (e-book): 978-1-946722-20-1

ISBN (paperback): 978-1-946722-22-5

Cover design by Laura Hidalgo, Beyond DEF Lit. https://www.beyonddeflit.com/

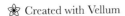 Created with Vellum

This one is for you, lovelies. The readers that make my dream of writing books (even dark and twisty ones) a reality. Imperfect Monster is the first book I've written in the first-person point of view, but it was how Andre appeared in my head, and once he started talking he didn't want to stop. I hope that you like this one, lovelies. It's exciting and dark and thrilling, and I have to say… nothing is better than how amazing it feels to be able to write for you.

Thank you all. <3

—

Author Note: *Spanish is used occasionally throughout the book, but not often. One word is 'cuadro' which is Columbian slang for friend, dude, bro, etc. My ARC team suggested I share that ahead of time so it doesn't distract you. Enjoy!*

ONE

Andre

"*Cabrón!* You're fucking cheating!" Diego threw his cards across the table, and the others laughed as José dragged the pile of wrinkled cash towards him.

"I don't cheat, *pinche idiota*. Maybe you wouldn't lose so much if you learned to bluff," José mocked him, smoothing out the bills one at a time to pile them in his hand. The insults continued to fly as another hand was dealt, but I was tucked on a couch to the side, nursing a bottle of tequila. They'd been gambling since mid-morning and drinking since breakfast, but time didn't matter much in this house.

Especially not when things were so quiet.

Paulo García had been keeping his cards close to his chest, not talking about his plans, not making any moves — that we could see anyway — which was fucking up all of *my* plans in the process.

Over two years.

Thirty-one months of my life spent with these assholes, and I still didn't have enough to get out.

Taking another swig of tequila, I let it burn its way into my belly, numbing me further. The warm metal of my gun dug uncomfortably into my spine, but even that was dulled by the alcohol as I adjusted my seat on the couch.

Screw it.

I had more than a decent buzz going, which wasn't strictly by the book, but I could no longer bring myself to give a fuck about the drinking. Not when the bottle did such a good job of taking my mind off the rest of it. Off all of the terrible shit I'd done before this, and now...

Now, I'd done so much worse working for Paulo.

"Andre, come play a hand!" Marco called out, all broad grin, friendly, but I just waved at him.

"I'm good, *cuadro.*"

"He's still pissed that I took all his money last week!" José laughed loudly, and the other men joined in.

Raising my middle finger in the air I felt my lips tilt up. "*Besa mi culo, puto.* You wish that was all my money."

Jokes came fast, the men nudging each other at the table as they continued to bet, but I just muttered under my breath as the brief smile disappeared. What was worse — having nothing to report, or actually liking the criminal fucks I spent my days with?

The only answer to those questions? *Tequila.*

I had just taken another long drink when a buzzing sound came from the area by the front door. Diego hopped out of his seat to check the security feed, his low whistle followed by a quiet chuckle. "Well, hello."

"Who is it?" Marco asked, the game stopping as the others turned towards the man.

"One hot piece of ass by the looks of it, and she looks *pissed*." Diego laughed a little louder as another buzz came through the security system.

"Is *jefe* expecting someone?" José was a lot more serious, glancing up the broad, curving stairs.

"Hell if I know, he hasn't told me anything," Marco added, but he stood as well, which left only me reclining on the couch — still not giving a single fuck.

The buzzing returned, longer this time, and there was a shout from the top of the stairs. Paulo appeared in a rumpled button-down shirt and linen pants, irritated. "Why the hell isn't someone handling the door?"

"We don't know if we should let her come up the drive, *jefe*."

"Her?" Paulo's expression changed, a hand pushing through his dark hair as he moved down the steps. When he approached the security screens, Diego stepped back to give him room. "Well, well… we should see what she wants."

"You know who she is?" José asked, and that was when I saw the gun in his hand, resting at his side. A soldier through and through, ready to protect his general.

"No, I don't, but let's see what fun we can have." The cold humor in Paulo's voice made my stomach turn. If this bitch had any brains at all she'd turn around and run from the ornate gate that barred the entrance to Paulo's estate before it even opened.

Just as Paulo moved towards the door, José appeared at his side, almost blocking him. "Allow me, *jefe*. She may be some *puta*, but I should still check her first."

Grabbing José by the back of the neck, Paulo tapped his forehead to his. "You always have my back, *hermano*. Of course, give her a thorough check before she comes in — then we can discuss what the little blonde wants."

The front door opened an instant later, but Paulo strolled into the sitting room, making his way to the wet bar. One of the most violent drug lords ever to come out of South America, and he looked like he was on vacation with his casual clothes, and falsely friendly demeanor. My grip on the tequila bottle tensed as I stared at the man, but I made sure my expression was blank. It didn't matter how much I hated him, I was his until the job was done.

"Not curious about the girl, Andre?" Paulo asked, tilting up his fresh drink to take a sip.

"Why should I be curious when I can get the play by play just from listening?"

"Well, José seems to think she's a security risk."

"If you need her handled, I'll do it, *jefe*. Otherwise, I see plenty of ass walking around Miami." I stayed still. Discussing shit like this was practically second nature now.

Paulo chuckled, leaning back with his elbows on the bar. "That's what I like about you, Andre. Cold as ice." He waved his drink at the men crowding the front door where a buzz of conversation had picked up. "The others are so hot tempered, they don't think. You *think*."

"Emotion clouds judgment."

"You're right. My father used to say… *mata a tu corazón, o te matará*. Do you know this phrase?"

I hadn't heard it before, but I knew what it meant, and it fit Paulo perfectly. "Kill your heart, or it will kill you."

A shark's grin spread across Paulo's features. "Exactly. Emotion makes you weak, and weakness is death."

"Your father was a smart man," I answered, voice on automatic, but the words were almost overridden by the feminine shout that came from the front door.

"Are you in there, Paulo García? HUH?"

The man's eyebrows lifted the tiniest fraction, his chilling smile not shifting. "Let her in, José."

"Keep your fucking hands off me." The blonde who stumbled into the room from the foyer was clad in shorts and a form fitting blue shirt that had some phrase across it in pale, swirling text. Male laughter followed her, and I forced myself to be still, not even breathing so I wouldn't move.

She was definitely American, and fucking beautiful. As I turned my eyes back to Paulo I knew the man smelled blood in the water. A wicked hunger waking up in those coal black eyes — the same hunger that I hated myself for feeling. "*Hola, señorita.* What can I do for you?"

"Do for me?" Her voice was practically boiling with rage, tanned cheeks flushing with it as she held out a thick envelope. "How about leaving my little brother the fuck alone? I've got your money, and I want you to take it and then never fucking speak to him again

5

— any of you! *That* is what you can do for me, asshole."

Marco and Diego started laughing behind her, amused by her little outburst as they looked over her curves, her strong legs, all the way down to the multi-colored running shoes on her feet. Even Paulo seemed vaguely amused as he spread his arms wide. "I have no idea who your brother is, *belleza*, but if he owes me money that was his choice."

"Fuck you! I know you hurt Chris, threatened him, but this is it. Take your money, and get out of his life!" She shook the envelope again, shouting, and my cock twitched at the same moment my stomach dropped.

José stepped up beside her, grabbing her arm in a tight grip. "You do not speak to him like that. Apologize."

The girl's eyes flicked to the gun in his hand, and she swallowed instead of shouting again, which was the first smart thing she'd done. José was as loyal as a dog, vicious as a pit bull, and almost as unpredictable as Paulo. "Look, I'm just here to deliver the money, and then I'm leaving."

"Of course. It's fine. Bring me the envelope, José." Paulo held out his hand, and the man released her arm to snatch the thick packet from her fingers. Crossing the tile, he delivered it and then stood at his master's side, glaring down the feisty girl who had more spirit than sense. Opening the flap, Paulo flicked through the money inside for a second before handing it back to José. "Count it."

"Look, you have your money, so now you can leave Chris alone. He's done with all of this." Her voice was wavering, and my eyes were glued to the shallow breaths making her breasts rise and fall. The fear was creeping in now that her rage was fizzling out, her eyes moving quickly over everyone in the room as she realized her situation.

That's right, girl. You walked yourself into the lion's den. Now, run.

"What is your name?" Paulo asked, and I cursed internally, struggling to maintain my cool composure. *He wants her.*

"You don't need my name."

"Oh, but I asked for it, and you're in my house." The subtle threat was there, Paulo García still wearing his shark's smile as Diego and Marco moved closer behind her.

She twisted at the waist to look at them, taking a few short steps into the room to gain some space, but they followed her. "I'm leaving, but Chris is done. Okay?"

"Chris who?" Paulo tilted his head, shrugging as he laughed softly. "I do not know his last name."

José slapped the envelope of cash onto the bar. "Twenty thousand."

Paulo's brows lifted a fraction. "This is a good amount of money for your little brother to owe me, especially when I do not even know his name."

"It's Chris Harris."

Faking confusion, Paulo turned to José. "Do you know this Chris Harris?" His eyes skimmed the rest of the room, touching on me for a moment. "I feel I should know this name if he owes me money."

"I don't know him," Diego answered, moving close enough to the girl's back that she jumped, taking another step deeper into the room.

"Me either." José shrugged, eyes sweeping her from top to bottom.

Finishing his drink, Paulo set it on the bar and then clapped his hands together. "Well, this seems unfortunate, *belleza*. I'll need to make some calls. You should sit, have a drink."

"No, I'm leaving." She turned and found herself looking at Marco's chest, his grin broad as he grabbed her shoulders.

"*Jefe* told you to sit."

"I need to go." The girl was either incredibly brave, or seriously stupid, but I was still impressed that she wasn't crying already. Diego had circled her, and now he approached her from the back. She stiffened, hands fisting at her sides as I forced down another mouthful of tequila, trying to prepare for what was going to come next. Trying to convince myself I wasn't tempted by her curves, her fire.

You should have run when you had the chance.

"But if you leave, how will I know whose account all this money goes to?" Paulo snapped his fingers, pointing at the wingback chair angled towards the couch. In a moment Marco and Diego had forced the struggling girl into the seat, a hand on each of her shoulders as she argued and then sputtered into silence.

Her wide, blue eyes landed on me, but I didn't react to her fear, her wordless, desperate plea — I just took another drink.

Approaching slowly, each step casual, Paulo made his way towards her. "Now, while I look into your little brother's account, you'll stay *right here*." He raised a hand when she opened her mouth to speak. "I just need to know your name so I can explain who I have as my guest."

"No," she whispered, and Diego chuckled above her.

Definitely brave, and definitely stupid.

"This is your last chance to tell me your name, *belleza*, before I have Andre ask you." Paulo's head tilted towards me, and I lifted my eyes to the man without a reaction. "And I do not think you want him to ask you."

The girl swallowed hard, clearly shaking in fear, the flush in her cheeks disappearing as her eyes went wide on mine. I knew what she saw. Tattoos, black muscle shirt, black pants, and an empty expression — because that's what I was, empty. I'd made full-grown men piss themselves in fear, and this little blonde didn't stand a chance if Paulo spoke the command.

Finally, she broke her gaze from mine to look back at Paulo, speaking softly, this time with much less venom in her tone. "It's Nicky… I mean, Nicole."

TWO

Nicky

"Nicole..." My heart was pounding in my ears, but nothing could block out the way Paulo García repeated my name, rolling it around in his mouth, thick with his accent. "Well, Nicole Harris, I will look into your brother and see what debts he may have. Until then, have a drink, relax."

One of the men beside the chair brushed his knuckles against my cheek, and I jerked away from him, only to be snapped back into the seat by a harsh grip on my shoulder. Pain radiated from where his fingers dug into my skin. When the man grinned above me I pressed my knees together, trying to shut down the fear.

This is for Chris. Just don't let them know you're afraid.

"I don't want a drink. I want you to accept Chris' payment so I can leave. Then you'll never hear from either of us again." As hard as I'd tried to sound confident, my fucking voice still wavered when the one with the gun approached.

Paulo shrugged. "It will depend on what I find, but my men will take good care of you. I have calls to make."

The one with the gun flashed his teeth in wh. imagined was supposed to be a smile. "Play nic for now."

For now.

The words planted ice in my veins, and I shifted under the grip of the men on either side of the chair, my eyes flicking between the man with the gun and the terrifying one on the couch who hadn't spoken a word. As soon as I looked at him, he lifted the bottle of alcohol and took another drink, those dark eyes never leaving me.

"Yes, *jefe*." The one with the gun nodded, and then Paulo García left the room.

Somehow, I'd actually felt safer with the drug dealer than I did now, and I berated myself for being so fucking stupid as to come inside. I could have stayed on the front porch, or in the damn circle driveway. Thrown the money at him and left, but, no, I needed to come in and let my temper loose.

God dammit, Chris. Who have you pissed off now?

"What would you like to drink?" The one who hadn't touched my cheek spoke, his grip on my shoulder easing slightly.

"I don't want a drink! I want him to clear Chris' debt so I can leave."

"You're not leaving until *jefe* says you can leave." Gun guy slipped the weapon into the back of his pants as he spoke. "So, you should have a drink as he suggested."

"No."

"Do you like tequila? Vodka?" The first man asked it

away from the chair I was still held in by
...ad dared to touch me.

...he drinks tequila. Probably grew up here
in ..viiami, didn't you?" Instead of brushing my cheek this
time, he grabbed my chin, angling my head back sharply
so I was looking into his dark blue eyes. Bottomless pools,
and I had no doubt what he wanted.

"Diego, *jefe* said to play nice." The guy who had stepped
away smiled as the one called Diego released my face, the
indentions of his fingers leaving ghost sensations on my
jaw. "But you should play nice too, Nicole. Tell us what you
want to drink. I'll make it."

Rolling my shoulders now that no one was pressing me
into the chair, I tried to stay calm, to keep *them* calm by
playing along as I scanned the bar from afar. "Fine, sure,
but I don't like tequila. Rum if you have it."

"Beach girl for sure."

"Wonder if she's tan all over?" the aggressive one with the
gun asked, his gaze threatening as his eyes roamed slowly
down my body. I sat up straight in the chair, pressing my
hands against the cushion, fighting the urge to cross my
arms over my chest. "What do you think, Marco?" he
asked over his shoulder.

Marco was the one walking towards the bar, but he didn't
respond at first. Instead, he stepped behind the bar and
pulled down a bottle, the clatter of ice filling the silence.

"*Cabrón*, you think she's tan all over?"

"I think that *jefe* said to get her a drink and have her
relax while he figures out the money. So, that's what I'm
doing, *José*." Marco's voice was quiet, but strong, and I

wanted him to come back. He seemed nicer, less scary, and, despite all my best intentions to show up like a badass and get Chris out of this shit, the others were scaring me.

Chris. My dumbass baby brother.

José laughed quietly, leaning on the matching chair across from mine. "Want to take bets on whether she has tan lines? Eh, Andre?"

All eyes went to the quiet one on the couch, and my stomach turned with the way he looked at me. His arms were covered in tattoos, with another one up the side of his neck, and his muscles more than filled out the shirt. Dark hair, dark eyes, I would have almost called him handsome, except he looked like a killer. Violence was etched in every line of his body, and when he continued to stay silent I felt a shiver rush over my skin.

"My bet is no," Diego answered instead, but he stepped away from the chair to drop onto the couch beside Andre.

"Oh, I'd bet she's got a few," José said, sinking into the chair to lean forward on his knees, eyes never leaving me. "Want to help us settle a bet, *belleza?*"

"Fuck you," I spat.

"Maybe later." The laughter came from Diego, and I swallowed hard, briefly wondering if I could make it to the door... and out of the long drive, before one of them caught me.

Not a fucking chance.

"Here. Drink it." Marco had returned, offering the glass of rum, another one in his own hand. I accepted it, and he caught my eye as he took a long drink of his own. Like some silent assurance it wasn't drugged.

Sure, Nicky. Just drink the strange drink the drug dealer's goons brought you. So smart.

But with all eyes on me, it wasn't like I had a choice. Finally, I took a sip, the sweet burn of the rum not setting off any alarms, and they all smiled — except the massive guy on the couch.

He just stared, took another drink from his bottle, and stared some more. Dark eyes burning holes in my skin.

So, instead of responding I looked down, avoiding all of them. Praying silently that Paulo García would accept the last of my parents' life insurance money, and let me go. Let Christopher out of his dumbass debt, and then I'd beat the shit out of him as soon as he was out of the hospital.

THREE

Andre

The first hour she'd sat in that chair, sipping her one glass of rum, the guys had circled her like wolves... but I'd refused to move. Mostly empty bottle of tequila propped on my thigh, fuzzy eyes glued to her perfectly pink lips, I tried to convince myself I was standing guard.

That as long as I was sitting close, the guys wouldn't do anything.

Not without Paulo's permission anyway.

I grimaced and upended the tequila bottle, swallowing one of the last dregs. Fortunately, alcohol was something Paulo had in spades.

Mercy, *unfortunately*, was not.

Which was a bad deal for Nicky Harris.

Not Nicole, *Nicky*. It was the first name she'd given, the one she was clearly more comfortable with, and while the others were calling her Nicole, I knew she was a Nicky. Too smart-mouthed, too brash to be a Nicole. Paulo kept calling her *belleza*, beauty, and it meant that the man had some of the same ideas I did about those pink lips — another stroke of bad luck for the girl.

Diego glanced over, and I focused on him. He was the one I needed to watch the most. He'd already touched her twice, looping closer to her every time he stood up from the poker table to get another drink. José was getting off on scaring her, Marco was playing some kind of knight in denim armor routine, and I was just watching her.

I could tell I was freaking her out, those blue eyes widening whenever she flicked them towards me, but that was for the best. She needed to stay far away from me. I hadn't been human in so long, I wouldn't know what to do with someone like her.

Someone good.

Someone innocent enough to think she could bully men like *these* and leave without repercussions. That didn't stop my cock from twitching inside my pants whenever she brushed the rim of that damn glass across her bottom lip.

"Andre." It was Paulo, speaking from the edge of the room, and I lifted my eyes from her to see the smile of the devil himself. "Walk with me."

Looking back at Nicky, I found her eyes already on me, the fear so clear that I could almost taste it.

As sweet as she probably tasted.

Fuck.

Standing, I adjusted my dick in my jeans to ease the pressure, and forced myself to walk to Paulo like a good little soldier. Anything to put some space between me and the girl, because right now she stood a better chance with Diego than she did with me.

Silently, we crossed the foyer towards his office, the French doors open on one side, and Paulo took one of his favorite positions — leaning against the front of his massive desk.

"She's interesting, don't you think?" Paulo had dropped the smile, his face as blank as what I imagined my own looked like, but I didn't really know. I'd been avoiding mirrors for years.

"She's stupid."

The edge of Paulo's mouth twitched. "For coming here? Yes. But her brother did owe me money, and I made calls. One of my men put him in the hospital."

"That's probably why she's pissed, *jefe*," I replied, deadpan, and Paulo simply nodded.

"Yes. There is only one problem."

"What?" I asked, feeling the cold settle deep into my bones. Paulo had a plan, I could hear it in his voice, and his plans never turned out good for the target.

"She only brought twenty thousand. He still owes five more." The man was still, unmoving, waiting for some kind of response, but I had no idea what he wanted to hear.

It was a shitty situation. She shouldn't have come here. She was innocent in this. A stupid, innocent, honey-skinned girl. But she'd already handed herself over to the devil to try and save her brother — even if she didn't realize it yet.

"How do you think I should get the rest of that money, Andre?" Paulo glanced down at his desk, adjusting a statue on it until the base was parallel with the edge, and then those soulless eyes were back on mine.

"Does she have any family to ransom her to?" I felt a flicker of something in my chest when I said the words, but I ignored it. Guilt was something I'd lost the ability to feel too long ago.

"Unfortunately, no. I made calls for that too. She is alone, with her brother. Bad for her… he likes the drugs. Wants to sell, but cannot keep his hands off the product so he makes bad choices." Paulo loosely gripped the edge of his desk, tilting his head. "I could sell her."

Another twinge somewhere under my ribs, a sinking feeling in my stomach, but then all I could imagine was her naked. Her thighs spread, back arching, with sweet, desperate sounds leaving those pretty lips. "You could," I acknowledged, choking off the visions in my head.

"Or I could keep her. Use her until I am bored of her." He inclined his head. "Until all of you are bored with her."

The vision was back, full force, and my cock grew stiff, pressing against my zipper. I could hear her whimpers against my ear, feel the way her flesh would give as I pinned her down. It would be so easy. And that was the offer on the table. *Her.* I wanted the final drops of the tequila in my hand to burn out the thoughts, but that would be a tell. Paulo would read my tension, my interest, instantly.

You're off the deep end, Andre. You're fucking gone.

"Do you want a drink?" Paulo asked, a hint of amusement in his tone, and I knew I had twitched. Imagining fucking the girl had broken my concentration, but I looked down at the bottle like I'd forgotten I had it.

"It's empty." Turning it up I swallowed the last bit of tequila, reveling in the burn, even though it didn't dim the vision of Nicky spread out in front of me. "See?"

Paulo didn't react at all. "So, how do I get the rest of my money?"

"However you want to, *jefe*."

Why the fuck are you asking me?

The man's hands tightened on the desk, a short flash of irritation that disappeared as quickly as it had appeared. "What would you do in my situation, *cuadro*?"

I swallowed with a suddenly dry throat. He wanted me to choose. Sentence this girl to being whored out in some shithole south of the border, or being a prisoner in this house with the same damn result.

All over five grand.

I knew Paulo didn't give a shit about the money. He'd lost ten times that when a runner had been picked up the month before. No, this wasn't about the money, it was about her. Nicky Harris. Her fucking attitude, her lithe curves, the fire inside her.

Paulo wanted to snuff it out, to crush it in his palm and feel it die… but I just wanted to touch it. To touch her. To taste her. To remind myself what *good* felt like one more time before this world destroyed her too, and I couldn't do that if she disappeared.

The decision was going to take another piece of my dwindling soul, another flapping scrap of my humanity torn away — which was exactly what Paulo wanted. He wanted this to be on me. For everything they'd do to her to be laid at my feet, and as the visions flickered inside my head again, I already knew the words that would leave my mouth. "I'd keep her."

The slow smile on Paulo's lips was a promise of hellfire, but I was already headed there anyway.

May as well reserve my seat with a little sweetness on my tongue.

Diego was squatting in front of her when we walked back into the room. He was hunched forward, trying to catch the girl's eyes as he taunted her. "*Mírame*. Give me a smile. Come on. I bet you're pretty when you smile."

My fingers twitched against the bottle in my hand, but I didn't do a damn thing about it, stopping my feet a half step behind Paulo's. I'd made the choice, and that meant Diego would get his hands on her sooner rather than later.

You shouldn't have come here, Nicky.

The burnt orange light of the evening sun filtered in through the windows, those elegant gauzy curtains glowing with it. It set the room on fire, made her blonde hair shine, and I knew Paulo saw it too. Took it in with the slow, thoughtful deliberation that made him so fucking dangerous.

"Ms. Harris," he purred, and she snapped to attention, her head jerking around to follow him as he paced deeper into the room so he could face her. I moved the other way, circling behind her chair to slip back into my spot on the couch, but I noticed the death grip she had on the leather seat. White knuckled, panic evident even as Diego backed off. "It seems we have a problem."

"What?" Nicky's voice cracked and she cleared her throat, the ice clinking in her glass as she shifted. "No. No, there's no problem. I gave you the money, and now my brother is clear."

Paulo shrugged a shoulder. "Yes, you gave me *some* money, but it is not enough." He lifted a hand when she started to sputter an argument, her cheeks flushing again as her temper spiked. "Your brother must have lied to you, *señorita*. I do not know what else to tell you."

"It's twenty thousand dollars!" she screamed, furious, and I was tempted to cover her mouth just to shut her up. "How the fuck is that not enough? He said—"

"What he *said* does not matter to me. You do not have enough, which is a problem. Well, *your* problem now." Paulo's eyes lifted over her head to meet mine, his mouth twitching like he was enjoying this cat and mouse game. Torturing the girl before he dropped the bomb and turned her over to every salivating bastard in the room. It would destroy her, ruin all the goodness in her... and all I could think of was how much I wanted her before Paulo obliterated her.

"How much more does he owe? Just tell me, maybe I can—"

"Five thousand dollars." He cut her off again, and I watched the color drain from her face. It was an answer without her even speaking a word. She didn't have the money, and even if she claimed to, I knew Paulo wasn't going to let her walk out of the house.

Too late, Nicky. Way too late.

The trap had long since snapped shut, but she was oblivious as she shifted nervously in the chair. Blue eyes flicking around the room. Seeking an escape that wasn't there. The ice in her glass rattled softly from the shaking of her hands, but I found myself drawn to the flickering pulse just under her jaw, the way her throat worked as she swallowed. Finally smart enough to be scared, and I wanted to press my lips to her skin, to bite down at the place where her neck met her shoulder and hear her scream.

"Do you like chicken?" Paulo asked the question casually, but she wasn't the only one whose head swiveled towards him in confusion, my eyes focusing as I tried to read him.

"Why the fuck does that matter?" she snapped, but he just gave his shark's grin once more. Baring his teeth like he planned to devour her, and I wondered for a moment if I'd even try to stop him — or if I'd just watch like I always did.

"We're about to eat dinner. You will join us." He crossed the space between them in a handful of steps, looming over her in his relaxed way, thumbs hooked into his pockets. "Then we can discuss your situation."

"I don't want to eat dinner with you." Nicky was clearly as stunned as the rest of us at the odd change of direction, but her voice was still too loud, too angry, too disrespectful.

She didn't know Paulo like I did; if she did she would have been crying already.

"You don't want to eat dinner?"

"NO!" she shouted, and Paulo's hand moved fast, tangling

in the hair under her ponytail as he ripped her from her seat. Her glass shattered on the tiles as her hands came up, reaching for his grip, but Paulo wasn't faking nice anymore. Nicky's yelp of pain, her curse-filled fury, all of it was cut short by the sight of the knife.

I hated myself for the way my cock twitched as Paulo dragged the dark blade down the delicate line of her neck. Tracing the same artery I'd been eyeing a minute before. He bent her head back, stepping closer so that his foot was planted between hers, and I could hear her soft whimper as the metal scraped over her skin.

For a moment I wanted to be the one holding the knife. Feeling her tremors of fear.

I wanted to see her eyes as the hope went out of them.

"Let me see if I understand…" Paulo's voice was dangerously soft as he turned the knife to trace back up her throat to her cheek. "You come to my house without an invitation, but I let you in. You are rude to my men, to me, and then you *demand* that I forgive a debt that is not even yours… but still, I listen. I make calls, I look into your brother's mistakes, and I tell you that *he* lied to you, but then you raise your voice to me, curse at me — and when I offer to discuss it over dinner? Offer to feed you at my own table? You refuse."

"Mr. García, I—"

"It is *Mister* García now, is it?" Paulo tsked, shaking his head slowly as he tapped the blade against her cheek in time. "I do not think you understand your situation, *Miss* Nicole Harris, but you will. It will just be explained without the courtesy of dinner."

He threw her to the floor hard, but she caught herself on her hands, panicked breaths making her stutter. "Pl-please, I didn't mean—"

"Take her to the storage room. We'll see if she feels more... accommodating after she has a few hours to think about my hospitality."

Paulo's command unleashed the hounds. José made it to her first, yanking her up by her arm, but Diego was barely a second behind as he wound his fist in her hair. She tried to fight, brave and stupid all at once, but when she tried to kick, José twisted her arm high behind her back. Another pretty yelp of pain, a whine as Diego's hand moved somewhere lower, and then they were forcing her forward. Towards the kitchen, and then the storage room.

I didn't move, didn't follow, likely didn't even flinch, as practiced as I was at watching things like this play out.

Marco's eyes landed on me, and I met his gaze for a long second before I turned to Paulo, awaiting his orders.

"You're out of tequila, *cuadro*. Join me in some rum?" The man stepped over the sparkling shards of glass on the floor, walking towards the bar without a second glance for the screams still echoing out of the hallway.

"Sure, *jefe*, whatever you want." I set the empty tequila bottle on the floor and moved to meet him at the bar. "Make mine a double?"

"Of course." Paulo smiled, cold and empty, just like me.

FOUR

Nicky

"You can't do this!" I yelled, my heart racing. The pain in my shoulder was intense, but I still tried to dig my heels in, to fight them, the rubber of my running shoes squeaking against the tiles as the two assholes shoved me forward again. Pleading, cursing, shouting — but none of it slowed them. I stumbled when the fucker called José took a corner too quickly, and the scream was unavoidable.

White-hot agony seared across my shoulders, only easing a little as he released my arm and I hit the floor, trying to bite back the shit I wanted to scream into their faces. We were in a kitchen now, a giant chef's island dominating the center of it, complete with a copper hanging pot rack above it. I could smell food, my stomach growling at the scent of spices in the air, but Diego had his hand around my throat before I could even regret refusing to eat.

He hauled me off the floor, my fingers wrapping uselessly around his wrist as I stood. Fetid breath puffing on my face as he laughed. "Oh, *puta*, I'm going to enjoy making you scream like that."

"Go to hell," I choked, but he just smiled.

"Downstairs, Diego. You heard *jefe*." The bastard shoved the shoulder he'd just nearly ripped out of socket, and I clenched my teeth, stifling the whine of pain. There was no choice except to walk. They paused in a small hallway off the side, near the pantry, but it wasn't the single door that José reached for — it was a seam in the decorative wallpaper on the opposite wall. Palm fronds and fucking tropical fruits done in a tasteful soft yellow against cream. The details of the wallpaper instantly evaporated from my head as the wall separated an inch, just enough for José's fingers to slip in and swing a panel of it out like a door.

A black hole loomed where the panel had been. Not enough light in the dimly lit hall to even illuminate the first few inches of the pitch black in front of me. My chest tightened, fear overwhelming me, and the two men behind me knew it. Diego fisted my hair, tearing most of it free of the ponytail as he attempted to shove me forward into the darkness.

"No!" I shouted, panic making my voice high-pitched, and the whimper as I braced my hand against the wall was even worse.

I'd wanted to be strong, to protect Chris, get him out of this bullshit so he could get better, make his life better — but I'd never planned to die for him.

"Let. Go." It was José who moved close, the heat of his body radiating through the back of my shirt.

"Please don't do this?" I turned, meeting empty black eyes, and I found no pity, no mercy. "Don't kill me." My words were so soft I wasn't even sure they could hear me, but the tightening of Diego's fist in my hair, accompanied by his low laugh, assured me they had.

"Why would we kill you when there's so many other things we can do?" Diego only laughed harder when I whimpered, trying to fight as José buckled my arm with ease and the two of them shoved me through the doorway.

The first wooden step made me gasp. *Not falling. It's some kind of basement.* The second step made a chill rush over my skin as the scent of earth and damp hit my nose. There was no light, not even a sliver, and I reached out to stroke the walls as Diego's hand forced me to take the steps faster and faster.

I am walking into my own grave.

The thought was completely unhelpful, but once it had appeared, I couldn't push it away. It smelled like soil and stale air, like the inside of a coffin. The vacuous darkness of being underground. My lungs couldn't get enough oxygen, my heart racing even though there was nothing to do but take the next step, and the next — until there wasn't even that. Flat, gritty concrete scratched under my shoes, and then someone slammed me into the wall.

My head hit in a stunning flash before I could bring my hands up to try and push back, but his weight was against me, crushing me. "You gonna scream for me?" Diego growled against my ear, huffing as one of his hands slid over my stomach, tugging blindly at my shirt until he found skin. I felt his fingers scratching, and wanted to throw up.

"STOP!" My voice tore with the effort of the shout, body shaking from the adrenaline. Desperate, trying to push his hand away and keep him from pinning me to the wall at the same time, but it was useless. He was bigger, so much fucking stronger, and all I could do was scream — just like he wanted — as he groped me, rubbed the hard ridge of his erection against my ass.

"That's it, fight me, *puta*. Make me work for it." Diego found the button of my shorts too fast, and we struggled as I kicked back from the wall. His laughter rebounded back in the space, louder, just before he landed a punch to my ribs. Pain starburst from the point, and I cried out, buckled, tears burning my eyes as he slammed me into the wall again.

"Please, please don't — *no*, stop! Just STOP!" I was panicking, grabbing blindly at his hands as the button of my shorts popped free and I felt the zipper give. Snapping my head back, I heard a grunt, a pained curse as his body pulled back from mine and I threw myself to the side. Away from him, deeper into whatever fucking room they'd brought me to.

Light flashed on, instantly blinding, and I winced and stumbled back further. "Shit…"

José was laughing, a huskier sound than Diego's menacing one. "She got you, did she, *cabrón?*"

"Fuck off!" Diego snapped, growling, and as my eyes focused I caught the swipe of red under his nose that matched the blur on his hand. His eyes found mine and he pointed at me. "I'm going to make you bleed, whore."

My stomach dropped, but José caught his shirt before he managed more than a step. "*Jefe* said she stays in here and thinks for now, but you know he will let us have her later." José's stoic expression turned into a smirk, the scar on his jaw stretching so I could see it. "And then we will see just how long she can keep fighting."

"And whether or not she's got any fucking tan lines."

"That's right, what *did* you bet me on that one?" José stood side by side with Diego, both of their eyes moving over me as they made their plans.

"*Nada*, but I'll bet you now that I fuck her first if she doesn't have a tan line." Diego groped the front of his pants as he said it, and I bit down on my tongue hard enough to taste blood just to keep from saying anything stupid.

Well, anything *else* stupid.

"Nah, I'll bet you a hundred she has at least one tan line, and another fifty that she's shaved."

I swallowed, eyes finally adjusted enough to look at the room. It was small, maybe ten feet wide, fifteen feet deep, but there was a table and some scattered chairs. Some odds and ends stacked in an alcove by the stairs. When I tuned back into them they were both staring, grinning, and I felt my hands clench into fists, the prick of my nails biting into my palms.

"Eh, Nicole? You want to play nice with us?"

"Never." I growled out the words, knowing I didn't scare them a bit, but when José pulled out his gun again I was terrified.

"Have you ever put a gun in your mouth?" he asked, walking towards me slowly, and when I stepped backwards he snapped his fingers. "Stop."

"What's the plan, José?" Diego was moving closer, a nervous glance over his shoulder at the stairs before he returned his eyes to me.

"Come here." Ignoring his friend, José pointed at the floor in front of him, beckoning me, but I didn't move. Not until he flicked something on the gun and I heard it click. "Now, *puta*, before I decide that shooting you in the leg is worth shortening our fun."

"You don't have to do this." I spoke softly as I approached, my body revolting at every inch I progressed. "I can get the rest of the money, I swear—"

José huffed as he grabbed my injured shoulder, digging his thumb in until I gasped in pain and he forced me to my knees. "You think money is what we want from you? What *jefe* wants from you?" He laughed as he ran the gun along my cheek, and when I jerked back he snapped it against the side of my head.

Fuck!

I flinched as the ache spread, a headache building behind my eyes as I refused to imagine what was next. If I thought about it, pictured it, I was lost. Dead.

"Open your mouth." José nudged the metal of the gun under my chin, lifting until I was looking up at him. His lips twitched and then he slapped me, the blunt, stinging force of it sending me to the floor as pain bloomed across my cheek, aching.

"Please, I just want to leave. You can keep the money, you can—"

"We can do whatever we want." José slapped me hard again, and I crumpled against the gritty concrete, cried out, pleaded nonsense words as Diego dragged me up by my hair, ponytail gone — and for some fucked up reason, that was what my brain focused on.

Even as the tears streaked my cheeks, and he ripped my head back harder and the pain spread, I wondered where the little hair band had gone. *Like it's going to fucking matter once Paulo says they can have you.*

I whimpered as reality set in, as my hopeless stupidity settled over me, and then José tapped my lips with the gun. "Open."

This time I listened, and before there was even enough room he pushed it in, scraping my teeth until I widened enough for it not to clatter against them. I wasn't strong anymore, couldn't fight while kneeling between them with a fucking gun in my mouth. No, I was losing it. I was crying, hot tears fighting the chill on my skin even though it was over ninety outside. Outside of this hellhole, where no one knew where I fucking was.

They're going to kill you when they're done.

"That's nice, looks good. Real pretty. You like the taste of my gun?" José smiled above me, rubbing the bitter weapon back and forth over my tongue, just at the height of his hips. "Answer me."

"*Oouhh!*" I tried to say no, but it was hard to enunciate with the thick, black metal pressing deeper into my mouth. He shoved it forward then, gagging me, but Diego jerked my head back into place when I flinched and I caught his eyes. Hungry, merciless, and the grin told me just how much he was enjoying this.

"This is good practice, *puta*. Keep your teeth off my gun and you might get to keep them when I fuck your pretty face." José pressed the muzzle down onto my tongue, forcing me to angle my head back as it pressed into my top teeth. "Wider. I better not hear teeth."

My jaw ached, but I stretched, gagging again as he slid it deep once more. The taste reminded me of blood and oil, metallic and greasy, and just the recognition had me swallowing to keep from throwing up.

Diego leaned down and licked the side of my neck, his tongue sloppy and wet. Then his teeth caught my earlobe, sharp pain making me whine against the gun while he chuckled. "You know what happens later? We will fuck your throat until you can't even scream anymore, fuck your pussy and your ass until you bleed." His tongue dragged over my cheek, catching the tears I wasn't fighting anymore, his mouth brushing my ear as I dragged in breaths around the metal pushed too far back. "But, personally, that's my favorite part, *Nicole*... because once you're bleeding we won't even need to use spit to fuck you anymore."

I choked, the retching sounds in my throat turning into sobs as José pulled his weapon free. The gagging didn't stop, the visions he'd planted in my head making me grateful I'd refused the dinner as I braced my hands on the floor. Diego shoved my head down as he used it to stand, and the both of them walked towards the stairs laughing low. "Look at that, she drooled all over it, but not a scratch on it. I guess she's had some practice."

"We will see..." Their voices faded as they climbed the steps, but under the buzzing, yellowish light of the ceiling, all I could do was curl into a ball, running my fingers over my bruised, chapped lips.

A heavy thud at the top of the stairs assured me they were gone, but it didn't bring me the relief I thought it would. There was no escaping what they'd promised, not with the taste of José's gun still fresh on my tongue. Broken, hushed sobs slipped out and I covered my mouth, trying to be quiet, to force them to stop — but the bruised spot on my ribs ached from the effort and eventually I gave up and let it out. Dragged myself into the nest of random shit in the alcove beside the stairs, where I curled up between boxes and imagined all of the places I should have been instead of here.

FIVE

Andre

It wasn't the fact that I'd gone upstairs to brush my teeth after dinner that bothered me.

It wasn't even that as I was standing in the dark, splashing ice cold water on my face, I hadn't been able to get the erection to go away. After the way José had described her crying as he fucked her mouth with his gun... the erection made sense.

The bottle of rum in my hand didn't bother me either. *That* was normal.

No, what bothered me was the pair of condoms tucked in my back pocket.

I barely remembered grabbing them in my room. Definitely didn't remember putting them in my pocket, but I could feel them. Had caught the edge of the foil when I'd tried to put my hand in a moment before — and now I was just frozen. Listening to the NFL game on the television, Paulo's cheers and curses as loud as José's. They were enjoying the blood sport. Something to fill the time.

Tossing back the rum again, I swallowed rough and stifled a cough, the flash of Nicky on her knees with tears in her eyes making my cock twitch. I brought my head back hard against the wall, feeling the snap of pain somewhere underneath the haze of the alcohol.

I had to get a hold of myself.

José and Paulo were fine, Marco was sulking in one of the big chairs, and Diego was —

Where the fuck is Diego?

Fire rushed through my veins as I stood up straight, straining my ears to listen over the booming surround sound of the game. Before I'd even made the decision, my feet were carrying me through the kitchen, to the storage room door that was slightly ajar.

Motherfucker.

Rage, dark and hot, flooded me. Burning a hole in my stomach, using the alcohol as a catalyst, and at the first pathetic scream from below I ripped the door wide. Stomping down the stairs, I could hear her desperate pleading over the heavy sound of my boots booming on the steps.

I made it to the floor just in time to see Diego throw her down on the table, her shorts tangled around her golden thighs, legs kicking. When she reached up to claw at his face he caught her wrist, twisted it, and then he backhanded her. Sent her back to the table with a thump and a choked off sob.

"STOP!" she screamed, but he almost had her shorts off, and there was no way she could fight him.

There was a roaring in my ears, the heat inside my chest burning the haze of the alcohol away, and suddenly all I wanted to do was hurt him. Break his face.

It only took a few steps for me to be beside him, surprise flashing in his expression just before I grabbed his shirt and hauled him off her, shoving him back harder than necessary. Diego stumbled, caught himself on a chair, his pants open, belt flopping as he shouted, "What the fuck, *cabrón?* What you think you're doing?"

"She's mine," I growled, and I felt darkness surging inside me. Lapping at the edges of my sanity, devouring it piece by piece.

"Like hell, this little *puta* is mine." Diego tried to step around me, to get to Nicky, but I caught him with a hand in the center of his chest and shoved him back once more. My fist tightened, arm twitching like I was about to knock his fucking lights out — which was crazy. I rolled my shoulder as he stared at me, as shocked as I was by what I was doing.

And what the fuck am I doing exactly?

Nicky's soft whimpers, her sniffling, trickled into my consciousness and I knew I was rock hard. Could feel the strain of my cock pressed against my zipper, wanting to be buried somewhere warm and wet. Wanting me to take Diego's place on top of her.

"Andre, move the fuck out of the way. You can have her next!" Diego took a step toward me, toward Nicky, but he froze in place when I flexed my hands and faced him completely. He'd seen exactly what I could do with my hands, exactly what happened when I let the darkness out of its cage, and I had no idea what he saw in my eyes… but he stopped.

"Paulo said I get her first." The low rumble of my voice was answered by a hiccupped sob from the table behind me, and it was wrong how much I enjoyed it.

Diego knew I was lying, his mouth gaping like a fish for a moment before he clapped it shut and cursed under his breath. "Fine, but I'm coming back later."

He moved towards the stairs, and I turned around to see Nicky leaned up on her elbows. Dirty blonde hair in a mussed halo around her face, feet tucked on the edge of the table, with only one of her shoes on. Her cheeks were flushed, still wet with tears, and she was biting her lower lip hard enough to make me wonder if it hurt — and if she liked it.

The shorts around her calves blocked my view between her legs, and I wanted to see. I promised myself all I wanted was to see her, but she didn't know that. Kicking out at me as I approached, panicked sounds filling the room. It took no effort at all to catch her foot, rip the last shoe off and throw it somewhere else. The shorts were next, her struggles actually helping the process, and then I was looking at pale blue panties.

"Please don't do this." Wide, terrified eyes, almost the same color as her underwear, but with more dimension. More vibrant from the tears.

I didn't answer her. I reached for the edge of the cloth and she fought me weakly, a useless punch landing on my shoulder, the heels of her hands pressing at me with what I figured was all her strength — as little as it mattered.

Grabbing her by the throat I slammed her back to the table, her sharp whine of pain making my balls ache.

She even sounds sweet.

"Don't move," I growled, and her eyes went wider. Frightened and fragile. Delicate. I could seriously hurt her. I could be the one to snuff out that light if I wasn't careful. Trailing my hand between her breasts, over her belly, I hooked my fingers into her underwear and slid them down shaking thighs. Her fear was tangible as I tossed them free, knees snapping back together like it could stop me.

But I just wanted to see.

I shoved her legs wide without a word, digging my thumbs into her flesh when she tried to fight me, gripping hard enough to make it hurt. Nicky whimpered, throwing an arm over her eyes as another sob shook her chest. I ran my tongue over my bottom lip as I focused on the trim, golden down between her thighs, imagining what she'd taste like. Would she be as sweet as I imagined? Would she taste like redemption even as I damned myself further?

"You gonna fuck her or not?" Diego was leaning against the wall at the bottom of the stairs, pants buttoned again but still deformed by his hard-on.

Sonuvabitch.

"Plan on watching?" I asked, digging my fingers in a little harder when she tried to twitch away.

"Doesn't seem like there's much to watch. You got a problem?" Diego dropped his eyes low with a mocking grin before he cupped his dick through his pants. "Because I sure don't."

Switching my hands to her hips I yanked her down the table, splitting her thighs around me, exposing her pink folds. Not wet. *Yet*. I could get her there. Nicky panicked when I ripped open the button to my pants, crying harder and trying to turn away. I almost flipped her onto her belly, but I wanted to see her face. Needed to.

I wrapped my arm around her thigh to hold her in place as I shoved everything out of the way, groaning as I wrapped a fist around the base of my cock. So tantalizingly close to her pussy. It would take so little effort to shove in, to hold her down… *condom.* After digging in my pocket I tore the foil between my teeth and rolled it on.

"No, no, no…" Nicky was pulling back, withdrawing, her eyes clenched tight as she shook her head back and forth on the table. "Why? I didn't do anything—" She was crying again, her voice tinted with the pathetic sound of it. "I didn't do anything to you!"

There was a twinge in my chest, somewhere inside the inky blackness eating away at everything except the urge to own her, to take her while she was still *her*. Before Diego could have her, before Paulo ruined her. Her next sob was like a ripple in the black, and I ripped her up from the table, fist buried in her hair. Eyes open, wide and afraid on mine.

"Please," she whispered, close enough to my face that I felt her exhale. Another shudder in the black, a flicker of something almost human.

I crushed her to my chest, my other arm moving around her waist to hold her in place so I could roll my hips against her, rubbing my latex-clad cock against her soft flesh. Her hair smelled like sunlight, warm and summery, and I clenched my jaw as I brushed my stubble against her neck. Women were always nervous in my bed, a hint of fear as they wondered what I'd do to them, and more often than not there was pain along with the pleasure. I didn't do gentle, I couldn't, but they always signed up for it. They wanted to taste the darkness. Nicky had just wanted to save her brother. Feeling the shiver rush through her muscles, the grip of her thighs around my hips, the hitched expansion of her ribs — it was perfect. *She* was perfect, and I didn't want to ruin it... did I?

More importantly, could I stop myself?

My lips moved to her ear, and I spoke as quietly as I could, cursing myself in the process for delaying the inevitable. "I'm not going to fuck you, but you need to fight me. Cry. Make it believable."

A feminine gasp was her only answer, and I wrenched her head back harder than necessary. The yelp of pain was authentic, not giving her time to react as I looked down, pretending to line up with her perfect pussy, but when I thrust my hips forward I slid outside of her. Through her folds, and her hips twitched as my cock brushed her clit.

Nicky just stared at me, lips parted. Maybe it was the shock finally settling in, but I could see Diego in my peripheral vision and he wasn't going to accept this quiet.

Pressing her down to the table I did what I'd wanted to all those hours before, I trailed my tongue along her throat, and then bit down hard at the beginning of her shoulder. She screamed, hands shoving at my ribs, but I caught them and pinned them to the wood above her head.

"Take it," I groaned against her skin, loud enough for Diego to hear, and swung my hips back and forward again.

"STOP!" she screamed, and I smiled before biting down again, reveling in the sharp cry she released. Hands trying to twist free of my grip, she was nothing against my strength with both her wrists pinned under one of mine. I knew I was leaving bruises as I mimed thrusts between her thighs. Torturing myself, wondering how much of her pleading was real, and how much was a show for Diego.

None of it mattered though, because I had my hands on her. I could taste her skin, and hear her whimpers beside my ear. With my next thrust I felt the slick glide of her wetness easing my path, and I buried my nose against her neck and breathed deep. Nicky was aroused, whether she wanted to be or not, and that actually made it hotter. Grinding my cock against her like a goddamn teenager, her quiet pleas for me to stop were constant, but I ignored them… kind of enjoyed them.

I shoved her shirt up with my other hand, her bra was next, her body torquing as she fought hard, begged. It only helped me though, her hips working my cock between our bodies, her arched back offering up a breast, and I drew the nipple into my mouth.

Fuck.

Every inch of her tasted incredible. So pure. The cries, the whines, leaving her lips a fucking symphony in my ears. I was lost, the darkness surging, a new wave with each jerk of her body against mine. Each wave larger than the last, threatening to drown me, to crack the last shred of self-control I had.

Because Nicky was heaven and hell in the same breath.

Diego was gone, I'd heard him stomp up the stairs, but it didn't matter now. The liquid heat between her thighs was spreading with each thrust through her folds, my cock straining, my body urging me to push her wider and take her, claim her while she was still the innocent warrior who had come to save her brother.

I wanted to be inside her. I wanted to hurt her again so she'd cry out, scream for me as I thrust deep. I wanted to drag her into the dark with me... just to see if she'd survive it.

SIX

Nicky

Hissing air between my teeth, I tried to fight the pleasure humming between my thighs. Stoked with every thrust of the powerful body above mine, which was only more confusing. The terrifying one, the one who had stared so intensely at me upstairs, had been the one to stop Diego.

Andre.

Tattooed, all solid muscle, and scary enough to make even the others back away — and now he was grinding against my clit with a kind of vicious precision that forced my hips to twitch to meet his. Arching, I yelped when his teeth nipped my breast, but he just did it again, and again, before switching to the other breast to start anew, and I didn't understand the heat coiling low in my belly. The flood of wetness between my thighs as he rocked his hips, hard cock gliding over my clit again, and again, and again.

Why is he even doing this? Why did he stop Diego? And… why is he still doing it now that Diego is gone?

I'd turned my head away, biting my lip to stifle a moan that had almost slipped out, but that was when I'd noticed the vacant space of wall where Diego had been watching.

Tugging at his merciless grip on my wrists, I tried to speak up but it came out on a whisper, "He's gone."

"I know." Andre surged above me, so big, and when he looked down at me, the thin barrier of the condom the only thing separating us, I couldn't hide my fear. His eyes were dark brown, almost black, and his hair was falling across his forehead, but there was nothing in his expression. No emotion. Not anger, not lust, nothing.

I flinched when he moved again, hating the way my body sparked, nerves lighting up to pulse tendrils of pleasure through every inch of my skin. My hips lifted without permission, and I had the strangest urge to wrap my legs around his hips and give in. Give in to the pleasure he was torturing me with, but — no. I needed to get out of here.

"Help me?" I whispered, terrified that someone other than the monster above me might hear me. "Please? Get me out of here?"

"I can't." His eyes shuttered, nose buried against my throat again as he rocked and groaned against me, slowing his hips into long, devious strokes. Back and forth, directly against my clit, his body heat scorching me as he held me to the table.

"After they go to bed. Please," I begged, the whine in my voice desperate.

"Shut up," he hissed, and his next mimicked thrust was rougher, less controlled, his hand gripping my hip tight enough to hurt.

Tears pricked my eyes even as the pleasure rumbled

through me. I wished that I could turn it off, ignore the constant stimulation, but his teeth nipped my shoulder again. Plucking the tension inside me like an instrument, amplifying the pleasure between my thighs, and I couldn't understand it. Any of it. "Why are you doing this?"

"Being merciful?" he asked, and the way he said it made me swallow.

"Yes," I whispered.

"I don't know." His hand slid up, cupping my breast so he could squeeze, and then he caught my nipple and twisted, the zing of pain rebounding inside me to join the heat pulsing behind my clit. "But I can't stop them, Nicky."

Tears burned my eyes as reality returned. Trapped in a basement beneath a fucking drug lord's house, which I had walked into like a fucking idiot. Being half-naked under one of his lackeys, or guards, or whoever the fuck Andre was … this was just the beginning. Diego would be worse, José would be worse. Paulo would probably kill me. The sob escaped, ending on a whine as I tried my best to stifle it, but Andre growled above me.

"God, you sound so pretty when you cry." Reaching between us, his thumb found my clit, rubbing fast until I was shaking my head, fighting the tension coiling at the base of my spine. His weight crushed my wrists to the hardwood, but I couldn't even bring myself to care as he wound me higher and higher. "So beautiful, so pure…"

"Fuck!" I screamed as he thrust inside me without warning, arching off the table, but he pulled back and went deeper with the next swing of his hips, a low rumble echoing out of his chest. It hurt a little, the width of him stretching me at the deepest point of his thrust, a twinge inside, but then he would withdraw and every nerve ending would light up like a fucking runway. Urging him to return, my hips lifting of their own volition to welcome him — and I couldn't fight it.

Couldn't fight him.

He was too strong, too much, and I was too tense anyway.

"Jesus…" he groaned, and released my hands, standing up between my thighs, his face unbelievably handsome as he stared down at me. There was a tilt to his lips, something almost like a smile, before he slid his thumb between us to find my clit once more. "Not going to beg me to stop?"

"Please——" I started to talk, but he yanked my ass off the end of the table. Buried deep, he held onto my hips, rolling his forward and back.

"Go ahead and beg, Nicky. I'm not going to stop." With that, he started to fuck me hard, every inch of his ridiculously strong body following through on each thrust. And it hurt, but in a way that was addictive, terrible and incredible at the same time. I dug my nails into my palms, trying to hold back, because I hated that I wanted him to keep going, to keep pushing me, keep talking to me in that low, rumbling voice that made me shiver.

Lifting my hips to meet his, I whined, the deep thrusts making it hard to breathe, but it suddenly didn't matter. He wasn't going to stop anyway, and I bit my tongue to keep myself from asking him to keep going. He was so terrifying. So intense.

And it felt so fucking good.

The orgasm exploded like a hidden bomb, shrapnel of light and heat rushing through every inch of my body, and on some level I heard myself cry out, curse — but suddenly I was outside of myself. Feeling the pleasure and the pain in one cataclysmic wave, unable to process the way Andre leaned over me, watching me fall apart. I was blurry with heat, a tingling ecstasy that crushed the terror, blurred the dark future that awaited me.

None of it mattered when his hands landed on either side of my ribs, his body working above mine to achieve his own pleasure, pushing one of my legs over his shoulder to angle deeper, to fuck harder — and I just spiraled again. Another crescendo of euphoria that had me breathless and pleading, the tears from before still drying on my cheeks.

Pulling him down toward me when I knew I should have been fighting, pushing him away.

A dichotomy I couldn't begin to process.

"Please!" I begged, and his hand landed on my throat, squeezing hard enough to make my pulse pound behind my eyes. Grabbing onto his wrist I struggled, arched my back, seeking air, but then he came with a shout, cock jerking deep inside me as his fingers tightened for a moment. My vision tunneled, ears buzzing, and I pressed my nails into his skin in a silent plea.

"Fuck, *belleza*…" Releasing my throat, he held himself still for a moment as I coughed, gasped, pulling in air that only seemed to amplify the spiraling aftereffects of the orgasms.

Delirious, exhausted, stunned.

Our harsh breaths intermingled, one of his hands braced beside me, the other trailing up my leg that was still caught over his shoulder. It was a brief brush with insanity that

had caused me to lift my hips to his, to let him have me —
but maybe it would be what fucking saved me.

He's already saved me once.

"A-Andre?" His name stumbled off my tongue, but I tried
to stay strong as he stared down at me, still buried deep.
"Will you help me?"

"You want me to help you?"

I nodded, rubbing my neck where I could still feel the
outline of his fingers, and for a moment his dark eyes
locked on mine, dark brows pulling together ever so
slightly. Reaching towards me, he brushed a thumb over
my lips, and then my cheek, and there was no urge to
pull away.

He'll help me. I know it. He has to.

Then he shook his head and slid from me, tossing the
condom on the floor as he tucked himself away. Eyes glued
to his black pants, he spoke low, gruff. "There's nothing I
can do. I already told you I can't stop them."

"No!" I shouted, his words shaking me to the core. "You
can't, you can't let them…" The sobs came back, my
breath coming short as I sat up on the edge of the table,
wheezing, my lungs tightening in my chest. All I could
think of was José's smirk as he shoved his gun into my
mouth, Diego's hands on me as he'd tugged at my clothes.
The things the both of them had promised to do. "Oh
God… they're going to kill me."

"I will *not* let them kill you." Andre was in front of me
again, broad and looming, and he grabbed my chin when I
didn't look up at him. "Got it?"

Shoving his hand away, I jerked my chin out of his grasp. "But you'll let them fuck me? *Rape* me?"

He stood frozen, that empty gaze burning as he breathed deeply, slowly, and then his eyes flicked away from me to the stairs. "You'll survive."

"I don't want to survive that! I want out! I want out of here, dammit! Just let me up, let me go!" I hit his chest, trying to push him back, to get him away from me, but he caught my wrists and tightened his grip until they hurt. The tears were scalding my cheeks, my sobs turning into hiccups, and I couldn't control it, couldn't stop it.

"You. Will. Live." Andre shook me by his grip on my arms. "Do whatever they say, and you'll live."

"NO!" I screamed, and when I couldn't break my arms free I tried to kick him square in the balls, but he blocked it at the last second with his thigh, and suddenly I was face down on the table, one arm wrenched high between my shoulders. Pain. His body weight pressed me down, my ribs aching, shoulder throbbing, and all I could do was cry. Scream into the wood of the table.

Rage peppered his voice, as cold and vicious as he'd been when he'd spoken to Diego. "Shut up. Right now. You need to think, be smart. You walked into Paulo *fucking* García's house, what the fuck did you think was going to happen?"

"I didn't even know who he was!" I sobbed, sniffling and twisting to try and ease the painful position. "My brother said his name when he woke up. I was asking him who hurt him, asking him *why*, and he said his name. I asked around his friends and got this address, and—"

"And no one thought you'd be stupid enough to actually fucking show up here." His voice was mocking as he crushed me to the table harder, his rage showing in the creaking of my ribs.

"*Andre, please…*"

"Don't say my name like you fucking know me. You don't know me." His grip tightened, shoving my arm a little higher on my back until I screamed. "I just fucked you. I did exactly what Diego was planning to do to you, why in the hell do you think I'd ever help you?"

Whimpering, I tried to breathe through the torment, asking as coldly as I could manage, "Do you really think that's how Diego would have fucked me?"

Silence reigned for a minute, his grip not loosening at all, and then finally a low growl rumbled above me. "You're too brave for your own good, *belleza*." His breath brushed my cheek, and I kept my eyes on the wall. "You walked into hell all on your own, and now you're expecting me to pull you out of the flames?"

"Yes!" I hissed, anger surfacing inside me through the fear and the lust and the desperation. "Why did you try to protect me from him if you didn't want to help me?"

"I stopped him because I wanted you first." His hips rocked against my ass, and I flinched, refusing to believe that. He would have fucked me immediately, wouldn't have bothered pretending at first if he was anything like the others. Wouldn't have told me to make it convincing.

"Liar."

"You don't know shit, Nicky Harris." Releasing my arm he stomped away from me, his heavy boots crunching over the gritty concrete. "You have no fucking idea what you've walked in to."

Gently lifting myself from the table I took the time to fix my bra, tugging my shirt back down, even though my underwear and shorts were somewhere on the floor. I could feel my pulse in my shoulder, wondering if something had finally torn as I stood up. He was pacing, one of those massive fists clenched in his hair as he wandered back and forth across the narrow room. It was worse because he looked so good doing it. All of that hard muscle I'd felt against me moving under his tight shirt, the long gait of each step due to his height. The bronze of his skin broken up by dark tattoos. Both arms, up his neck — he looked every bit the killer, the monster I'd believed him to be… but I was definitely hoping I was wrong.

"Are you really going to let them do this?" I asked softly, and his boots crunched to a halt. The grit on the floor scratched as he turned towards me. I could feel his eyes boring into me, as intense as they'd been before everything had gone to hell.

Nothing. There is nothing behind those eyes.

No remorse. No concern. Nothing.

He stayed silent as he marched towards the stairs, my lips parting to call after him, but I didn't get a second glance as his booming steps moved upward. The hard clap of the hidden door was his answer and in a flash, my world collapsed.

The others would come next, and Andre's words came back like a curse: *You'll survive.*

As if I'd even want to when they were done.

SEVEN

Andre

My heart pounded, body still humming from the argument, and I stayed in the kitchen to calm down. Unsteady for the first time in years.

No one had ever affected me like Nicky Harris.

The fucking innocent Valkyrie. Impossibly tempting. Impossibly sweet.

Jesus Christ, you fucked her.

Everything spun as I leaned my head back against the wall, staring up at the ceiling like it could hold some answers. Back when I'd gone to church regularly like a good Catholic boy, I would have known the right prayers to say — not that God would listen to a monster like me. Especially not after what I'd just done.

Wiping a hand over my face, the idea that had hit me downstairs grew stronger, and I knew I needed to be steady to make it happen. The bottle of rum I'd abandoned on the counter was still there, and I took a few swallows.

Letting it wash the taste of Nicky from my tongue, even though nothing could touch the memory of her cunt squeezing me when I slid deep, the whimpers, the way her eyes clenched tight when she came.

Shaking my head, I stepped into the bathroom in the hall and checked my reflection. Dark scruff on my cheeks, my black hair a touch longer than it should have been, and empty eyes. I always called Paulo the devil, but that was exactly what I looked like. Looking in the mirror was something I avoided for a reason, and this was why.

I hated the man in the mirror as much as I hated Paulo.

I wanted both of us to burn.

The rum on my tongue wasn't enough, and so I swallowed another mouthful, and then another, before I adjusted my clothes to look more presentable. I deserved hell, I deserved fire and damnation — but stupid, brave Nicky? She didn't.

Flipping the light off in the little bathroom, I avoided the mirror so I could face Paulo easier. There was laughter in the living room, jokes, but what had made me smile that morning now made me nauseous. Pushing all the bullshit away, I stood in the doorway, watching them. Marco was still in his chair, Paulo and José on opposite ends of the couch, and Diego was laid out on the other sofa, head propped up on the armrest.

Grow some balls, cabrón.

"*Jefe*." I raised my voice just enough to be heard over the surround sound, but all four heads turned to me.

"What is it, *cuadro?* Come to join us?" Paulo was smiling,

deep into his own bottle of rum, but there was still nothing real behind the tilt of his lips.

"I need to speak with you." The seriousness of my voice perked his ears and he sat up completely, dropping the smile like he'd never even attempted it.

"Problem?"

"I hope not, *jefe*."

He stood without another question. One benefit to always doing what Paulo García commanded was that he tended to listen when I spoke — mostly because I never did. Unfortunately, the same was not true for Diego.

"You all done?" Diego asked, swinging his legs to sit up on the couch, and *his* grin left no questions as to his thoughts.

"No. I'm not." I could hear the tinge of rage in my voice just remembering his hands on Nicky, the darkness bubbling down deep where she'd pushed it with all her sweetness.

Paulo caught the edge in my tone as well, and his gaze landed on me as he stopped in front of me. "My office?"

"Lead the way, *jefe*." I waited for Paulo to start walking, keeping my eyes on Diego until he muttered under his breath and dropped back onto the couch. Only then did I follow, trying to organize my thoughts, which were way too fucking scattered to be facing off with the devil himself.

Soon enough we were taking up the same positions we had earlier, only this time it was a bottle of rum in my hand instead of tequila, and there was plenty left. Paulo gestured towards me as he got comfortable leaning against his desk. "Well?"

"I want the girl." The words left my mouth too quickly, and Paulo's lips twitched.

"Then go have her."

Fingering the bottle in my hand, I shrugged, mimicking one of his colder smiles. "I already did."

A chuckle was his only answer for a moment. "I see." Paulo crossed his arms, evaluating me with those coal black eyes. "You know, *cuadro*, I was starting to think you were some kind of *maricón*. You never touch the girls that come here."

"I'm no *maricón*, *jefe*. I don't fuck men." The insult made me twitch, but I kept the rum at my side.

He shrugged a shoulder, not seeming to care either way. "So, if you've already fucked her, what more do you want?"

"I don't want to share her." I let the disgust show on my face. "I'm not interested in having her after Diego is done."

Paulo only nodded, resting his palms back on the smooth surface of his desk. "And what about me?"

My stomach twisted, but I forced my expression to stay blank. "Do you want her, *jefe?*"

"I might, but tell me what your offer is, *cuadro*. I'm listening." The man looked at me like we were discussing the weather and not the body of a young woman trapped in his fucking basement.

"You said she still owes five grand. I'll cover it in exchange for not having to share her."

Paulo clicked his tongue, shaking his head slowly. "You

don't touch a single girl in front of us, in all the time I've known you, but *this* girl you want to pay five thousand dollars for? Why?"

"She sounds pretty when she cries, and even better when she screams." *Not a lie.*

Black eyes glittered at my words, and Paulo leaned forward slightly. "Did you make her scream, *cuadro?*"

"More than once." I shrugged, ignoring the twist in my stomach. "She reminds me of my neighbor growing up. I used to make her scream too."

Real laughter came from him then, not the friendly kind he'd been choking out with the others — no, this was sinister, twisted, soft. "This is why I like you, Andre. You don't hide the monster within, you don't put on some sheen of civility for the bastards."

"No, *jefe*. I don't see the point."

"There is no point in hiding who we truly are, it always comes out in the end." Paulo clapped his hands together and walked to the small liquor stand stuck between two bookshelves. "She's yours, just give me the money in the morning. Now, we should drink. Good stuff, not that rum, put it on the desk."

I obeyed, like I always did, and waited for him to hand me a crystal glass filled with the amber tequila of Casa Herradura, the *Seleccion Suprema* was one of the bottles he kept in here. Away from the open bar in the front rooms. "*Gracias, jefe.*" Inclining my head towards him as he lifted his glass.

"To your new *belleza*." He clinked his glass against mine,

and then continued. "All I ask is that if you kill her, you handle it away from my home."

Something swished through the darkness inside me, hungry, itching at my skin to be released — but it wasn't aimed at Nicky, it was focused on Paulo. I wanted to break the crystal glass and slice his throat open with it. Watch his pale shirt and linen pants get soaked with his blood. Beat his face in while he was still choking for air. Ruin him in his last moments as much as he'd ruined me.

Instead, I nodded.

"Of course, *jefe*. When I'm done with her, I'll handle it." We drank then, peaceful sharks drowning our appetites in tequila. Very expensive tequila, because I couldn't deny how good it tasted, but as much as I wanted to blame all my shit on Paulo García, I knew that was pointless. I'd made all my choices, for all my own reasons, and as bitter as my past tasted… at least I had Nicky now.

But what the fuck am I going to do with her?

"I need to tell the others. Diego was quite frustrated that you interrupted him."

I almost choked on the tequila, but managed to swallow it down, offering my empty glass to Paulo with a steady hand. "He got in my way."

"So, you did go downstairs to find her."

"I told you earlier that I'd keep her, *jefe*."

He plucked the glass from my hand and set them both on his desk for the cleaning crew in the morning. "Well, she's yours now, *cuadro*. But, maybe I will have some fun with her too?"

Paulo smiled as he passed me, heading for the door, but I couldn't even muster a response. Just the idea of him between her thighs, his hands on her — it made my mind bloody with visions of destruction. The things I wanted to do to him for all of his sins.

But I wasn't going to do anything.

I snagged the rum before I followed him. The football game was still on when we came back to the room, and Paulo headed towards the couch calmly. "What's the score?"

"Twenty-seven to twenty-four. Is everything okay, *jefe?*" José glanced back at me for a second, before returning his gaze to Paulo.

"It's all good. The girl belongs to Andre, no one touches her, understand?" It was cold, quick, to the point, and even though the others glanced at me, no one spoke a word against Paulo.

A chorus of, "Yes, *jefe*," echoed around the room, and I felt the darkness calm a little. Diego was furious, taking a long draw on the Corona in his hands, but I didn't give a shit.

I had to get back downstairs.

My feet carried me back to the hidden door, and when I popped it open I expected to find her waiting at the bottom of the stairs, a ball of tears or fury — instead, it was empty and quiet. Moving down slowly, I hit the concrete and started to turn when something sharp was pressed to my throat.

"Move, and I'll kill you."

"Really?" I asked, looking over at her. Her blonde hair was

a wrecked halo in the buzzing, yellow light of the storage room. My bite marks showed red and splotchy on her skin, purple in places where bruises promised.

"Yes. I won't let them have me. I'll kill all of you if I have to." Her voice was meant to be strong, but she wavered on the last bit, losing her confidence. It was almost cute how brave she was — still so stupid considering I could break her arm in an instant... but cute. When I didn't even flinch, she seemed to lose more of her nerve, but then she spoke again. "Or I'll kill myself. But I—"

Grabbing the arm holding the broken edge of a ceramic vase, I spun her away from me, twisting her wrist until the sharp little fragment fell to the floor and she yelped in pain.

Fuck, I love that sound.

I shoved her forward until she was pressed to the wall by the stairs, one of my hands keeping her wrist twisted, and the other in the center of her back, holding her in place. She was whining, all her bravado melting away in a series of muttered curses.

"None of them will touch you, and you will *not* kill yourself."

Nicky went rigid against the wall, the muscles in her back tensing, and *that* was when I noticed she'd restored her clothes and her shoes. "What?"

"You're mine now. Paulo agreed to it." I couldn't resist pressing myself against her back, so much smaller than me, so fragile. A little bit of innocence, caught amidst the monsters — at least for a little while longer. Running my lips across the side of her neck, I smiled when she angled her head away to give me access. "Which means you are not allowed to hurt yourself, do you understand?"

"How am I yours?" she whispered, and my cock twitched.

"I paid for you. The five grand your brother still owed." My tongue flicked out to taste her skin, but she jerked away from me, tucking her head to block my access, and I growled.

"That doesn't make me yours, that makes me in debt to you."

"And how the fuck do you think I want to claim that debt?" I couldn't stop myself, grinding my slowly hardening cock against her ass, and when she tried to rip her hand from mine I squeezed hard enough for her to whimper. I already wanted her again.

"I have to leave, I need to—"

"You *need* to shut up. We *need* to go upstairs to my room, and I'd prefer it if you didn't attract any more attention from Diego." It was cruel, but I forced her head to the side so I could press my lips against her ear. "Unless you want me to withdraw my offer and let him have you?"

"NO!" Her panicked cry woke my cock up the rest of the way, and I contemplated tearing her shorts back off to fuck her against the wall. Take her ass with the last condom in my pocket, but there would be time for that after I made contact.

"Then will you behave on the way upstairs, or do I need to haul you over my shoulder?" The picture was something I wasn't opposed to, even if it would be exhausting carrying her up all those stairs, and it would *definitely* attract attention. Still, having her struggling form completely under my control was… tempting.

"I'll go with you." Her quick acceptance ruined the ideas in my head, but it opened up the door for a lot more. So many things I could do to her while everyone figured out how to handle the situation.

Shifting my hand into her hair, I made a fist at the base of her skull, the hiss of air between her teeth telling me it stung. "Same rules as before, you've got to cry. Make it believable."

"Going to fuck me again?" she muttered through clenched teeth as we started up the stairs, and I laughed low, knowing I wouldn't be able to resist with her body in my bed. No use fighting the temptation when I was already damned.

And I've done my good deed for the year.

"I think you want me to fuck you again, *belleza*. You made the best sounds the first time." *That* shut her up, and as we left the storage room I clicked the hidden panel back into place, pushing her through the kitchen so I could grab my rum off the counter. Everything was good until we got to the base of the stairs. It was the sudden shudder of Nicky's shoulders that alerted me to the fact that something was off.

Diego.

He was lurking near the bottom step, eyes devouring her curves. "Going to share?" he asked, and I stared at him as I shoved Nicky onto the first step, where she whimpered like I'd told her to, or she was actually terrified.

"You remember what I did to that fucker who stole cash from Paulo's storehouse?"

"She's not worth half a million, Andre," Diego spat.

"That's not what I asked you, *cuadro*. Do you remember?" I shifted my body until I was between him and Nicky, so that his eyes had to meet mine — and I saw the recognition in them.

"I remember... no need to threaten me with that shit. After all, there's plenty of pussy around. I'll get mine." Diego shrugged and stepped back, moving towards the hall. "*Buenos noches*."

Ignoring his attempt to pacify me, I shoved Nicky up another step, catching her arm so she had to follow me. Down the right hall, I pulled a key from my front pocket and unlocked my room. As soon as we were inside, she stood right behind me as I flipped the deadbolt, and then locked the rest I'd installed that had no external access.

"You're safe in here," I muttered, and then shrugged as I met her wide blue eyes. "Well, safe from everyone but me. Now, go sit down on the bed and shut up. I need to handle something."

"Andre?" The way she said my name made my cock twitch, and I growled because I really *did* have shit I needed to do before I took her in a bed.

"What did I say?"

Nicky made a face at me, but she moved towards the king-sized bed and dropped onto the edge of it, her feet dangling as she watched me, but I couldn't keep looking at her. Not with my dick pressed against my zipper, begging to get wet again, to make her scream again. Stalking to my desk, I slammed the rum down, flipped open the laptop, and typed in a web address I had long-ago memorized.

"Porn?" she asked, her voice irritated, and I glanced back to see her twisting so she could see my screen.

Ignoring her, I passed over the various videos on the screen and clicked the contact feature on the page, typing in my normal phrase. Barely a minute later my cell phone buzzed in my pocket and I answered fast. "Hello."

"Hello, sir, you requested a customer service call. What seems to be the problem?"

"I placed an order."

"For what?" the calm voice on the other side asked.

"Forty-two credits, yesterday."

"One moment." As the voice paused, I heard the huff from Nicky, but I kept my eyes on the screen. I needed to focus. "Can you verify the last four of your credit card?"

"Two-seven-nine-nine."

"Please hold." There was *actual* hold music for about thirty seconds, and then I heard the clicking of the routing, and then Nathan's voice came on. My handler. My lifeline to the real world.

"You there, Andre?"

"Yeah." Relief washed over me, and for an instant I felt normal, even though everything about my life was so far from normal that it was a fucking joke. It had been too long. "I've got a problem."

"Give me your codes."

"Bravo. Zulu. Charlie. Quebec."

"Must not be that big of a problem for you to be bothering me with no emergency. What's up?" Nathan dropped the formality and I could hear him settle into wherever he was sitting. Probably at home with his family, bored in his suburban oasis. *Fucker.* "Line is secure, but you know we have to keep this short, so hurry."

"There's a girl here."

"A girl?" He chuckled. "So?"

"It's…" I trailed off, remembering that Nicky could hear me. *Shit.* Maybe I should have left her downstairs for this.

"What is it, Andre? Is there a problem?"

"Yes."

"Are you trying to tell me this girl is in trouble or something?" Nathan sounded irritated, and I wasn't far behind him as my teeth ground together.

"*Yes.* That is what I'm saying."

"Well, maybe the bitch shouldn't have shown up at Paulo García's house." His handler made a disgusted noise. "If you're trying to suggest getting her out of there—"

"You don't understand, Paulo is focused. This won't end well."

"You're fucking with me, right?" Nathan turned his TV on in the background. "We're not wasting three years of work on some random girl. Deal with whatever the problem is and stay focused on the mission."

"I can't." Glancing back at her, I found her wide blue eyes on me and that only made my voice more intense, because

I wanted her on her knees looking up at me like that, and I wanted to do a lot more than that — she needed away from me as much as she needed out of this fucking house. I was going to destroy her if someone didn't stop me. "Give me something here."

"Not fucking happening. It could blow your cover. Do what you have to do, Andre. But I don't wanna know, got it?" Nathan ended the discussion before it could even begin, and as images of the basement flashed in my head, I knew exactly what kind of shit Nathan *didn't* want to know.

It had been a gamble, a Hail Mary — and it had failed. I swallowed hard, and felt the darkness purr deep in my chest. "Yeah. I got it."

"Don't seek contact again unless it's a real emergency, or you've got what we need. This is too important." The line went dead a second later, and I stared at my phone, clenching my jaw.

Thirty-one months of my life and they couldn't even give me this.

Couldn't even save one fucking girl from Paulo García.

Wouldn't even save her from me — because God knew I couldn't resist her. I'd tried so hard in the basement, tried to be the good guy, the hero, but I wasn't. I had fucked her even though I'd told her I wouldn't. Ignored her pleas, held her down, taken her like any other monster in the house would have.

And now she's mine, and on my fucking bed.

Slamming the laptop closed, I laid my phone on top of it and stood up to face her. "Strip."

"Who was that?" She shifted on the bed like she knew what kind of threat I was. "Are you trying to help me?"

"There's no helping you, *belleza*. I'm the only thing standing between you and the rest of the guys here, so… do you want to strip, or do you want me to put you in the hall?"

Nicky stood up, ripping her shirt over her head. Now wearing just a bra, those little shorts, and her multi-colored shoes. *Not* naked, but definitely pissed off. "Who were you talking to? You told someone I was here. Who was it?"

I moved closer, reveling in the way she twitched back and then chose to hold her ground. Still afraid of me, yet so damn brave at the same time. "No one." Running a finger under one of her bra straps, I pushed it off her shoulder. "And I think I told you to strip."

"I don't deserve to be here," she whispered.

"None of us do." Grabbing her hips, I shoved her back to the wall, pressing close to her. "But I just spent a lot of money keeping you away from those fucks downstairs who you are so afraid of, and that means I want my money's worth."

A dirty ploy. Conniving. Evil. And it worked.

Nicky's blue eyes were fierce as she unbuttoned her shorts, shoving them down over her hips along with her underwear. She toed her shoes off to rid herself of the clothes that pooled next to us, and I reached behind her to unsnap her bra, drawing it over her arms. Then I stepped back to look her over. My golden Valkyrie, so stupid, so brave, and so irresistible.

Scooping her up, I tossed her onto the bed, and she let out

a squeak as she bounced. Her knees parted, showing me the still glistening petals of her pussy. When I pulled off my shirt, I heard her gasp, and I wasn't sure if it was from all the ink, the scar across my ribs, or the abs — but no matter what, it made me smile. Pants, boxers, and everything else was on the floor, condom tucked in my hand as I climbed between her thighs.

"Going to fight me?" I asked low, and she bit her bottom lip. "It's okay if you don't want to fight me right now, I'll figure out something to make you struggle tomorrow."

Nosing my way into her hair, I breathed in summer and let it push back the darkness for now. No Paulo in this room, no more handler shit, no undercover BS for a case they'd never make — it was just Nicky's sweet skin, her tight cunt, and the noises she made. I nipped her just to make her yelp, and when she tried to twist away I dropped my weight over her, pinning her to the bed.

"See? I'm already figuring out which buttons to push."

Golden brows pulled together as she looked up at me, pretty pink lips pouting. "I remember what you said downstairs, and I heard you on the phone. You're trying to help me."

"You don't know what you fucking heard."

She caught my face between her hands, and I clenched the condom in my fist as her blue eyes locked on me. "Who are you, Andre?"

"Don't ask stupid questions." I tore the foil on the condom, flipping her to her stomach as I rolled it on. "I'm going to make one thing very clear, Nicky." Pulling her hips high, I lined up with her cunt, eyeing the little star of her ass with a smile. *Next time.* "I'm not a good man. I can't save you, and honestly, now that I have you, I don't really want to."

Reaching forward I grabbed a fistful of hair and wrenched her head back, her back arching as she whined in pain.

With that pretty little cry, I thrust deep, and she groaned. "Fuck, yes…" I growled, feeling her sweet pussy grip me, pull me deeper. "So, I made a phone call… that doesn't mean shit. You belong to me, and I belong to Paulo García. Welcome to hell."

Another hard thrust and she whimpered, her hands braced on the bed to try and ease the grip I had on her hair. "Paulo?" she managed to croak out the name through the strain on her throat, and I rewarded her with another stroke, feeling her slick cunt tighten down.

"That's right, *belleza*. That was one of the agreements I had to make when I bought your debt." I slammed into her to drive the point home. "If he ever decides he wants you, he gets you."

She started crying again, and I released her hair so I could hear it better. Nicky folded forward, and I bruised her hips with how hard I gripped them, the soft sound of her sniffling interrupted by every thrust. I wasn't sure how I'd react if Paulo said he wanted her. It was a fifty-fifty chance that I'd finally snap and shoot him myself… or hand Nicky over like a good little soldier.

All I knew for sure was that she was mine, and neither of us were getting out of hell any time soon, but with my cock buried deep inside her — for the first time in a long time, I wasn't sure I wanted to leave.

EIGHT

Nicky

I woke up hot, covered in sweat, and it took a second for me to recognize the heavy weight of a man's arm draped over my ribs. *He* was pressed against my back, approximately a million degrees of male body heat. I moved my legs under the sheets, feeling the tender ache between my thighs just as everything from the day before slammed into me like a fucking train.

Taking the money out, driving to Paulo García's house, and then... everything else. The men, the threats, Paulo, José, Diego...

Andre.

Twisting at the waist I leaned up just enough to look at his sleeping face, slightly less terrifying in the dim light drifting through the wooden blinds. Still, my stomach tightened when I remembered that I was trapped here. In a fucking drug dealer's house, in the bed of a man who might be trying to help me, or could just as easily use me and kill me.

Andre wasn't exactly making his intentions clear.

First, he'd protected me from Diego, told me to fight him, to make it believable as he'd rubbed his cock against me — but then he *had* fucked me. Which was confusing enough because it had been good. *Too good.* And then he'd, what? Bought me? Was that what he'd fucking done?

I had the strongest urge to find something to stab through his throat, but then I'd still be two floors up and in the house with a bunch of killers.

My bladder nudged me, threatening, and I went to get out of bed when his arm tightened and pulled me back. His voice was rough with sleep as he spoke. "What are you doing?"

"I need to pee."

Andre huffed and lifted his arm, rolling to his back so that the sheet slid down toward his waist. Firm chest, rolling abs, all of those muscles and tattoos shifting as he groaned and stretched. "Bathroom is by the door."

"Thanks," I muttered, all too aware of my nudity as I scrambled for the door and shut myself in. It was a small bathroom. A tub with a plain white shower curtain, a sink with cabinets underneath, and then a toilet beside it. As I settled on the toilet I could hear him moving in the room, and it made me want to hide in the bathroom until… until what? No one was going to look for me until Christopher was out of the hospital, which would be another week at least.

Four broken ribs, bruised organs, a concussion, a fractured jaw, a broken nose.

He'd looked like some kind of extra in a zombie movie as

I'd sat in his hospital room, with his brain swelling, in and out of consciousness. I was already stressing about the medical bills that would show up — and then he'd started babbling. About Paulo García, about his debt, so many useless apologies that didn't mean fuck all.

Twenty thousand. That was what he'd said. Not twenty-five, and we didn't have that much anyway. I had *maybe* another twelve-hundred in savings, three hundred in my bank account, could possibly borrow a few hundred more from friends, but five grand? Impossible.

Without my parents' life insurance even the twenty thousand would have been unreachable, and now I was trapped in this fucking house. All because I'd wanted to get him out of trouble, *again*.

The bathroom door opened and I clamped my knees together with a snap. Andre's eyes roamed over me, and then he blinked against the light in the bathroom. "Finish up, I need to piss."

"Sure," I mumbled as he walked away, leaving the door open. Quickly wiping and flushing, I was washing my hands when he walked in behind me wearing dark jeans and a heather gray shirt.

"You need to not draw attention to yourself." Andre mumbled while staring down at the toilet, the loud sound of liquid hitting the water telling me he was peeing right next to me. I felt the heat in my cheeks as I stepped out and sought refuge by leaning against the bit of wall between the bathroom door and his bedroom door.

"How do you expect me to do that? I never *tried* to draw attention to myself."

A rough laugh came from the bathroom just as the sound of him flushing the toilet obscured the end of it. "Sure, showing up at Paulo García's house, shouting at everyone, *that* wasn't going to draw attention."

"I was trying to help my brother, asshole."

"Well, how did that turn out?" he asked as he leaned out of the doorframe.

"Fuck off."

"Watching your mouth would be a good first step to not drawing attention, *belleza*. Paulo and José are pretty sensitive to disrespect." Leaning back into the bathroom, he kept talking. "And I won't tolerate it either. Come brush your teeth."

Stepping inside, I paused next to him and looked over the counter and only saw the single toothbrush at the edge of the sink. "Do you have another toothbrush?"

"No," he replied as he walked out of the bathroom.

Glaring at the sink, I scrubbed his toothbrush with toothpaste first, rinsed it, and then reapplied to brush my teeth. It felt good to rake the toothpaste over my tongue. The memory of gun metal made me shudder, and I kept scrubbing until the urge to vomit passed. Andre wasn't good, but he had still protected me from Diego and José. Had taken me out of the basement.

But he also said that if Paulo wants you, he gets you.

Just the idea made my stomach turn again and I spat out the suds of toothpaste, gathering water in my hand to rinse before I cleaned his toothbrush and set it back on the side of the sink. Staring at myself in the mirror, I winced.

There was a bruise on my ribs, a pale one on my left cheek, and my wrists had small dime sized bruises over the bones.

Still, I knew if Andre hadn't intervened it would have been worse. Much worse.

Taking a deep breath, I forced myself to walk out of the bathroom and found my clothes picked up from the floor, draped over the end of the bed. Andre was sitting in his desk chair, playing on his phone, not even looking at me. I grabbed my bra and put it on, then my underwear as the silence stretched. I was waiting for him to speak, to explain what was going to happen, but he just continued scrolling through something on his phone, which reminded me... "So, José has my phone."

"And?" he asked without lifting his eyes.

"I want it back. I want to check on Chris, to see if he—"

"You're not getting your phone back."

"You can't keep me like some prisoner here!" I snapped.

Andre was out of the chair in an instant, towering over me, and I stumbled back a step before I remembered to hold onto my anger, to stare into his hard face and hide my fear. He reached forward slowly, brushing his thumb across my jaw before he rested his grip on the side of my neck. "Do you even remotely understand your situation?"

"I *understand* that you paid off the rest of my brother's debt, and I appreciate that, but I think we're even now. Don't you?"

He laughed. Fucking laughed, low and under his breath, as he traced his thumb over my lips until his hand wrapped around my throat and tightened. "Even?" he mocked.

"You fucked me. Twice." *And I already feel like a whore.*

"And you think that makes us even? You think you're worth five grand for a couple of fucks?" Andre pushed me backwards until I stumbled into the wall, and then I felt the constriction of my airway, the pressure building behind my eyes as his grip tightened further and my fear returned.

"Stop," I hissed.

"You don't make the rules here, Nicky. I do." He shook his head a little before those dark eyes bored into mine again. "Paulo does. And if you don't want to end up back in the basement, getting fucked by every dick in this house, you'll fucking listen to what I say and maybe, just *maybe*, you'll leave here in one piece. Understand?"

I jerked my head in a nod and he let go of me, leaving me to slump against the wall as I coughed and dragged in air.

"Put your fucking clothes on. We need to go down for breakfast. You'll sit next to me." Andre's gaze roamed over my body, and then he pointed at me, his voice rougher. "Don't lift your eyes from the table, don't even *look* at anyone else. Before you answer anyone, you'll look at me first to make sure I want you to answer. Got it?"

"I get it."

"Good," he growled, and then he walked into the bathroom and slammed the door.

I was screwed. Totally fucked, and I had no idea how to get out of this situation. Would Andre kill me if Paulo García ordered it? Would he hand me over to him if the bastard, or someone else, asked? Those questions made my stomach sour as I pulled on the rest of my clothes.

When he stepped out, he looked me over with only a flicker of the lust from the basement, and unlocked the series of bolts on the door. Finally, he held the door wide and I stepped out, only to watch him relock the single one visible from the hall.

"Come on," he summoned, and I followed him down the stairs. The sound of people talking in the kitchen preceded our entrance, and I caught sight of Paulo and José before I dropped my eyes. Andre slid into a chair near the middle of the dining table beside the main kitchen, leaving me an outside chair… directly across from Paulo.

"*Cuadro*, how did you sleep?" Paulo smiled, vicious and cold, and Andre made a low sound in his throat.

"*Bueno, jefe,* you?" Andre seemed perfectly comfortable as he took food from the family style dishes on the table to add to his plate and mine. I got a scoop of some kind of egg and meat scramble, and a sausage, before he put all of that and more onto his own plate.

"Well. Very well." Glancing at the older woman bustling around the kitchen, Paulo nodded to her, and then cups of black coffee were sat in front of both of us. Despite my best attempts, I couldn't get the woman to make eye contact with me. Surely she knew I wasn't here by choice? Wouldn't she help me? Save me?

As I watched her return to the sink to continue washing dishes, I realized it was hopeless, and dropped my eyes to the plate in front of me.

"Did you have a good night with the girl?" Paulo asked, and I cringed at being talked about like I wasn't there.

"Yes," Andre answered, short and abrupt before he pushed a forkful of food between his lips.

"Does she have tan lines?" José asked, smirking, and I made the mistake of looking up at him just in time to catch his eyes glaring hungrily towards me.

"Yes," Andre replied, and I blushed, heat rising in my cheeks.

"Shaved?" José asked again, and Paulo stopped drinking his coffee to listen.

"No," Andre answered quickly, like he had catalogued my naked body with his mind. More than anything I wanted to reach across the table and drive my fork into José's hand, the one resting beside his plate, but just as I gripped my fork, Andre's hand landed on my thigh and squeezed.

"Well, not everyone's perfect. She must be a good fuck for you to want to keep her to yourself." José nudged his plate forward and sat back. "Maybe when you're bored with her we can all have a go? See what she has to offer?"

"Maybe." The short word felt like a death sentence as Andre continued eating, offering the cream for the coffee like *that* would make this all okay.

I took the creamer and set it beside the coffee, staring down at my lap as if I could block them all out if I just ignored the vulgar conversation, but Andre wouldn't allow it. His fingers tightened on my thigh, half on my skin and half on my shorts.

"Eat," he muttered, and I glared at him.

"I'm not hungry," I hissed back, but the growl of my

stomach betrayed me a second later and his eyebrow twitched.

"You still don't want to eat at the table?" Paulo asked, tilting his coffee cup side to side. "Then put her on the floor, Andre. Feed her like a dog if she can't be grateful."

Before I could react, Andre's fist was in my hair, yanking me painfully from the chair as I fell to the floor beside his seat with a yelp. "Don't fucking move," he growled, and the sound of male laughter from above made my skin itch. "Eat."

A sausage appeared in my vision, but I stayed still, fists clenched at my sides until his hand jerked my head back and he pressed the meat against my lips, smearing grease over my skin. I ripped it from him and wiped my mouth on my arm before taking a bitter bite.

"Having trouble with her?" Paulo asked smoothly, but I knew better. He had ordered them to take me downstairs the night before in the same casual tone. I had no doubt he'd ordered men killed in the same relaxed voice, and so nothing about it was comforting.

"She's fine," Andre answered, handing down a cloth napkin as I slowly devoured the sausage. Conversation continued above my head, and after a few minutes a cup of coffee, already tan with cream, appeared in my line of vision.

I stared at it, burning hate building in my stomach as doom settled over me. This place was a death sentence, and I was already kneeling for the executioner.

What the fuck would come next?

NINE

Andre

I held the cup beside my thigh, trying to pay attention to the random discussions between José and Paulo, but Nicky wasn't taking the coffee. Glancing down at her, I nudged it closer and she finally snagged it.

"Look at that, the *puta* is on her knees this morning!" Diego laughed as he walked into the room. "You teach her a lesson, Andre?"

"I think he's still having trouble with her," José answered, smirking, and I felt my blood heat.

"Oh? That's funny. *We* didn't have any trouble with her, not after we showed her who's boss. Right, José?" Diego was smiling as he took the chair to José's left, and I wanted to tell her to go upstairs, to lock herself in my room, but she hadn't had enough to eat.

"*Puta* knows her place, don't you?" I grabbed her chin, tilting her beautiful face up just enough to catch those pretty blue eyes — but all I saw was hate. "Drink your coffee," I ordered her and let go of her jaw, looking back up to the others.

The sound of sipping filled my ears, and I fought not to watch. Not to ensure she was drinking the coffee, I just blindly filled a fork from the food on her plate and offered it down to her. It was strangely sexual to glance down and see her lips close over the fork, pulling back to chew and swallow what I'd provided. I hadn't expected it, hadn't planned any of this shit, but now she was mine. Mine to feed, mine to use, mine to protect, mine to fuck.

It was the kind of shit I was supposed to avoid, and I had *tried*. I had called Nathan, tried to get her out, but he'd ignored it. Left her with me, left her *here*, and that meant I had to figure it out and try not to destroy her in the process. But I wasn't even sure I was capable of that anymore, wasn't sure that some dark part of me didn't want to feel her break.

"What do you want with her, *cuadro?*" Paulo asked, lifting his lips in that shark smile that made my skin cold.

"I'm just enjoying myself, *jefe*." I kept my answer short, like I always did, offering her another bite of food because I wanted her fed. I wanted her strong. If there was a chance for an out, I wanted her to take it — but at the same time I didn't. I wanted her in my bed, I wanted her to be there tonight. I hadn't slept that well in months, with those feminine curves against my front, and I didn't want to just give it up.

Did that make me evil? Maybe. But it didn't change the situation, and the way Diego and José and Paulo were looking at her, I knew if I even tried to show her the door they'd drag her back inside and fuck her in the foyer just to make the point that she wasn't free to leave. The only chance she had was for me to act as possessive as I felt.

Even if she hated me for it.

"*Buenos dias*," Marco mumbled as he stumbled into the kitchen, dropping into the last open chair beside me. Even his eyes tracked to her though, the pile of blonde hair atop her head, and I felt that flicker of rage I shouldn't feel. Not *here*, not with them. Not yet.

"Morning." Sliding my fingers into her hair, I dragged my nails over her scalp, feeling her stiffen at my side as I listened to whatever bullshit Diego was spewing about the plans for the day, for once it seemed to include something other than hanging around this house, and then Paulo spoke just as I reached over to fill another fork with food for her.

"Andre, I want you with me today." It wasn't a request, and that meant leaving Nicky here. Alone. Unprotected. But I had no choice.

"Okay, *jefe*." The food on the fork hovered by my thigh, untouched, and I risked a glance down at her. Blonde hair hung down on either side of her face, the coffee cup resting between her knees, delicate fingers holding the cup upright. She wasn't eating, and I knew she should, knew she needed it, but I couldn't draw attention to her.

It would only make things worse the moment I was out of the house.

"We have a meeting. Come heavy, understand, *cuadro?*" Paulo clarified before drinking the last of his coffee.

"*Claro, jefe.*" I nodded, and forced the fork against Nicky's lips so that she had to take it from me and feed it to herself.

Grabbing my own bite as she chewed, I felt an urge to hurt her when she kept the fork in her hand. Defying me in front of Paulo? Stupid.

"Want me there, *jefe?*" Marco asked, mouth full of egg.

"No. José and Andre will be enough." Paulo pushed back from the table and stood, giving a passing glance to Nicky. "We leave in an hour."

"Yes, *jefe*," I answered, along with the others around the table. As soon as Paulo left the room I looked down at Nicky and held my hand out for the fork, and when she didn't move I felt the darkness surge. Inky black waves painting my insides as I tore her head back and stared down into pale blue eyes. "Are you done eating?" I growled.

"I can feed myself," she hissed.

"I can feed her something." Diego laughed, cupping himself under the table, and for a second I was tempted to let him, just to get her to understand the fucked up situation she'd put herself in… but the flash of fear in her eyes made me hesitate.

"Fork. Now." I kept my hand steady, and eventually her gaze flickered away from mine and she handed up the utensil in silence.

Releasing her hair, I made a point to eat a few bites on my own, watching as José kept his gaze glued to the top of her head peeking over the edge of the table even as Diego and Marco continued chatting like it was a normal morning.

"Teresa! Any more *huevos?*" Marco thumbed the edge of the empty platter, and the older woman walked over in silence to take it back to the stove.

"I can keep Nicole busy while you're out with *jefe*, Andre. Make sure she doesn't get lonely." Diego smiled at me, and I piled more food on a fork for her and offered it down, satisfied when she ate without a single remark.

"No."

"No?" Diego huffed. "What the fuck good is she if we can't have some fun with her?" He laughed along with José and I hated Paulo even more for taking me away from the house today. It was on purpose, I wasn't stupid enough to think otherwise, but I had no idea if *she* would be smart enough to stay in the fucking room.

If I found her a cum-soaked bloody mess on the floor when I returned, I'd know she was an idiot.

And then I'd probably give in and finally snap and kill them all.

Perfecto.

"She's mine," I growled, feeling the fork as she pressed it against my thigh. Instead of taking it, I handed the plate down to her so she could finish eating.

"Paulo said she eats like a dog," José sneered, leaning back to glance under the table.

"She's on the floor."

"Dogs don't have forks."

"Like I said, she's mine. She isn't eating at the table, and as soon as she's done I'm putting her back in *my* room until I return." Glancing around the table I met each of their gazes, tempted to give them a reminder of just who they were fucking with. "Have a problem with it?"

"Nope," Marco answered before snagging another hearty

spoonful of eggs from the fresh platter Teresa sat on the table. But he was the only one who answered, Diego and José simply leaned back, watching Nicky as she started to eat.

They looked like salivating wolves, and I felt a growl in my chest. Darkness swirling. Angry.

Possessive.

Protective.

Shit.

Shoving Nicky into the room ahead of me, I heard her stumble as I turned to slam and lock the door. Cursing under her breath, she glared when I turned around, but I strode past her to the dresser to pull out two of my guns and a few extra clips.

"What the *fuck* was that?" she finally managed to spit through the huffing and puffing.

I ignored her as I filled clips and slid them into my back pockets, the weight tugging at my pants. Grabbing the shoulder holster, I adjusted it before I added the guns and then went for the closet to grab a lightweight jacket that would still make the Miami heat unbearable but would effectively hide the weapons.

"Andre!" Nicky shouted, and I turned as I slid my arms into the jacket.

"Stop using my name like you know me."

"You have to get me out of here." She took a step forward,

and then stopped, her blue eyes striking in the sunlight inching through the blinds. "You can't leave me here. With *them*."

"All you have to do is stay in this room until I come back."

"And then?" she asked, exasperated, and I brushed past her to drag out the duffel under my bed, digging through until I found the dark zippered bag that held wads of cash.

"Then, I'll be back," I answered, counting in my head as I laid hundred dollar bills on the floor beside my boot.

"What the fuck will that do for me? Are you going to get me out of here when you come back?" Panic was creeping into her voice, desperation, and I wanted to make her stop asking questions. I wanted to shut her up, to fuck her, to hurt her. The urge was almost uncontrollable, but I needed my head on straight. Needed to not get me, or Paulo, killed during whatever-the-fuck was about to go down. He was the key out of this, and Nicky... she was just a side note. A post-script. A footnote in the history of this clusterfuck of undercover work that would probably end up with both of us dead on the wrong side of the border or at the bottom of the gulf.

"Count this," I demanded as I stood and slapped the wad of bills into her hands.

"Andre!" She called after me as I stomped into the bathroom and shut the door, leaning back against it just in time to hear her grumble and curse. My heart was racing, beating at the inside of my chest like it wanted out of this shit as bad as I did, but there was no out. No exit. No extraction.

The only way out is through. Isn't that a famous quote from some pompous white guy?

Leaning over the sink, I splashed cold water over my face, swallowing a handful and then another. As I twisted the water off, I stared into the mirror again and saw myself clearly. The monster. Guns peeking out from beneath the edges of my jacket, dark and shiny and metallic. Scruff on my cheeks, the tattoo crawling up my neck that reminded me of bitter memories that *this shit* was supposed to ease — but it was only making it worse.

Making me worse.

I wasn't good, no matter the lies I told myself. There were bruises on Nicky's wrists from my hands. I'd pinned her to the fucking table, bent her over in my goddamned bed to fuck her. I hadn't saved her. At best I'd given her a stay of execution, just held off on the inevitable until it would be that much worse when Paulo pulled my fucking strings and took her for himself just to prove he could.

And as I looked into the mirror, I saw the same empty eyes I hated in him. I knew that if it came down to it I would have to let him have her, because there was no saving either one of us.

I'd only made shit worse showing any interest in her. Giving her any hope at all.

"Andre?" A series of knocks accompanied her soft voice, and I grabbed the towel to wipe off my face before I ripped the door open.

"What."

"It's five thousand." Her delicate hand held out the stack of bills and I took them, tucking them into my front pocket as she stood there blocking the door and staring at the guns hanging against my ribs. Eventually, she blinked and looked into my eyes. "You're really leaving?"

"Want me to fuck you before I go?" I asked, nudging her out of my way as I stepped back into the room to snag my phone from the desk.

"No."

Turning around, I once again found her between me and the door. "Then get out of my way."

"What am I supposed to do while you're gone?"

"Read a book." I tilted my head toward the stack of paperbacks on the side of my desk, and then shrugged. "Or sleep. Masturbate. Meditate. I don't give a fuck as long as you lock the door after I leave."

"Why do you care if I lock the door?" she asked, her chin lifting just enough to show me that steel backbone that had helped her waltz into Paulo García's house in the first place, but it only made the darkness purr.

Striding forward, I snagged her hair and slammed her into the wall before she could react, planting my knee between her thighs so she could feel me against her. "You know that Diego is going to come for you, right?"

"*Don't*," she whimpered, and I tightened my fist in her hair to shut her up.

"The second I leave this house, he's going to come check that fucking door." Leaning down I took a deep breath of the summer sun that seemed to live in her skin. "If you want to end up under him, that's your choice. Leave the fucking door unlocked. Try and run. He'll take you on the fucking floor, and leave you bleeding until we get back so that they can pass you around until you stop fighting, until you beg them to—"

"Stop!"

"Well, you'll beg for that too, but by then you'll mostly just beg for them to kill you." I wanted to kiss her, to take her mouth, to feel her fight as I nipped her lips, her tongue, but I didn't. Releasing her, I shoved her back into the room. Then I ripped open the bedroom door, holding onto it for a second until I found the self-control to look at her again. "It's your choice."

I forced myself to step into the hallway, slamming the door, and I had barely taken a few steps before I heard the clatter of the locks sliding into place. The fact that it gave me some small amount of peace should have given me pause. It should have made me think about Nicky Harris, about what she could mean to me in some situation that was more normal than this fucking hellhole, but I didn't have that luxury. Paulo had told me to come heavy, to be ready to kill, and that was what I needed to think about.

Death. Murder. Not her soft skin, or her sweet cries, or her tight, grasping cunt.

And definitely not her bravery, her iron-clad will that had kept her alive and somehow still delicate and strong and beautiful.

Fuck.

Stomping down the stairs, I ripped the zipper up on my jacket to hide the guns. When I came to the last steps I saw José at the door talking quietly with Paulo, and when both of their eyes lifted to me I felt a chill on my skin, like death was breathing on the back of my neck.

"Ready, *cuadro?*" Paulo asked, that false smile making his lips curve upward.

"Whenever you are, *jefe*."

TEN

Nicky

──────────

I felt like I had ants crawling over my skin. A nervous, anxious energy crackling over my nerves until I found myself pacing back and forth, jumping at every creak of the house flexing in the heat and humidity.

Andre was gone, and I didn't know how to feel about that. Relieved? Afraid? Fucked in the head? He made no sense. Simultaneously terrifying, and strangely concerned for me, and still so fucking hot that I had trouble not staring at him when he stood near.

Which possibly said more about my mental state than his — but *he* was the real question.

Was Andre really the monster he seemed to be? Was he actually trying to help me? Or was he just a killer with a conscience when it came to women he wanted to fuck?

The last option seemed the most likely, and no matter what I was trapped in his fucking bedroom. Andre's room, where I'd counted out fifty of those one hundred dollar bills that he was probably handing over to Paulo at this very moment. The five thousand dollars that he'd used to pay off Christopher's debt, to buy me, to take me out of the basement, to keep me for himself.

"You're safe, sure… until Paulo wants you," I mumbled under my breath, cracking my knuckles one at a time.

You belong to me, and I belong to Paulo García. Welcome to Hell.

The door knob turned, creaking and rattling, and I stumbled back from it as it snapped back into place. Heart pounding, mouth dry, I felt my nails digging into my palms. A heavy thud against the door rattled the various locks, and then Diego's voice came through the wood. "Unlock the door, *puta*."

"No!" I shouted, and everything rattled again. Then again as he slammed his fist against it, or kicked it, and I cowered back against the blinds, hearing them clatter.

"You got the door barricaded? You think that's going to stop me?" he asked, a low laugh in his voice that made me tremble. I felt the panic clenching my chest tight, the dread settling deep like it had when I'd first realized how fucked I was standing in Paulo's sitting room.

Another hard slam against the door, and I wondered how long it would hold against a full-grown man hitting it like that. When the next hit came I slid to the floor and screamed, "STOP!"

"Just open the door."

"FUCK OFF!" I shouted, and listened as Diego attacked the door, making it shake in the frame, jarring the series of locks that made me grateful for whatever drove Andre's paranoia against these other monsters.

"I know that *maricón* Andre didn't really fuck you downstairs, but I can. I'll fuck you until you're screaming my name." The door rattled, shaking violently against the frame. "Come on, I'll even let you go when I'm done with you."

"I belong to Andre, asshole!" The words came from my panic, and I hated them even as I held them up like a shield.

"He didn't fuck you, *puta*. We both know he didn't."

"Yes, you motherfucker! He fucked me! In the basement and in here, and he'll fucking kill you if you touch me!" I was shaking, back to the wall, head against the window sill, and *that* felt true. Whether or not he'd do the same with Paulo, I couldn't say, but I'd seen the way he'd reacted to Diego touching me — and that he wouldn't allow. He'd kill him, and for once I didn't even flinch at the idea. I'd watch him destroy Diego with a fucking smile on my face.

There was no answer. No more slams of a heavy, male body against the door, and I held my breath trying to listen for noises outside the door.

Nothing.

Eventually I slumped, the tension in my chest caving in until I felt the pain of it, and I felt the tears on my cheeks before I realized I was crying. Brushing at my face I heard the first, pathetic croak of a sob and I had the urge to burn the fucking house down around me. I didn't want to be the girl crying in a room. I didn't want to be trapped. I didn't want to be afraid.

I didn't want to be *here*.

The memory of Christopher connected to all of those

tubes, the sight of his body wrapped in gauze, the swollen shape of his face that I knew well enough to know it was seriously *wrong* — it appeared behind my eyes and I still wanted to help him as another sob choked past my tightened throat. I wondered if some other goon of Paulo's was sneaking into the hospital to end him. To erase the only connection that anyone could use to find me. To kill my little brother that I'd spent my entire life trying to help, to support, to fix.

My friends had probably called my cell phone when I hadn't shown up at the bar for work last night. But how many times would they call? How many times would they swing by my apartment and knock? Would anyone even call the cops?

For the first time in years I wished my parents were still around. They'd never had much, never had *enough*, but they had still been parents. There had been birthday parties, and Thanksgiving, and Christmas, and someone to give a shit if I fell off the face of the earth. But would anyone do that now?

I shook my head, trying not to run through my friends in my head and gauge their willingness to look for me. I needed a distraction. Something to keep my mind off this nightmare.

Standing up I went for his desk chair, pulling it out and opening the laptop as I sat down. I tapped the spacebar and it woke up to a locked screen. *Of course it had a password.* This guy had six different locks on his bedroom door, why had I even thought his laptop would be unlocked?

Fucking stupid.

Swiveling back and forth I snagged the first book on the short stack of well-worn paperbacks. It was thick, a book called *'Last of the Breed'* by Louis L'Amour. A western of some kind. Setting it aside I went for the next. *'Brave New World'* by Aldous Huxley, which felt familiar, but I laid it atop the first. Then there were two by James Patterson, macho-guy action books, and finally *Harry Potter and the Sorceror's Stone.* Just seeing it on his desk made me smile, a slightly hysterical laugh creeping up my throat until it came out in a series of huffs. Andre the tattooed badass liked to read Harry Potter?

So weird.

But if he could escape into Hogwarts and a world of magic, then so could I. At least it would distract me from the real monsters roaming the house.

Andre

José was driving, and Paulo had tilted his head towards the back of the SUV for me to sit with him in the black-on-black Land Rover with custom bulletproof glass. There was no seeing into the windows in the back, and even the front windows were probably tinted darker than legal. It was a luxury fortress on twenty-two inch wheels.

As we pulled out onto the road, Paulo shifted in his seat to face me. "Do you have something for me, *cuadro?*"

I nodded, lifting my hips from the seat to grab the wad of cash from my front pocket. "Of course, *jefe.*"

Paulo took it from me, flicking through it for a second

before he tucked it into a bag between the seats. "*Gracias*, Andre. I do hope you feel she's worth the expense?"

"So far," I answered before muttering under my breath, "Mouthy little puta, though."

A low chuckle left him, but there was no humor in it. "You surprise me, *cuadro*. This Nicole Harris caught your eye quickly. She will not be a distraction, will she?"

"No, *jefe*. I don't get distracted." Something felt off, but I couldn't pinpoint it. Paulo liked to take me out on meets, but normally Diego or Marco were in the car as well. The temptation to ask a question plucked inside me, but I pushed it away. Asking questions never got me anywhere, it would be up to Paulo if he shared or not.

"I am glad. Some new opportunities have come to light, and I will need all of you at your best. I have also called in a few others." The man was glancing out the window, watching as we moved onto the highway and the engine purred.

"Who have you called in?" *That* was something I could ask.

"Luis, Samuel, and Nicolás." He waved his hand. "It is just a precaution."

"Good men." My stomach tightened with the knowledge that they would be in the house. Luis was loyal, handled a lot of the border work, but it was Samuel and Nicolás that would be the concern. A pair of brothers that were ruthless to the core.

"Yes, they are." His cold smile spread across his face as he turned to look at me again. "Do not worry, *cuadro*, I have brought my best men with me today."

"*Gracias, jefe.*" I nodded at the compliment and settled back in the seat, noticing José's eyes on me in the rearview mirror before he returned them to the road.

The uneasy feeling wasn't fading, and I couldn't figure out what it was. Some instinct, some sixth sense warning me of danger — I just couldn't tell if it was for me, or Nicky.

Almost an hour later we pulled up outside a nightclub, but José wove the large SUV into an alley that ran behind the building. I leaned forward, hand gripping the leather of the passenger seat, and shook my head as I saw the alley bend ahead. "This isn't good, *jefe*. Do we know if there's an exit to this, or is it a dead-end?"

"There's an exit on the other side. Trash pick-up for the buildings." José grinned, turning the car off as he faced me. "You look nervous."

"I don't want *jefe* trapped if the meeting goes to shit." *And I don't want to be trapped either, asshole.*

"We will be good," Paulo answered with that cold smile. "Come, we do not want to be late."

José climbed out on his side, opening Paulo's door as I stepped out and shut my door, feeling for the zipper on my jacket to ensure I could react if need be. "Guns out?" I asked Paulo as we moved toward the backdoor of the club.

"No. Just be ready if they do not like my terms."

With a nod, I watched as José unzipped his jacket, then pounded a fist on the door. I opened my jacket as well, but tucked my hands into the pockets to keep it closed over the guns. A moment later the door opened, and we moved inside.

The interior of the club was quiet, but I could hear men talking as we walked through the back halls and onto the main floor. The lights were all on, and a group of five men sat around in chairs, looking at us as we arrived. *Fuck.* With the sixth man that had brought us from the back, we were completely outnumbered. Two to one. Not good odds.

"Carlos, I am glad you found time to meet with me." Paulo walked forward, wearing those light linen pants he loved, and an off-white button down with the sleeves rolled up to his elbows. If he'd been in sandals, he'd look like he'd just walked off the beach. Every other man was dressed in darker clothes, and at least three of the men were carrying, one of them cocky enough to have the gun tucked into the front of his pants. *Idiota.* The man in the center stood and nodded, moving forward to shake Paulo's hand.

"Of course. I am always happy to meet with a business associate such as yourself," Carlos answered in a neutral tone. He snuck a glance over his shoulder to check on his men. Nervous.

Paulo didn't even tense up as he spread his arms. "What do you say we start with a drink? I hear such good things about your club from my men."

"*Si*, that sounds good." Snapping his fingers, Carlos gestured at one of his men. "Manuel, get us some tequila and glasses for everyone. Top shelf."

The asshole with the gun in the front of his pants stood, showing off a gold grill on his front teeth as he smirked. "Sure thing, boss."

"You said you wanted to meet in person. May I ask why?" Carlos settled into a chair.

Paulo took the seat across from him, rapping his knuckles on the table. "I had some things to discuss that I do not like to discuss over the phone."

He continued to tap his knuckles on the table. Slowly. *Thump… thump… thump.*

"Is— is there a problem?" The club owner asked, and the slight waver in his voice betrayed the answer. He knew why Paulo was here, which meant someone was going to die.

I glanced over at José, and the man inclined his chin just enough to confirm that I was right. The man may be a bastard, but I knew he'd have my back if, or when, shit went south. He'd done it before, and the pussy back at the house didn't factor into situations like this.

Paulo laughed softly as Manuel returned with a bottle of tequila under his arm, and four glasses in each hand, his fingers stuck inside them to hold on. "*Gracias,*" Paulo said as the man set it all down, but Paulo took the tequila before he could pour.

Manuel stepped back behind his boss, watching as Paulo poured an inch or more of the amber liquid into each of the glasses. I hadn't had a drink all day, and so when Paulo tilted his head for us to come over, I readily snagged one from the table, using the opportunity to take a position behind Paulo, leaning against the rail overlooking the empty dancefloor.

We were one glass short, and another man had walked over to the bar to get a glass for himself, which Paulo filled like the perfect fucking host — even though he wasn't the host, and definitely wasn't generous. When he was nice like this, it was dangerous.

He leaned back in his seat, taking a sip of the tequila, and as if Paulo's movements had given everyone permission we all followed suit. "Ah, this is good Carlos. *Muy bueno. Gracias.*"

"*De nada*, Paulo. I am grateful for our partnership, my club is doing very well." The man's thumb was running over the rim of the glass, back and forth, a subconscious nervous tick he probably wasn't even aware of. But if I had noticed it, so had Paulo.

"Yes, I am also grateful. We do good business here, and your men have served our mutual interests well for years." Paulo tilted his head, still relaxed against the back of his chair. "Which is why I wanted to have this conversation in person."

"And… what conversation is this?" Carlos asked.

Paulo took another drink. "One I wish I did not have to have with you, Carlos, but… the numbers simply do not add up."

"Numbers?"

"*Si*. You know that I pay attention to the movement of my product, to the debts owed to me." As he spoke, Paulo glanced back at me, and I felt a cold pit form in my stomach. "Unfortunately, your club has shown some… discrepancies."

"I'm sure there has been some kind of mistake, Paulo. I would never—"

"Never steal from me?" Paulo asked, and everyone in the

room tensed except for him. His voice was still soft, unerringly calm.

"Steal? No, Paulo. No, no, no." Carlos shook his head, sitting up in his chair. "We accept the product from you, we sell it on the premises, and we pay you. On time. Every dime, every month."

"This was true, until six months ago." Lifting his glass, Paulo took another sip, finishing the tequila so he could reach for more. Refilling his own, he added more to Carlos' even though the man still had plenty. With a smile on his face, he turned and offered it to me. I took the bottle, poured, and passed it along. Paulo laughed low. "I did not want to damage our business relationship, and so I waited to see if it was a, let's say, *accidental* error."

"I'm sure—"

Paulo raised his hand to cut Carlos off. "Unfortunately, while the errors were small at first, last month they were more substantial. I'm sure you understand that a ten-thousand-dollar mistake is one I cannot afford to ignore. If I let your operation get away with something like that,"— he shrugged—"what would the rest of my business partners think?"

"Paulo—"

The sharp snap of his hand slamming flat onto the table cut Carlos off once again. "They might think I was weak. They might think that they could take advantage of me as well, take advantage of the business relationship we have cultivated. I'm sure you understand why *that* is something I simply cannot allow."

"I swear to you, Paulo. I will look into this, I will identify who has betrayed your trust, *my* trust. It will be dealt with." Carlos leaned forward on the table, nodding as he continued. "They will die, *patrón*."

"There is no need to look into it. I already know who among your men has been selling my product on the side for his own profit." Paulo snapped his fingers, and José drew his gun, which caused me and each of Carlos' men to do the same.

"Wait, wait, *por favor*." Carlos lifted his hands, gesturing to his men, and for the moment every gun was aimed at the floor — but that didn't mean a thing. Anyone with experience could lift and fire in a breath.

"José, if you will?" Paulo spoke steadily, still so calm, so steady, and José walked around the table to grab one of Carlos' men by the collar, pressing his gun against the base of his skull as he jerked him away from the group to stand beside the table. The others twitched, but no one intervened.

"Fuck you, this is bullshit. I haven't done anything." The man's eyes were wide, his hands raised to his shoulders, gun loose in his hand. José reached over and disarmed him, setting the gun on the table in front of Paulo.

The weight of the weapon in my hands was a comfort, but Paulo was still too exposed. Facing four men with guns. Carlos seemed panicked, and he shook his head. "*Por favor, patrón*, Francisco would not do this. He is loyal to me. I knew his father."

"Francisco?" Paulo asked, tapping his glass against the table in a patient rhythm. "Do you have something to say?"

"Yeah, I didn't do shit. I wouldn't steal from Carlos or the club. I'm no traitor." Francisco's chin was lifted, bold and full of machismo.

"*Por favor*, let me speak with him, find out what has happened. I know we can make this right." Carlos was begging, but I already knew that there was nothing that would satisfy Paulo except for blood.

"You want to hear it from his lips? Okay." Paulo snapped his fingers again. "Andre, talk to the man."

Cold poured through my veins, a dark, chilling ichor that tainted me from the inside out. I put my gun back in the holster and pulled my jacket off. No need to hide the weapons now. Clenching my fists, I felt my knuckles pop just before I tilted my neck and felt the vertebrae do the same.

Francisco looked me over and raised his hands. "Hey, hey, this wasn't me!"

I shut him up with a hard right hook, and he almost stumbled, but José had him. Gun hand in the man's short hair, the other fisting the back of his button-down shirt. Without waiting, I landed a left hook as soon as he was upright. Francisco spit out blood, cursing through the pain.

"Carlos! This wasn't me!" He continued to plead his case, as I brought my fist into his stomach, and José let the man fold over before ripping him back up by his hold on the shirt. There was a retching, groaning noise, and I silently hoped he wouldn't hurl all over my shoes.

"Paulo, I can handle this internally."

"You should have been watching the numbers, Carlos. It should have been handled five months ago." The cold voice behind me held no mercy, and I waited for his command as Francisco breathed hard, spitting again. "But, since I had to come out here to handle it myself, my men will make sure it is done right."

"I didn't do *shit!*" Francisco shouted as he wavered back upright, sniffing hard as he stared past me to glare at Paulo.

"Find the man a chair, José." Paulo commanded, and José leaned back to drag a chair over and force Francisco into it. "Help him be comfortable."

"Yes, *jefe*," José answered with a dangerous grin, and he pulled out a pair of handcuffs from his jacket pocket, bending Francisco forward enough to drag his hands behind his back. The man struggled, shouting and cursing about his innocence, but I brought my fist back and hit him again so that José could get his wrists cuffed behind his back. The hit was a dull ache across my knuckles, but I barely felt it as I went cold, let the darkness swallow me whole.

"Ready to confess?" Paulo asked, casually sipping his tequila as I watched him, looking for his direction.

"Fuck you!" Francisco shouted, but I didn't move.

"Andre, if you will."

"Yes, *jefe*." Turning, I waited for José to get a grip on the man's shoulder, his gun hand back in Francisco's hair to lift his head upright. Then I hit him, feeling the impact of his cheekbone in my fist and the ache continued to fade as I focused. Another hit to the stomach, then the other side of his face, this time across the jaw.

Francisco shouted in pain, grunting, but he just spat out

the blood as José pulled him upright again. The look he gave me was a challenge, a silent promise that I wouldn't make him crack.

Over the next thirty minutes, I hit him until he'd lost a few teeth, and his face had become a swollen, bloody mess. The hits to his sides had probably cracked a few ribs, if not straight up broken one or two by the rough sound of his breathing. Paulo had asked a few more times, but the man had only muttered curses and insults.

My knuckles were split in spots, reddened and angry, but I hit much harder than José. He didn't have my build, my weight to put behind it. *This was the kind of shit Nathan didn't want to know about.*

"Francisco…" Paulo sighed and stood. He placed a fresh glass of tequila in my hands, and I took a drink, watching the smears of blood mar the outside of the glass as I finished it off and welcomed the burn into the swirling black inside me. "You have a daughter, yes?"

Francisco jerked, looking up with his one good eye, the other already swollen shut.

"She is eleven. Very pretty, or so I'm told." Paulo grabbed the man's chin as his head wobbled, lifting until he met his stare. "I know you don't want anything to happen to her… and so many bad things could happen to her. And your wife."

"Boss!" Manuel spoke up from behind.

Carlos raised his hand fast. "*Cállate*, Manuel," he ordered, jaw clenched tight as he told his man to shut up. He watched Francisco with empty eyes as the man shook his head over and over, pulling free of Paulo's grip.

"No, *por favor*, don't hurt them. It was me, it was." Garbled words, but we all heard them.

Paulo wiped his bloody fingers on the traitor's shirt and stepped back, locking those coal black eyes on me as he nodded slightly. Then he returned to his seat, and I hit Francisco hard. He almost fell out of the chair, would have if José hadn't held him in place.

"See?" Paulo said. "He stole from me, and from *you*, Carlos."

"Don't hurt my little girl…" Francisco's words were slurred, altered by the mess that his mouth had become. "Or Anna, *por favor*."

"Where is the money?" Carlos asked, a coldness to his tone that made me aware of how he would have handled the situation if he had truly known.

"It's gone. I—" Groaning, sloppily spitting out more blood and drool, he let out a pathetic sound. "I sent it to my mamá in Cuba. She needed it, boss. Was going to lose her house. Carlos, *por favor*, give me a chance. I'll get you the money back. I'll do whatever you want!"

Ending on a shout, it was clear he was looking past me to Paulo now, pleading with the man really in charge. I set the blood smeared glass on the table and shook out my hands, waiting for Paulo's order.

"*If* that's true, I understand why you did it, Francisco." Paulo sounded empathetic, which was impossible. It was fake, a blatant lie, but the poor fucking idiot in front of me still looked up with hope in his good eye. "But you can't steal from me. The others need to know that. Do you understand?"

I watched as the reality of death settled inside him, for a moment he cried, cursing as he slammed his shoe onto the smooth, black concrete under him. Then he nodded, tongue running over his split lip. "*Sí*, I understand. Just… just please don't hurt my family. They didn't know, I swear, they didn't know, *patrón*."

"Twenty-three thousand dollars' worth of product, Francisco." Paulo sighed. "I may have let you live for less, let you earn it back, but this I cannot forgive. You have a choice to make."

I glanced up at José to see him grinning, holding Francisco's head up as he twisted in the handcuffs. I should have felt something, but all I could feel was the cold darkness that filled me up. The emptiness that told me what was coming before Paulo even spoke.

"You can choose death, and Andre will shoot you in the stomach. Let you bleed out on the floor here in front of Carlos and the others. It will be *very* painful, *cabrón*." Paulo took a slow breath. "Or, you can choose to sell Anna and Luisa to me, and I will make my money back that way. I'm assuming Luisa is still young enough to be a virgin, yes?"

Francisco stiffened, rage making him jerk against José's hold on him, but he was too weak to get out of the chair. "Don't touch them!" he shouted, breaths strained from the pain of his ribs and the blood in his mouth.

"Your choice?" Paulo asked, voice as calm and steady as ever.

There was a low whining groan from the man, and José let him buckle forward as he started crying. Almost everyone broke at the end. I could count on one hand the number of men who had faced death without pleading, without crying. Most of those didn't have a family though.

Francisco sniffed hard, sucking his bloodied lip between his teeth for a moment before he forced himself upright and stared at Carlos. "I'm sorry, boss. I swear, I never meant for this to happen. Please, *por favor*, tell Anna I'm sorry. Don't tell her what I did. Let her think it was an accident, something Luisa can live with."

"I will, but I will not support them for you. You betrayed me, *traidor*." Traitor. Carlos' tone was cold, and I knew I should feel for the woman and her child, but I was too far in to react like a human.

"Andre," Paulo said my name, and it was an order. An order to kill. Not the first time, and not the last. For some reason, as I drew my gun, I saw Nicky in my head. I couldn't refuse. Refusal would mean death for me, and then they'd have her. All of them.

I'd never had something to live for before, but the idea of going back to her, of hearing her cries against my ear as I buried my cock inside her… that was worth living for. Worth killing for. What was one more mark on my ruined soul anyway?

I pointed the gun at his stomach, just like Paulo wanted, and flipped the safety off. Francisco drew himself up as much as he could, fighting the pain in his broken ribs, and I stared into his bloodied, swollen face — and pulled the trigger.

The *boom* of the shot echoed off the high ceilings and all that concrete, and there were several low sounds from Carlos' men. José showed no expression, he just let him go, let him tumble from the chair to the floor as Francisco curled around the wound, groaning in pain.

"I can trust that there will be no further issues with the numbers, Carlos." Paulo was staring at the other man whose eyes were glued to the dying man on the floor.

"There will be no issues, patrón. I will monitor it personally from now on."

"*Bueno.*" Clapping his hands together, Paulo turned with that cold smile and nodded. "Thank you for the tequila. I will leave you to decide what to do with the body."

Paulo walked around Francisco's writhing form, and José fell into step beside him, but I kept my gun out, walking backwards until I was sure Paulo was securely in the hall. Only then did I turn and catch up with them, exiting out the back into the sweltering midday heat.

The SUV was boiling when we climbed inside, the leather hot enough to bleed through the denim of my jeans, and I felt sweat breaking out all over my skin. None of it could touch the cold core inside me though, that empty black that filled me as I added another death to the tainted weight of my soul.

José cranked the air conditioning as we settled into our seats, and I dragged the seatbelt across me on automatic. Barely aware of the low words he said as he guided us around the end of the alley and out the other side. There was an exit. Bright sunlight, blue skies, and traffic.

"*Gracias, cuadro*. You did well." Paulo spoke low, nodding at me with a slight smile. "I knew I brought the right men to deal with this issue."

"*De nada, jefe*," I replied. *It's nothing.* Nothing to beat a man, nothing to take a life. What bothered me more than anything was that I wasn't sure if I felt any guilt or remorse at all, or if I was just thinking of how I *should* feel something. Francisco would be dead soon. Carlos wouldn't dare seek medical attention for him, and he'd probably end up in the swamps, or the gulf — but as I clenched my bloody fists, I felt nothing. Nothing except an urge to get my hands on Nicky again, so that I could feel something as I fucked her. Something to placate the darkness, and she was innocent enough to be the perfect outlet for all of the evil inside me.

ELEVEN

Nicky

I was lost in the magical world of Harry Potter when I heard a heavy fist on the door, and my stomach dropped. *Had Diego come back?* Sitting up on Andre's bed, my heart pounded against the inside of my chest at a much more rapid pace than the second round of knocks.

"Nicky, open the door." It was Andre's voice, and I shoved a scrap of paper I'd found into the book to mark my place and left it on the bedside table before moving to the door. I fumbled with shaking hands through the locks, but finally opened it and he pushed both me and the door aside as he walked in. I caught the masculine scent of sweat and the outside as he brushed past, but managed to shut the door tight as soon as he was inside. Redoing all of the locks.

"What happened?" I asked, but Andre was silent. Removing his guns to set them on the top of the dresser beside his closet. Then the jacket came off, and then the holster thing that wrapped across his back and chest to keep the guns against his ribs. "Andre?"

When he turned around, I stumbled backward until my legs hit the bed behind me. He looked like he had the day before, when I was caught in that fucking chair, waiting for Paulo to decide my fate. Empty, dark brown eyes, a frightening expression on his face that sent fear thrumming through me.

He didn't look human.

"Andre?" I repeated, voice wavering, and he stalked forward. So tall, so broad, and when he grabbed onto my waist I flinched. He squeezed hard, pinching my skin before he ripped my shirt over my head, forcing me to duck my head through the hole as he tossed it aside. I couldn't even react because his hands were already at my shorts, the button popped free and the zipper down. Then he grabbed me under the arms and tossed me onto the bed hard so he could roughly yank the shorts free.

Fuck. What was wrong with him?

I was afraid. No other reaction was really appropriate as he planted one knee on the end of the bed, and I scrambled backward but he caught my ankle and yanked me flat. He was still clothed, sweaty and silent and terrifying. "Don't hurt me," I whispered.

Something in his expression faltered, but then his eyes dropped to my chest and he grabbed my shoulder to jerk me onto my side so he could undo the clasp of my bra. He tossed it aside, immediately palming my breasts as he straddled one of my thighs. Thumbs rolling over my nipples, I could barely process that they were already hard and peaked before I felt him tighten his grip and pinch them both.

"FUCK!" I screamed, whimpering as the pain shot like

bolts of lightning through my breasts, forcing my back to arch in an effort to ease the strain. But Andre didn't back off, he twisted them further and I felt tears in my eyes, grabbing onto his arms and digging my nails in as if it would make him stop.

Leaning over me, he bit down on my shoulder and I screamed again, pleading with him to stop, pushing at his ribs as he released my tender nipples — and then he had both his legs between mine. Spreading me, digging his knees into my thighs so I had no way to stop him, but I could barely focus as his teeth pressed in harder.

"Please, please, please!" I begged, whining when he finally took a breath and released me, his dark eyes staring at the place his mouth had just been. Then he looked between us, and he growled like an animal as he grabbed my panties, tearing the pale blue fabric, biceps bulging from the effort. The fabric burned against my hips as he ripped it, yanking the remnants out from under me so he could throw them aside. "Andre?"

His name didn't seem to affect him at all as he slid his fingers between my legs, forcing two of them into me where I wasn't wet in the least. I cried out and lifted my hips off the bed, but he ran his thumb over my clit as his mouth moved to my breast, sucking on the tender bud as he stroked me below. For a minute, every shift of his fingers seemed to burn and ache, and then my body finally caught up, lubricating around his harsh touch. There was pleasure and pain as he opened me up, warming my body for what I knew would come next. It was almost cruel how deft his touch was, the way his thumb swirled over my clit, his mouth sucking and nipping at my breast, sending zings of sensation through my body.

I wanted to fight, and I didn't. I wanted to give in, and I wanted him to take me by force.

Thought was something I couldn't effectively manage as he stroked his fingers in and out, wetting them as I grew slick, as my whimpers turned to moans. Then he grabbed my thighs and bent them towards my chest, staring down at my open pussy with the look of a desperate, dangerous man.

I was afraid to speak, afraid to struggle against his strength as he tucked my heels over his shoulders and opened his jeans to shove the fabric out of the way and free his cock. I had stared yesterday, but in this position he somehow seemed larger, especially as he moved closer to my entrance, erection bobbing at his hips. Watching him wrap one fist around it, I opened my mouth to argue, but he lined up and drove home hard, stealing the words away as I cried out.

It was painful, the sudden, brutal stretch as he bottomed out in one thrust. With my body bent he slammed even deeper on his second drive, and I felt the sharp ache as he hit my cervix, tears burning my eyes. "Please," I whimpered, reaching past my legs to dig my nails into his arms, but there was no reaction.

Andre braced his hands on either side of my ribs, folding me as he used every inch of power in his body to fuck me. It hurt, it felt good, and I couldn't think straight as he continued to move. My breaths were short, a consequence of my ribs being compressed, and that wasn't helping the dizzying effects of his thrusts. Pleasure blurred the aches and pains, made me forget the threat of the man above me as I sank into it.

Soon, I was crying out, moaning, saying his name even though I knew this was wrong. Everything about this situation was wrong. This house, the fact that he'd paid for me, the fact that… "Condom!" I shouted as his breaths shortened and my mind cleared enough for me to remember that he hadn't put one on as he'd climbed atop me.

That seemed to make him shudder, and he slammed deep once more and growled, a low, feral noise that made me whimper. When he spit on his fingers, I was confused for half a second, until he pulled out and began to rub my asshole.

"NO!" My scream didn't mean anything, especially when I tried to twist free of him, and his other hand dug furrows into my thigh, painfully gripping me as he bent me further.

He shoved two fingers deep in my pussy, gliding along my g-spot as I shuddered, and then he pulled back to press one of them against my ass. I squirmed, flexed my legs to try and force him back, but he dropped his body weight against me and I buckled just as his finger forced past my tight ring.

"AH! DON'T!" The shock was worse than the pain, but he only stroked a few times before his second finger was working its way inside my ass, and the dull ache spread. My quiet pleas ignored by the monster above me.

Shifting again, he pulled his fingers free and planted that hand against the bed so he could guide his cock to me with the other. I shook my head, I tried to struggle, to fight as he pushed himself against the ring of muscle — but he was too strong. With a sharp pain he was inside me, sinking deeper as he groaned above me, and I couldn't speak, couldn't scream as the burn intensified. "Yessss," he growled as his hips met my ass.

He was inside me, fucking my ass, and I whimpered because I'd only tried anal once before with a boyfriend. It hadn't gone well, I'd cried and made him stop, but that wasn't an option now. Andre wasn't going to back down. His hips pulled back, and then slammed forward, making me squeak. *Don't...* I wanted to tell him to stop. I'd rather have him come inside me than this, but I couldn't get the words past my lips.

Nothing was working, nothing except my body as it fired the sensations of pain and fullness as he stretched my ass with each new thrust.

Andre

I heard her scream, but surged forward anyways. Her ass was so tight, only growing tighter with each pain-filled cry, and I didn't even have to hold her down. The girl's calves were over my shoulders, pinned in place by my weight, by each thrust as I forced my way into her ass.

Delirium.

I wasn't thinking straight, wasn't thinking clearly at all. She'd been the one to shout out about the condom, and it had been the first rational thought I'd had since she'd opened the door and I'd seen her again. Immediately, I'd felt the urge to take her, possess her, but the weight of the guns and the extra clips had held me back. I needed them off, I didn't want to kill her. I'd done enough killing, I needed something else.

Escape. Control. Satisfaction.

That's what her body was — satisfying. As I sank in, I felt the darkness purr. It swelled, blocking out anything resembling morality. I'd tried to warm her up, but my tingling balls and aching cock were impatient. The darkness was hungry, and I knew I'd started fucking her ass before she was ready, but a part of me reveled in the pained expression on her face. The quiet squeaks of agony as her nails bit into my arms, digging in, making me want to slam into her harder. So, I did, and she screamed.

Beautiful. Belleza.

There would be no doubts in anyone listening in the house, she'd screamed loud enough for everyone to hear, and I slid back and forward again just to replicate it, but she only whimpered. Tears tracking across her nose with her head turned to the side.

This is wrong.

The black inside me rumbled, waves crashing, and I leaned down to kiss her throat, keeping still inside her as I nipped and licked my way to her shoulder and then to her breast. Sucking her nipple into my mouth, flicking the hard bud and drawing on it until she squeezed my cock and moaned softly. My hips jerked against her ass on instinct, and she yelped, but I shifted my weight to one hand so I could reach between us and find her clit. It took me a few rubs before I felt the hardened nub, but the bucking of her body confirmed I'd hit the right spot and I honed in on it. Switching to her other breast as I worked her and continued to move my hips, feeling the tight grip of her ass as she whimpered and started to moan.

"That's it," I whispered, growling as she leveraged my

shoulders to lift her hips into my cock and fingers. It took every shredded scrap of my concentration to focus on rubbing her clit as I moved in her ass, thrusting again and again, but her muffled cries of pleasure were worth it.

She made the best noises.

I wanted to make this last, to make the distraction stretch into the infinite, but my balls tightened and lightning stroked up my spine, sending heat mirroring downward in response, and I came deep inside. Everything disappeared, whited out, the world evaporating for a glorious moment of pure bliss — pure escape.

Her whimpers drew me out of my haze, my weight crushing her legs to her chest, and I clumsily pushed myself up, cock slipping free of her ass as I rolled myself to the side. I laid out beside her, breathing hard, hearing her groaning and panting as I tried to return to reality.

"Did you come?" I asked, and she shifted on the bed but didn't respond. "Answer me, Nicky."

"No," she grumbled, and it was a prick to my pride. Grabbing her thigh, I turned her on the bed, and she gasped as I ran my tongue over her pussy. Swollen, red, she was soaking wet now and still needy. I could feel her desperation as I flicked over her clit, hips bucking, her sweet whines louder when I pulled my mouth away.

"Beg."

"What?" she asked, more anger than pleasure in her tone, but I was sated and content to wait her out.

"Beg me to make you come, *belleza*." Speaking the words directly against the golden down between her thighs, I leaned forward and breathed in the scent of her. It made me salivate. She smelled like sex, all female wetness, but I wanted her to ask for it.

"You hurt me," she whined, accusing, and I nodded, nuzzling her clit with my nose but not offering my tongue.

"Yes, I did." Burying my face against her cunt, I let the scruff on my chin scrape over her sensitive parts, and her hips jerked, but I forced her to be still, digging my fingers in at her hips. "Now, beg me to make you feel good."

"You're an asshole," Nicky growled, fists clenched in the sheets on either side of her, breasts aimed to the ceiling as her back arched off the bed.

"So?" I chuckled. "Do you want to come or not?"

Just as I flicked my tongue against her clit, she hissed and nodded. "YES! I want to come!"

"Then beg," I demanded, already salivating at the movement of her sweet hips against my grip. She had the slightest softness to her belly, enough weight on her hips that I'd been able to squeeze her flesh, and now all those curves were writhing above me. Another delicate flick of my tongue and she buckled.

"PLEASE! Andre, please, just… just do it. You had me, please?" Nicky pleaded, whining as her hips twitched, seeking my mouth, and I almost wished I hadn't come already, just to feel her cunt reaching for my cock. But, having her desperate was fun either way. The darkness inside me seemed to abate as I licked between her thighs, swallowing her wetness as she moaned and whimpered. When I sucked on her clit she jerked off the bed, pushing up onto her elbows for a moment, cursing and crying out.

It was perfect.

I strained to remember which fingers I'd shoved into her ass, and then remembered so that I could bury the other hand between her thighs and focus my mouth on her clit. Two fingers, then three, and she was practically screaming her pleasure to the house. How long had it been since I'd had a woman like this? Something more than a drunken one-night-stand? I wasn't sure on the timeline and didn't care as she started to twitch her hips, writhing, whining. The time didn't matter, because I still remembered how to bring a woman over the edge. Curving to match my fingers to the place where my tongue focused, she jerked, thighs squeezing at my shoulders, and then she shouted and came hard.

Body shuddering, legs spreading, feet planted to lift her cunt to my mouth, I rode out her orgasm as her liquid heat pooled against my fingers. Licking, stroking, slowing down until she was twitching and satisfied — as sated as my dick was. I wanted to make her come again, but I was dizzy and my own orgasm had caught up to me. Giving her one last long lick as I slid my fingers free, I turned her on the bed so she was laying the right way and then moved beside her.

"Good girl," I mumbled, drawing her against my front as she panted, breathing hard, and I licked my lips, savoring the taste of her.

It was some time later when my heart had stopped racing, and I roused from my half-asleep state to take a deep breath of the tangled hair in my face. *Nicky*. My innocent warrior, my brave Valkyrie, *mine*. Pulling her closer to me, I buried my face against her neck and nipped her flesh before I kissed her soft skin. Licking over the fading imprint of my teeth in her shoulder, which would definitely bruise.

She squirmed, making quiet sounds in her sleep, and I propped my head up so I could look down at her. We were still on top of the sheets, but the air conditioning wasn't strong enough to make us cold with the afternoon Miami sun battering at the windows. Stroking along her side, keeping my touch light, it took a few minutes for my actions to catch up with me. But it wasn't the beating or the murder that weighed on me… it was what I'd done to her.

Nicky hadn't signed up to be in my bed, had never agreed to choose me over the other monsters in the house. No, I had chosen for her. I had decided I was a better option for this golden skinned beauty. My *belleza*. *Mine*. The word echoed in my head again, and I felt the sickening pit in my stomach as I recalled Paulo's addendum to our agreement. Yeah, I could have her, I could keep her from everyone else in the house, and any of the men he was bringing in — but I couldn't keep her from him.

Fuck.

I hadn't thought of anything but touching her on the long ride home. Knuckles bloody, the smell of gunpowder on my hands, and I'd gone straight for her. Didn't even wash my hands before I climbed the stairs to seek her out. As I looked her over, I could see blurred smears of red on her thighs, her hips, her breasts… all from me. I'd tainted her, and I needed to wash it away. Needed to wash it off of me.

Leaning down, I tilted her face towards me so I could kiss her softly. Nibbling her lower lip, I felt her wake, the twitch of her body as she curved towards me, leaning into my mouth for just a moment, but then she jerked back.

Her blue eyes would have singed me if she'd had the ability to turn that glare into fire, but she didn't, and so I simply sighed. "*Hola, belleza.*"

Twisting away from me, she gained a few inches as she turned onto her back, but it only gave me an excellent view of her naked body. The death glare didn't change though. "Is this how it's going to be?" she asked, and I felt my stomach tighten.

"Nicky…"

"Don't say my name like you know me," she snapped, throwing my words back in my face.

"You're beautiful," I replied without thinking, landing my hand on her thigh as she bent her knees and brought them together.

"Is that supposed to make me feel better?" Shifting her gaze, she grabbed at my hand and pried it off her leg, but she didn't let go. "And what the fuck did you do this morning?"

"What I was told to."

Her expression tightened, tension etching a furrow between her brows, and then she brushed her thumbs just below my bruised, split knuckles. "Paulo made you do this?"

"I work for him," I answered, trying to end the discussion, but she tightened her grip on my hand as I attempted to pull it away.

"And, what? You went and beat someone up for him?"

The truth weighed heavy on me, on my fucked up soul, and I confessed to her like it could somehow ease me. "Yes, and then I shot them. Killed them for him."

Nicky jerked, her reaction one of shock and confusion and a hint of concern. "You *killed* someone? This morning?"

"Yes," I answered, unable to lie to her about it, and I found myself leaning forward to capture her mouth — and she let me. The kiss was rough, messy, but still perfect. Her warm lips parted and our tongues met in a clash, the softest of moans rumbling up her throat until I could feel the buzz as I pulled her closer. It was good, too good for someone like me.

Then she broke the kiss, exhaling against my lips. "Are—are you going to kill me?" she asked softly, the hint of fear in her tone sending a dark, twisted thrill through my veins.

"I don't want to."

"But…" Nicky licked her lips, drawing her bottom lip between her teeth for a moment, those sweet blue eyes pleading with me to lie to her. "But you will? If Paulo tells you to?"

Burying my face against her shoulder, I pulled her harder against me, breathing in the summer scent of her hair. "I don't want to," I repeated, because I had killed this morning at his word, and Nathan had already told me that one girl's life didn't matter to him. Didn't matter to the department. The only thing that mattered was Paulo, and his connections in South America. He was the highest point on the food chain in Florida, and unless I could take him down, there was no way in hell they were pulling Nicky out. One sweet, innocent, warrior-like girl didn't matter to them, but she *did* matter, and I wouldn't feed her false hope.

"I just… I only wanted to save Chris," she whispered, and I felt her shudder as she stifled her tears. On instinct I wrapped my arms around her, pulled her tight to my chest. All of those soft curves conforming to my hard edges as she started to cry.

"I know, *belleza*," I whispered, but I couldn't offer any other assurances. I had pulled the only string I had, and Nathan had told me no. The only hope I had was that, eventually, everyone in the house might stop caring about her and I could take her outside without an argument. Let her go, let her be free… even if I never could be.

TWELVE

Nicky

_____

Standing in the warm shower with Andre was an odd, soothing experience. His hands expertly slid over me, gliding the soap into every nook and cranny, not leaving anything to chance, and as I braced my hands on the tile I wasn't sure I could really challenge him. Part of me craved his touch, the gentle, soothing strokes of his palms over my soaped flesh... but the other part wanted to shove him away, scream and rail at him until he left me alone.

I felt better when I plucked the soap from his hands and returned the favor. Gliding the stiff soap over all of his hard muscles, feeling his chest and the ridges in his abs, slipping my fingers between his thighs to move the suds over his cock and balls. His soft groan had me hiding a smile in my wet hair. Even flaccid he was impressive, which made me wonder how I'd ever taken him into my ass. Every inch of him was muscular and intimidating. So much of his chest, neck, back, and arms covered in ink.

Dragging my thumb over a scar across his ribs, I looked up at him and broke the stoic silence. "What is this?"

"A scar."

"I know that. What's it from?" I asked, running my hands across his back, pulling him closer even though I wasn't completely sure I wanted it. The dull sound of the shower filled the silence for a moment as he closed his eyes, and then opened them to stare down at me.

"It was a knife. Someone pulled one in a fight, cut me to the bone. Twenty-two stitches."

I couldn't help but gawk at him, my eyes glued to the long scar over his ribs, extending over the top of his ripped abs. "But you survived," I whispered, using his word from the day before, and his hand cupped my chin to make me look at him.

"Yes, I did. The *pinche pendejo* didn't stab me, he cut at me, but I killed him." Andre had a slight tilt to his lips, a hint of pride, and then he shrugged. "And pain is just pain."

"Is that why you do all of this? Because you don't care about pain?" I kept my eyes on him as he flinched a little, those dark brown eyes averting for a moment as he shifted me under the showerhead.

"I do what I have to do, *belleza*. Right now, I need to wash your hair." Without another word, Andre leaned away to snag a bottle from the corner of the tub. I couldn't deny the pleasant sensations as he turned me around and started to shampoo my scalp, working the lather to the ends of my hair before sliding back up. He massaged, fingers digging in to relieve the tension at my temples, caressing the base of my skull until I felt my body turn to liquid.

"That feels so good," I murmured, and he huffed.

"*Bueno*." When he shifted me again, putting my head under

the stream of water, he was sure to brush the water back, washing the suds from my hair, squeezing as he went, and after a few movements he tugged me out of the stream. Pressed against the tile, I could only open my mouth and breathe in the steam as he looked down at me. So much taller than me, so muscular and broad, I didn't understand why he'd chosen me. I was no one special, not very interesting, and I came with the baggage of my little brother so most men didn't bother with more than a fuck. Yet, Andre hadn't just fucked me — he'd paid off my debt, protected me, kept me from the others.

And hurt you.

My head focused in on the pain. How rough he was, the way he bit and hurt me over and over, and I couldn't deny how much the assfucking had hurt… but he'd also made me come, held me as I cried, kissed me softly, and now he was gently showering me like we were lovers. It was confusing, and weird, and there was no way I could make sense of it.

The whole situation was mad.

"Do you hate me?" I whispered, and his hands froze as they glided across my waist, his body keeping me against the wall.

"No…" Andre caught my chin again, forcing my face up so I looked at him. "Why do you think I hate you?"

"Because of… how you were before. Because I showed up and yelled at your boss, caused issues… and because I cost you five grand." The weight of that debt settled on me, and regardless of how many times he'd fucked me, regardless of everything he'd done, I still felt like I owed him. *How fucked is that?*

Andre's lips tilted into almost a smile. "I don't hate you. Actually, I'm enjoying myself, *belleza*. I can't control everyone else, or what they do, but I can make sure I enjoy *you*, and I can try to make you enjoy it too."

Because I don't have a choice in the matter.

"Right." Swallowing, I pulled my chin out of his grip and nudged him back to step to the other end of the tub. "I'll get out while you finish your shower."

"Nicky—" He caught my hand as my other reached for the shower curtain. For a moment we just stared at each other, and then he clenched his jaw and let me go. "Don't leave the room."

"I'm not an idiot," I muttered as I stepped out, snagging the towel from the rack. "You've only got one towel out here, by the way."

"There's more in the left cabinet under the sink." A low chuckle echoed from inside the shower. "And I'm not so sure you're as smart as you think you are, *belleza*."

Rubbing my skin dry, I glared at the shower curtain. "You're an asshole."

His laugh was a little louder. "You were the one that stormed into Paulo García's house like a fucking Valkyrie. Not many people would call that smart."

"And you fucked me without a condom. How smart are you?" His silence had my anger snapping back, all of the soothing caresses evaporating from my mind. "I swear, if you gave me any kind of—"

"I'm clean," he answered in a rough tone, all of his laughter gone.

A frustrated scream escaped me as I stomped out of the bathroom, shouting over my shoulder, "Yeah, sure, Andre. I believe that, because I have so many reasons to fucking trust you!"

Scrubbing at my hair, squeezing as much of the water out as I could with the towel, I stared at the ripped scraps of my underwear on the floor. The memory of the rough way he'd taken me on the bed, of the pleasure and the pain... it brought back the tingling heat between my thighs, but the anger I felt was inextricably wound up in it.

I heard the water turn off, and the metal scrape as he yanked the shower curtain back. Wrapping the towel around me, I listened as he slammed the cabinet door, and then he stepped out of the bathroom, rubbing the towel over all that gorgeous, toned flesh. *Fuck, he's hot.*

And a total bastard.

"You don't have to trust me, but I didn't lie about that. I get tested because I'm *not* an idiot." He growled. "And not using a condom was a mistake I won't repeat."

Rolling my eyes, I muttered under my breath, trying to bite my tongue and ignore the way his muscles moved under the ink on his skin.

"Want to yell at me some more?" he asked, and I actually did, but his tone was dangerous. Borderline threatening.

"You ruined my underwear."

"You don't need underwear." Andre rubbed the towel over his hair, leaving all of his skin on display. I shouldn't have stared, *definitely* shouldn't have stared at his cock, but I couldn't stop myself.

He was a walking, talking, seriously attractive specimen of pure alpha male. In another life he could have been some kind of model. A scary one... maybe for motorcycles or something.

Get your head on straight, Nicky. He's the fucking enemy.

I growled, gesturing at my clothes scattered on his floor. "I don't have any clean clothes, and *sorry*, but I actually like to wear underwear."

"You can wear mine," he gruffly answered, digging in a drawer of his dresser to pull out a pair of boxer briefs.

"I have a feeling we don't wear the same size, and you probably don't have a clean bra in there." It was meant to be sarcastic, but as he turned around I saw the hunger in his gaze.

"You don't need a bra either."

"So I'm just supposed to walk around this place in one of your shirts, and nothing else?" Another thing meant as sarcasm, but it only made his eyes darker, hungrier. "Andre, I'm being serious."

"So am I." He took a step toward me, the towel over one shoulder, and the boxer-briefs still in his hand, leaving him very naked, which made it very clear that his dick was about to re-join the party.

"Stop!" I raised my hand and he actually stopped, barely two steps away with his long legs. "I have clothes at my apartment, if you would just take me—"

"Not a chance," he growled.

"Then what the fuck am I supposed to wear, Andre? I can't just stay here forever, never wearing clothes!"

"I don't see why not…" He trailed off, tongue tracing his lower lip as his eyes moved down my body, sending a shiver through me, but I pushed back the arousal and stood my proverbial ground. There were a million good reasons, but I knew what would make him listen.

"Diego." It was just one word, but the way he jerked it was like I'd hit him, or called his mother a whore.

"Fine," he growled. "I'll go to your apartment and get you clothes."

"And my toothbrush!"

He smirked a little. "Don't like using mine, *belleza?*"

"Please."

Sighing, he turned around and pulled the boxers on. "Fine. Make a list of what you want, and write down your address."

"My keys are—"

"I know where your keys are. Marco moved your car last night." There was a dark edge to his voice, and the words brought back the reality that I was a prisoner here. In this room, this house, and Andre was my jailer.

No matter how hot he was, or how good in bed. He was still dangerous, he'd still hurt me more than once, and no matter how many orgasms he gave me… there was nothing *good* about this situation. It was fucked. Totally fucked.

Just like me.

"Wear this for now." He tossed black fabric towards me, and I spread it out to see what looked like a t-shirt for a giant with some logo on the front. Still, it was clean. Turning my back to him, I dropped the towel and pulled it on, feeling the hem brush the tops of my thighs. Andre was staring as I faced him again, but then he nodded and pulled his own shirt on. "Make the list, I'm going downstairs to get us something to eat. I'll drive to your apartment this evening. Okay?"

"Okay," I agreed, because it wasn't like I had any other options. Moving over to his desk to grab a pen from the coffee cup on it, I couldn't find any other scraps of paper. "What do you want me to write it on?"

He muttered under his breath as he walked over to the closet and opened it, digging through something before he came back with a sheet of paper he'd torn from a yellow notepad. "Use this, and don't forget to lock the door."

"Right." I swallowed, and stood back up to follow him to the door.

"Listen, Nicky..." Andre started to talk, but then he trailed off and just stared at my face, dark eyes flickering over me before he clenched his jaw and turned away. "Just don't leave the room."

"I'm not going to, trust me." *Not after Diego tried to get in here.*

"Good. I expect a list when I get back up here."

"You *expect* a—"

"Yeah, I do, because if I'm going to run errands for you, I'm going to fuck you again before I leave." Without another word, Andre unlocked the door and stepped out, slamming it hard, and I was left staring at the wood.

That shouldn't have turned me on. It definitely shouldn't have turned me on.

So... why was I so wet?

Andre

I cursed myself as I stomped down the stairs barefoot. *What the fuck was that?* It was like every time I tried to be nice to the girl, I ended up being more of an asshole. But staring at her wearing only my shirt, hanging barely to her thighs, I'd almost snapped and taken her on the floor.

Nicky was every temptation I was supposed to avoid. She was every dark thought, every fucked up thing I'd wanted to do since I got to this hellhole, and now she was mine. I'd lied to myself saying I wanted to save her, bullshitted myself about protecting her from Diego — no, I had just wanted *her*.

And isn't the road to hell paved with good intentions anyway?

She'd never had a chance, and neither had I. Cursing under my breath as I stormed into the kitchen, I heard the clatter of a pan and looked up to see Teresa wide-eyed and terrified. Standing by the sink, the older woman dropped her eyes and turned around quickly to keep washing dishes, and I forced myself to breathe.

Teresa was one of many beholden to Paulo García, and it was her day to cook meals. Tomorrow would be Laura, the next day Anna Maria, and then Teresa would be back. Then there were those who cleaned the house, ran the errands, did the laundry, did the shopping. It was a fully functioning estate, only none of them slept here.

Which was a blessing to them.

I walked to the counter that separated the kitchen from the dining room, giving the woman some space from the aggression I knew was radiating off me. Then, I did my best to speak softly. "Teresa, is there anything left from lunch?"

"*Claro, Señor Andre.*" She stood still at the sink for a moment, and then she pulled off the gloves and wiped her hands on a towel to move to the fridge. "How much you want?"

"Enough for me and the girl, and some silverware, *por favor*. We'll eat in my room."

Teresa nodded and moved silently, opening containers and taking down plates, but when I saw her turn the stove on I spoke up.

"No, Teresa. Just microwave it, you don't need to heat it on the stove."

"*Si, señor.*" Clicking the stove off, I watched as she portioned out the meat and veggies onto two plates, adding a spoonful of elote that had my stomach growling. I bit back a smile when I saw her add a second helping of it to one of the plates.

Her elote was a house favorite.

Popping the plates one at a time into the microwave she still ignored my comment about the stove and heated up a pan to spin the corn tortillas around in. She used her hands, like my mother used to, and if I squinted I could almost imagine the woman was my mother. If her hair were darker, and her waist a little wider, and if she had the radio blaring, singing every song that came on.

I shook my head, breaking away from bitter memories and the distant echoing laughter of my siblings. Too much darkness separated me from the cramped, sun-drenched kitchen of my childhood, and there was no use remembering something so lost. It took a few more minutes before Teresa had the plates settled on a tray, two glasses of water balanced on either side, with a nest of napkins and silverware in the center. I nodded at her and took it. "*Gracias*, Teresa."

"*De nada, señor.* Do you need anything else?" Her accent was thick, but she spoke English as much as the rest of us in the house. A skill Paulo insisted upon. Glancing up at her face, she looked almost concerned before the expression was wiped away.

"No. This is good."

"*Cuídese, Señor Andre*," Teresa replied as she moved back to the sink to continue cleaning. For a moment I was too surprised to move, but then I forced myself to walk towards the stairs.

In all the time I'd been staying at Paulo's house, I had never, not *once*, heard Teresa tell any of us to *take care*. The fact that she'd used it with me was even… stranger. Something felt off again, that same feeling that had crept up my spine in the SUV with Paulo and José that morning, and I didn't like it.

Detouring to the front room, I thought it was empty until I walked toward the bar and caught the shape of someone in the same chair Nicky had been put in. I relaxed a little when I recognized Marco, but his stillness unnerved me.

Never one to break a silence, I let him have his as I grabbed a bottle of rum and two short glasses to add to the tray.

"José and Paulo listened to you." His words came out quietly, slightly slurred, and I glanced over, catching the glint of light on a bottle between his legs. He was drunk. *Perfecto.* Marco tilted up the tequila, swallowing before he hissed between his teeth as he set it back down. "They laughed when she screamed."

A purr rumbled through the darkness inside me remembering the way she'd cried out under me, but I also remembered the fear in her as Paulo had traced the knife over her throat, remembered how I'd wanted to be the one holding the knife. The one feeling her tremble. I was no better than him, just a different brand of monster.

"Guess you proved them wrong, eh, *cuadro?*" Marco was still talking, having a one-way conversation because I wasn't planning on responding. Not about Nicky. He laughed roughly, low and without any real humor. "Not a *maricón*, eh? Is that why you hurt her? To prove it to them? Prove you didn't want to fuck men?"

I clenched my jaw, moving my gaze to the floor because getting into it with a drunk Marco wasn't going to do anyone any favors. Mostly it would just end up with him bleeding on the floor, and me having to explain it to Paulo. The tile was shining with the afternoon light coming through the windows, almost that perfect burnt orange that would appear in a couple of hours. She'd dropped her empty glass just *there* yesterday when Paulo had ripped her from the chair. It had shattered, but the glass was cleaned up now, which meant the cleaning crew had been by while we were out.

Everything pristine again, smooth and shiny. Just like Paulo liked.

There was no erasing her bruises though, or my bloody knuckles, or the things I'd already done to her. No denying the things I'd still do either.

You're still a monster.

Lifting the tray, I made sure it was balanced as I walked toward the doorway, but he stood as I approached, holding onto the chair with one hand to keep his balance.

"What did you do to her, Andre? Why did she scream like that?"

"Move," I growled.

"Did she tell you Diego tried to get in your room? Tried to break down the door? He wanted to hurt her. Hurt her just like you did." There was accusation and disgust in Marco's tone, still trying to be the knight for her, but the fact that he was shitfaced and sitting in the chair she'd been in was just proof that he couldn't have protected her anyway. He was too weak. Too weak for this fucked up world, no matter how many times he'd pulled the trigger at Paulo's command. Nicky needed someone strong, someone that the others actually feared, and no one feared young and friendly Marco.

But they were afraid of me.

And you really think you're protecting her? I wanted to tell my own head to fuck off, I wanted to find Diego and dig his spine out of his fucking body for even trying to get to her, but the surge of rage came out against Marco instead.

"Listen to me, *cabrón*, the girl is mine, and if you don't want me to remind you why *jefe* takes me on the meets instead of you, I suggest you shut the fuck up, sit back down, and keep drinking." The words had come out calm, deadly quiet, like I'd taken a page out of Paulo's fucking book, and I saw a flash of something in Marco. A hint of the soldier, the man who had killed just as willingly as the rest of us at Paulo's orders — but he also knew my reputation. Knew what I was capable of.

"*Chingate*, Andre." His face contorted with anger as he glared at the tray in my hands. "At least you're feeding her, *pendejo*." Marco was already walking away when he finished the insult, muttering under his breath as he left the room with the tequila at his side. Black rage flickered inside me like flames, and I had to fight the urge to follow him and put him on the fucking floor for challenging me, for getting in my face about Nicky.

He wanted her. I'd known it since he'd watched her sitting in that same goddamned chair. But she was *mine*. I'd made sure Diego knew it, and I could help Marco learn that lesson if he needed it.

They laughed when she screamed.

His words echoed in my head, and the fact that my cock twitched against my thigh told me more about how far I'd fallen from the boy who used to watch his mother sing and cook than anything else in the world could have.

"Fuck," I growled, walking toward the stairs with my eyes glued to the bottle on the tray. I needed a fucking drink, and I needed it now.

THIRTEEN

Nicky

The food was delicious, that was something I couldn't deny, and if Andre kept feeding me like this I'd probably be the only person in history to actually *gain* weight while being held captive. But something was wrong, all of the weird sexual tension was gone. Andre had barely looked at me when he'd returned, leaving me the tray on the bed as he took his plate to the desk.

Along with his water, one of the short glasses, and the *entire* bottle of rum he'd brought upstairs.

For the last fifteen minutes, it had been nothing but awkward silence with the scratch and scrape of silverware on the plates as we ate. It was weird, and I wanted a fucking drink. Popping the last bite of elote between my lips, I started tapping my fork on the plate until it irritated him enough for him to look over at me. "You going to give me some of that rum?"

"Depends, are you going to explain why you didn't tell me what happened when I was gone today?" Andre didn't flinch as he asked it, and I wondered if someone had told him, or if Diego had mouthed off about it... or if he had some kind of surveillance set up in or around his room. The latter wouldn't surprise me considering his security measures on the door, but none of that really mattered.

I huffed. "Did you really give me an *opportunity* to have a chat with you about the other assholes in this house when you got back?"

"There have been opportunities," he growled, pointedly not apologizing, and it cranked up my anger another notch.

"When?" I asked, voice dripping with rage-fueled exasperation. "When you were showering me after you pinned me to the bed and fucked my ass as I screamed and told you *no*? Or when you called me an idiot for coming here to save my brother? Or, wait, maybe you mean when you brought the food back and looked like you wanted to murder someone, *again*, and then sat your ass down over there to glare holes in your fucking desk?"

"What did he do, Nicky?" The question was a low rumble, threaded through with the violence that his body projected so clearly.

"He tried to get in. Right after you left, just like you told me he would." I fought the urge to shiver, remembering the raw fear as the door shook and Diego shouted. Shoving my hair back over my ears, I met Andre's dark eyes. "I want some fucking rum."

The way his body unfolded from the chair felt threatening, but he snagged the bottle of rum and brought it over to the bed, moving along the side until he was almost uncomfortably close. His gaze never left mine as he unscrewed the lid and took a drink directly from the bottle. I wanted to growl, to mutter about hygiene and backwash, but when he planted a hand on the bed beside me all of those words left me. Andre let his gaze roam over me with no shame, lingering on the spot where his shirt ended high on my thighs.

Swallowing, I tried to summon the ability to speak from wherever his overwhelming presence had banished it, but all I managed was a heavy exhale as he finally shifted his eyes to the glass on the tray and poured a hearty amount.

Andre planted the bottle on the other side of my thigh, caging me in with his arms. "I will kill him if he touches you, Nicky. Do you understand that?"

"That's what I told him," I whispered, aware of just how close he was.

"Did you mean it?" he asked, and his face was only inches away, his dark brown irises almost swallowed by his pupils.

"Yes."

"Have you ever killed someone, Nicky? Have you ever even seen someone die?" His voice was soft, but that *edge* was still there. A subtle threat, and for the moment I couldn't tell who it was for — so I just shook my head slowly. Andre's tongue snuck out over his bottom lip, and with his exhale I could smell the sweetness of the rum on his breath. "Would you watch if I killed Diego, *belleza?* Or would you turn away?"

"If he touched me again… I'd watch every minute of it."

A low groan escaped him just before his lips captured mine, the salt of our food mixing with the sugar of the rum and that overpowering richness of *him*. I moaned into the kiss as I felt his weight dip the edge of the bed, his hand moving to cradle the back of my head, fingers tightening to control the depth of the kiss. Tongues and teeth at war, nipping, tasting, devouring each other. Slowly, he leaned me back onto the pillow, and I felt the shirt riding up, over the tops of my thighs, and my only comfort was that I had my legs together, even though part of me wished I didn't.

As soon as I was laid back, he changed the angle of the kiss, growing more aggressive as he bit my lower lip, thrusting his tongue into my mouth again as I gasped. It was dizzying, consuming, and I couldn't deny the outbreak of heat between my thighs, coiling upward into my belly as I managed to move. Fisting his shirt with one hand to pull him harder against me, moaning softly as his weight pressed me into the bed. An almost feral sound tore out of him and he sat up suddenly, practically launching himself off of me as he stood and then tilted the rum back.

Stunned did not even begin to describe my headspace. We had gone from arguing to… whatever the fuck that was so fast that I'd never even caught up, and then it had all stopped. "What the fuck, Andre?"

He huffed out a laugh, but it sounded bitter before he cut it off with another drink. I pushed myself upright on shaky arms and grabbed for my own glass, needing… something to help me process this fucked up situation. Unfortunately, the burn of the liquor didn't give me the clarity I'd hoped for.

"Andre!" I raised my voice this time, and he turned to stare at me, a wild look in his eyes. My mouth hung open, because I honestly couldn't think of a thing to say to him.

"I don't know what to do with you, *belleza*." His lips tilted up in a wry smile, and then he stared up at the ceiling before he cursed under his breath and walked away, swallowing another mouthful of rum.

I took the hint and drank as well, shrugging as I offered a suggestion. "Let me go?"

Another huffed laugh, Andre shook his head as his eyes moved around the room, landing on everything *but* me. "You still don't get it, do you? Paulo isn't going to let you go, Nicky. I couldn't let you go even if I tried."

The words caught me by surprise, and I felt darkness creeping in, but I fought it. "That's… that's bullshit. You could at least *try!* Honestly, you could walk me out of here right—"

"Do you honestly think Paulo doesn't know where you live? Know the hospital room your brother is in?" Andre wiped a hand over his face, pacing the bit of floor between his closet and desk. "Fuck, Nicky, he probably knows your entire life by now. There isn't anywhere you could go where he wouldn't find you and fucking kill you."

Panic exploded inside me, spreading fast through my veins as I shook my head. "No, no, you bought me. You own me, right? Isn't that the deal? That means YOU can let me go! You can—"

"*Paulo* owns you, Nicky. I told you that last night. He owns me, he owns you, he owns this house and every man in it." Another harsh laugh that held no humor. "And if you think he doesn't pretty much own this fucking city, you're delusional."

I was spiraling, breaths coming shorter as I tried to wrap

my mind around what he was saying. It wasn't real, didn't *feel* real, but I had to say the words aloud, to make him confirm them. "He… he's never letting me go. Ever."

Andre's jaw was clenched as I looked up at him. Rough, terrifying, and for a fraction of a second he almost looked sorry. But then it was gone, and he jerked his chin toward me. "Drink the rum, Nicky."

It was like he'd let the air out of the room, and I followed the direction gladly. Not even tensing when he moved close again to refill my glass, carrying his own.

Nudging the tray out of his way, he took a seat on the edge of the bed, both of us drinking in silence for a while as I let the impossible settle inside me. *Never. I'm never getting out of here.* And as much as my mind tried to fight it, I couldn't deny the logic of it all, because there was no way that I'd grow old in this house. I wouldn't be like that woman making breakfast this morning, becoming some odd fixture of this place.

I was a toy, a plaything, and for right now I was *Andre's* toy, but Paulo could come by at any time and take me. And I had a very strong feeling that Paulo didn't take good care of his toys.

"I'm going to die here, aren't I?" It was barely a whisper, but I knew Andre had heard me because he took another long drink from his glass. When I looked up at him, his eyes were glued to the rumpled sheets. "Tell me the truth."

"No one knows the future, Nicky."

"Then tell me your fucking prediction," I snapped. "I'm not talking about whether or not I'll get married someday, or have kids, I'm asking about your fucking boss. Will he let me live or not?"

"It's…" He stopped, stealing another drink as he avoided my gaze. "The safest place for you is here." Andre spoke to the bed, not lifting his eyes at all, and my rage burned through all of the nihilism to find its way back to the surface.

"Why can't you just give me a straight fucking answer?" I shouted.

That brought his eyes up, but he seemed to be without any more bullshit answers. Everything about him closed off, shut down, until he was that empty, terrifying robot I'd seen the day before. Hot, cold. Violent, tender. On, off. Andre was made up of extremes, and I was lost in the middle somewhere.

Fucking drowning in the void.

"Why did you help me?" I asked quietly, feeling like something was tearing inside my chest. "Why didn't you just let them have me?"

"I don't know."

"Just leave. Can you just leave? Can you just — fuck! — can you just go get me some clothes? I can't — I don't *want* to be around you right now."

Tall, dark, and silent, he got up from the bed without another word. I watched as he set the glass down on the desk, tucking the list I'd hastily written into his pocket before he moved to his dresser to grab socks and then his shoes. I finished off the rum in my glass, and reached for the bottle on the tray to refill, already planning on getting completely drunk in his absence.

Once he finished tying those heavy boots, his phone went into a pocket, and then he grabbed one of the guns to tuck into the back of his dark jeans. The fact that grabbing a gun was as natural to him as his phone was not lost on me as he moved to the door, but he stopped at the edge of the wall for the bathroom. For a moment I wondered if he'd recalled his threat from before he'd brought lunch, his promise to fuck me, but he didn't even look at me.

"Don't forget the locks," he mumbled. Then he moved to the door and I listened as he opened and shut it.

A moment later I followed to lock myself into my own prison cell. My own fucking coffin. Quite possibly the last place I'd ever see alive.

Yeah. I was definitely going to get drunk.

FOURTEEN

Andre

I braked hard a few blocks away from the house, pulling to the side of the road to turn the fucking truck off. My hands would have been shaking, but I was too practiced in hiding everything I felt for something so physical to occur without my permission.

Still, I could feel the urge.

Everything was crumbling, falling the fuck apart, fraying at the edges, and I had no control over it. I wanted to help her, but I wanted to keep her. I wanted to call Nathan back and explain it all, explain it right fucking now, but I knew he wouldn't care. There was no hope for Nicky. Or, rather, *I* was Nicky's only hope — which was actually worse.

"Fuck!" I slammed my hand against the steering wheel and leaned back to the headrest, forcing breaths that didn't smell like her, because everything else did. My bed, my clothes, my fucking skin smelled like her. *This is all wrong.* I searched the cab of the truck for what I needed and then climbed out, welcoming the blast of humid heat that rebounded off the road as I paced to the back and leaned against the tailgate. With a sigh, I flicked the lighter and lit a cigarette.

The first inhale of nicotine was a balm to my raw nerves, and I closed my eyes as it rushed through me. I'd quit smoking a hundred times over the years, but then something would happen and I'd find myself digging out the emergency pack of stale cigarettes from the glove box. There was a reason I never threw those fuckers out, why I replaced it if it got empty, and *this* was it.

For completely fucked up situations like this. Situations like Nicky Harris.

"*Belleza…*" I muttered as I tugged the list she'd written from my pocket. Staring at the smooth loops of her handwriting, with all of the things she wanted written neatly in a column, I tilted the paper so that the wind would stop folding it. Her handwriting was so… feminine. Pretty. Infinitely better than any confusing scratch I was capable of, and staring at the rounded edge of each letter seemed to drive home how wrong all of this was. Not just the obvious shit — the fact that Paulo had imprisoned her in the house, the fact that the others had hurt her, the fact that *I* had hurt her more than once — but the other things.

She was just a girl, an innocent woman. Nicky was the kind of woman that fought for her family, her little brother, as fierce as a lioness. She was almost foolishly brave, no matter what was around her. Hell, I'd just basically told her she was going to suffer and die in that godforsaken house, and she'd still had the balls to yell at me to get out.

But worst of all, or best of all… she was good. So authentically fucking *good*.

Better than I deserved in my bed. I wished I were the kind of man who could be some kind of oasis for her, a safe harbor, but I wasn't. I could barely keep my fucking hands off her when I was in the room. I *hadn't* been able to keep my hands off her. I'd kissed her, wanted to push her knees apart and taste her again, fuck her again, make her scream in pleasure instead of pain... but even that was wrong. I knew it on some level, even as the darkness swelled at the idea of having her pinned underneath me, mouth open as she cried out.

All of this was fucking wrong. All of it was evil.

And I didn't want it to end.

Yet another reason I was damned. Taking another long draw on the cigarette, I let the nicotine flood my veins and push back the tension in my shoulders as I skimmed the list of items. I found her address and the directions for finding her apartment at the complex written at the bottom. She had even provided a description of where it was in relation to the pool as if I'd never had to find an apartment. With one last drag on the cigarette, I dropped it and stomped it out before climbing back into the truck. As soon as her address was set in my phone, I started driving. The sooner this errand was over, the sooner I could be back at the house.

Which meant I could drink, confront Diego, and then fuck her again.

I shook my head, a bitter laugh leaving my lips because my priorities were so fucking skewed. The first thing on that list should have been figuring out why the fuck Paulo thought he needed to call in extra men — but, no. It was all about Nicky, about making sure the others knew who she belonged to, just so I could be the one to hurt her.

"Marco was right. You're just another one of the monsters now, Andre," I growled, tightening my grip on the steering wheel as the black purred deep in my chest. Hungry, waiting, and never satisfied.

———————

Nicky's directions *had* made her place easy to find, which I admitted to myself with a smirk even though I'd never tell her that. The complex wasn't in the best part of town, but it wasn't the worst either. Her place was up a flight of concrete stairs, apartment 218, a tiny studio apartment. From the second I walked in I smelled her, and the fact that my cock twitched just thinking of her told me how far gone I was.

The apartment was boiling, just the single window unit, but it was off. Fake wood floors stretched until it reached the linoleum of the kitchen. One big room, she had a futon for a bed that I assumed she turned into a couch when she had company. A small flat screen TV on one of those Ikea things sat across from it, next to a dresser covered in picture frames.

The opposite wall had a hanging rack filled with clothes, the floor under it covered in shoes. No table, not like there would have been much room if she'd put one in. The place felt like a shoebox. Her entire apartment was maybe a couple hundred square feet larger than my room at Paulo's house, and both of them had a bathroom. It seemed like most of the extra space was taken up by the tiny galley kitchen.

Curiosity tugged at me, and I walked over to the dresser to look at the photos. Right in front was one of her making a ridiculous face with some guy. Her arm was around his shoulders, and they were obviously on the beach. He was bare chested, skinny, and she had on a black bikini top, her breasts pressed together to give her ample cleavage. For a flash I wondered if this was some boyfriend, my fist clenching tight enough to reopen one of my knuckles, but then I saw another picture just behind it. Nicky looked younger in it, maybe twenty, and the same guy was with her, but he looked about sixteen. Dressed like a junior thug, he had a forced smile on his face, while Nicky's was beaming. *This* was her brother. Chris Harris. The first picture was clearly a selfie, but the one of them younger was taken by someone else. There were other pictures too, including a family one that confirmed it for me. Mother, father, Nicky, and Chris. They looked happy, and I felt my stomach turn.

The other pictures had Nicky with friends, and one of her at Walt Disney World in Mickey ears, looking way too hot for as young as she probably was in that photo. I turned away before I felt even more fucked up than I already was — not like it really mattered. I'd looked at her driver's license when I'd got the keys from her purse. She was twenty-seven, so Nicky was more than legal now.

As if the shit you've done to her is legal.

Cursing, I yanked out the list and started to pull out her drawers, grabbing a few handfuls of multi-colored underwear to toss onto the futon, tossing a couple of bras and bundles of socks to join them. She'd actually listed *pajamas* on the paper, but I laughed under my breath as I shut the drawers. No way in hell was she wearing clothes in my bed.

Crossing to the hanging rack of clothes I flicked through them and grabbed the black yoga pants, a few pairs of shorts, and a random set of shirts and tank tops. There was only one little closet but she'd said that's where her duffel bag was, and I opened it and crumpled the list in my hand as I caught a stack of boxes that threatened to fall. Shifting the precarious tower backward, I leaned in to pull the bright purple duffel out and toss it behind me.

I was about to close the door when I stared at the boxes again. They were all liquor boxes, of different shapes and sizes, which explained the unsteady nature of her makeshift tower. But why did she have them crammed in the only closet she had in this shithole, and have all of her clothes hanging outside?

And where the fuck did Nicky get twenty-thousand dollars if this is where she lives?

"Please tell me you're not fucking with the drugs, *belleza*…" My stomach turned, images of Francisco's ruined face and the memory of pulling the trigger to kill him flashed behind my eyes as I grabbed the top box and set it on the floor. It was taped shut, and I'd left my knife in the truck, so I wandered to the kitchen to snag one.

"You're smarter than this, Nicky. *Por favor*, tell me you're smarter than this." Cutting the tape, I flipped it open and found plastic grocery bags, and inside the top one was pictures. Hundreds of photos. I grabbed a handful as I sat down on the floor, flipping through until I stopped at one that was clearly Nicky as a round-faced little kid. Blonde hair, blue eyes, covered in mud, grinning like she was fucking proud of the mess.

The dark shuddered inside me, like a miniature earthquake that started deep down and shook out until I saw the photos waver in my grip. *Fuck.*

I tossed them back in the bag like they were toxic, which they may as well be. I didn't need to think about her as a kid, or her fucking family. I closed the box and grabbed the next one. This one had blankets, a little stuffed dog and frog, and I shoved it aside too. The next was heavier, but it was just framed pictures and a jewelry box that I left alone. With one box left I leaned forward to drag it over, already knowing it didn't hold drugs, but other than getting the irritating reminder that Nicky had a fucking family, I hadn't found a single explanation as to how she had twenty thousand dollars to hand Paulo.

Unless her brother had it stashed somewhere?

But if he did… why hadn't he paid when Paulo's street guys had come to fuck him up? Nothing made sense, and I was developing a damn headache as I sliced into the last box. This one had yearbooks, a tassel from a graduation cap, and a bunch of other keepsakes that gave me no answers. It had been a mistake to go through the boxes, and I couldn't even tape them back up.

Will it matter if she never comes home anyway?

"*Que Dios me ayude,*" I whispered, wiping the sweat off my forehead as I laid back on her floor. A bitter laugh rumbled up my throat as I stared at her watermarked ceiling. Who was I to ask God for help? I was the monster in all of this, and did it really fucking matter how she got the money?

Paulo was taking his vengeance on her regardless — by letting me have her.

I knew that wasn't all he had planned though. Eventually he'd come for her. Whether it was because he actually wanted her, or if he just wanted to test my loyalty, I knew it would happen. Sooner rather than later. He'd already questioned me about whether or not she was a distraction, and here I was in her fucking apartment getting her clothes.

"And a toothbrush," I mumbled, shoving myself off the floor to reassemble her tower of memories in a more secure way, and then I shut the closet. Snagging the duffel bag I tossed the clothes into it, and then went to the bathroom. It had an awful pink tile in it, a dingy yellow light over the narrow mirror, and I shook my head.

The girl lived in a shit hole while her fuck of a brother squandered tens of thousands of dollars in drugs or drug money. It only took me a minute to grab the little bag from under the sink and fill it with all of her requests. As a last thought I opened her shower curtain and grabbed some of those things too.

"You really think she wants to shave her legs for you, *cabrón?*" Talking to myself was pointless, but it distracted me from the shit I'd seen digging through her life. Still, I made one last sweep of the shoebox she called home, and picked up a few random items before turning off the light in her bathroom.

Then someone knocked on her door.

Fuck.

Stepping back against the wall, I stayed still. There was

only one window above the air conditioner unit buried in the wall beside her door, but the blinds didn't provide perfect cover. Another round of knocks came, and then I heard a feminine voice.

"Nicky! Girl, are you in there? It's Elise!"

Moving quietly, I tucked myself against the door to her closet to stay out of sight in case she tried to look through the window. It put me closer to the front door, and I could hear the woman talking outside.

"—at Nicky's and she's not answering the door. Has she called you back?" There was a pause, and I was glad I hadn't given in to the heat to flip on her air conditioner, it would have been a dead giveaway to anyone with half a brain. "Shit, I don't know. Her car isn't here though, she's got a spot."

The sound of the door knob made my heart race and I lunged around the corner of the closet to grab onto it, biting down on the curses I wanted to shout. I'd left the fucking door unlocked. *Pinche idiota.* Keeping my head away from the peephole I stared at the deadbolt and debated how quietly I could turn it, because there was no way I could explain my presence here. No way I could let this girl see me and report it to the police.

So what are you going to do? Kill her?

No. No, that was not an option. Drug peddling thugs? Sure, I'd killed my share. I'd killed in self-defense, and I'd killed other killers… but I wasn't pulling the trigger on some random girl checking on Nicky.

"No, I don't have her brother's number. I don't even know where he lives."

Just give up and go. Leave.

"Okay, but when has Nicky ever missed a shift? Seriously, that's bullshit, Antonio. Fine… yeah… Then maybe you should…" The girl's voice faded, and I could hear her moving away on the concrete walkway outside. When I was sure she was gone, I sagged against the door, carefully flipping the deadbolt before I stepped away from it.

This entire trip had been fucking stupid. I had more than enough money to get her whatever the fuck she'd wanted from a store, and I wouldn't have had to drive halfway across Miami in afternoon traffic. Sweat rolled down my back, making my shirt stick to me, which was never good because the gun would show. Yanking it from the back of my pants, I unzipped her bright purple duffel and threw the weapon inside.

Standing in the middle of her shoebox of an apartment, I didn't know what I was going to do, but I knew one thing for sure. I wasn't perfect, and I hadn't been good in longer than I could remember, but Nicky was going to come back here. She was going to survive this, get back to her brother, her friends, her fucking life — and I would just be a bad memory.

Possibly a dead, bad memory depending on what I had to do to get her out, but she had something to live for. She had a life to return to, and I didn't.

I don't have anything but her.

FIFTEEN

Andre

It was evening when I got back to the house, the orange-gold light painting the pale façade, but there was something menacing about it. As if the spacious lawn was on fire and the flames were creeping toward the house, preparing to engulf it and return everyone inside to Hell. A fitting end to all of the devils inside, but I'd need to be in there for it to be right.

And she'd need to be out here. Alive and free.

Wishful fucking thinking. Digging in Nicky's bag, I returned the gun to the back of my pants and climbed out of the truck. I had to get my head on straight. Walking into Paulo García's house with anything less than complete focus would be suicide, and that meant I had to stop imagining killing them all.

The second I opened the front door, I heard the laughter, the loud voices in the front room — too many voices. Stepping past the entryway, I saw them around the poker table and let the cold wash over me and erase everything I'd seen in Nicky's apartment from my mind.

"*Hola,* Andre! Join us!" Samuel was grinning, leaning back in his chair to wave me over, and there was no way to avoid it. As much as I wanted to go upstairs to Nicky, I had to make an appearance or I wouldn't be able to figure out what the fuck was going on.

"*¿Qué onda, güey?* What's with the purple bag?" Nicolás asked as I approached, and a second later everyone was looking at me.

"Clothes for the girl," I answered, keeping my voice level as usual. Having the brothers here already wasn't a good sign, it meant Paulo was planning something soon. Very soon. As I looked around the room I saw Luis on the couch with Paulo in the chair closest to him. They'd clearly been talking. *Shit.*

"Yeah, we heard about this girl. *Muy bonita,* yes? Diego says you won't share her?" Samuel laughed.

"No, he won't," José answered for me. "We didn't even get to have any fun with her yesterday. Just scared her a little." He leaned forward on the table, lifting his chin a bit. "Why does the *puta* need clothes, *cuadro?*"

"I tore the ones she was wearing."

The brothers laughed loudly, José chuckled, and I even caught the hint of a smile on Paulo's face, but Diego sneered. "She's just a set of holes. Why you getting shit for her like some little bitch?"

"Diego, you still got blue balls?" Nicolás grinned, but Diego growled and shoved himself back from the table to head to the bar. The look he gave me promised pain — for him, if he was dumb enough to make a move.

"*Cuadro*, come and sit." Paulo beckoned and I obeyed like a good little soldier. Luis gestured to the couch beside him, and I dropped Nicky's bag to the floor.

"*Hola*, Luis." I shook his hand when he offered it and sat beside him.

"It has been a while, Andre. Six months?" Luis was stoic, level-headed, and not a man I minded spending time around. It was always easier when someone didn't fill silence with empty words.

"*Si*, about six months."

"Well, I do not like to take him away from his work if I don't have to. Luis handles the border well, eh?" Paulo took another drink, and it seemed that he'd had a few already. More relaxed, but that could be an act.

"My men make it so, *jefe*," Luis answered, humble and respectful as always.

"Yes, yes, *claro*. Andre, you do not have a drink. This is not right." Turning, Paulo saw Diego still lurking at the bar and smiled. "Diego, bring Andre a glass, and a bottle of the Casamigos tequila."

I couldn't fight my own smile as Diego's face went dark at the order, but he didn't dare speak against Paulo and brought it over without a word. As he set them on the table, his eyes met mine and I leaned back on the couch, making it clear he didn't worry me.

"Problem, *cuadro?*" Paulo asked as soon as Diego returned

to the poker table, but the shark's grin on his face told me that all he wanted to know was if blood would be spilled.

Shrugging a shoulder, I leaned forward to get the glass and pour. "We will see, *jefe*."

"*Bien*. I am glad you returned when you did. I have been telling Luis that you are the right man to accompany us to our meeting. I mentioned an opportunity to you this morning, do you remember?" Paulo was still smiling, the expression as empty as he was.

"Yes, *jefe*. What do you need me to do?"

"That is what we have been discussing. *Jefe* told me how you handled the accounting issue this morning, and that kind of loyalty is what will be needed." Luis always spoke so carefully, looping around the subject. No wonder Paulo kept him so fucking close.

"I understand." Taking a sip of the tequila, I savored it for a moment, because what I really wanted to do was toss it back and pour another, and then another. I was too sober for this shit.

"I will cut straight to it then. There have been some changes south of the border, and I believe our enterprise can benefit from them. Some interested parties are arriving in three days, and I need to be sure we are... prepared for the meeting." Paulo sat back in the chair, resting his hands on the arms, his glass dangling from his fingers. "There are so many ways meetings like this can go, as you know, *cuadro*."

I nodded, focused on keeping my breathing steady and even so that I didn't betray my sudden racing pulse. *Fuck*. Could this finally be it? Thirty-one months of this hellhole and I could finally get the names of the bastards serving up drugs by the plane and truckload? Too many thoughts hit at once, and so I shut them all down, let the black swallow me whole, just like I had that morning. "What is your main concern, *jefe?* Your safety, or the potential… consequences the changes may have on those at the meeting."

The edge of Luis' mouth lifted a bit. "They want to meet with *jefe*, Andre. He's allowing the meeting, I do not think they would risk the business relationship."

"Exactly." Paulo shrugged, looking every bit the king overseeing his empire, turning the wingback chair into a fucking throne. "How the meeting goes will depend on if their terms acknowledge our position here, or if they are insulting."

"This is why you asked Samuel and Nicolás to come in." It wasn't a question, and the slow smirk crossing Paulo's lips confirmed it before he spoke.

"I want the best with me, *cuadro*, and that includes you."

"*Gracias, jefe.*" For once, I actually meant those words. If I was with him, I might finally have the information to get the fuck out. To take him down, to burn them all down.

"Then it's settled! Time to drink. *Salud!*" Paulo raised his glass, and Luis and I did as well, echoing him, and I finished the rest of my tequila in one sweet, burning swallow.

I refilled all of our glasses with the Casamigos, and over the next hour we steadily drank. Luis talked about his children, Samuel and Nicolás joined for a bit to thank Paulo for the invitation and try the tequila, and Marco's absence was finally explained — he'd been drunk when the brothers had arrived and was already in bed. *Not surprising.*

The haze of the alcohol settled my head, but every time I looked down to see Nicky's bright purple duffel my cock throbbed. There were still conversations I needed to have with her, things I had to get answers to, but they could wait until the morning. As could the report to Nathan. I just needed the opportunity to step away without it being disrespectful.

As the buzz of conversation hit a lull, Luis stood and nodded to Paulo. "I had a long trip, *jefe*, I'm going to sleep. *Gracias* for the drinks as always."

"*Buenos noches*, Luis." Paulo raised a hand as Luis nodded to the others and headed to the stairs. My gaze followed him as he walked up, into the dim shadows at the top, and when I turned back to the group Paulo was smiling at me. "You want to go make *belleza* scream again, Andre?"

Leaning back in the seat, I let a smirk pass over my lips, the darkness surging its own acceptance of Paulo's offer. "She does sound so pretty when she screams, *jefe*."

A low laugh rumbled out of him, sinister and soft. His real laugh that matched the emptiness of his eyes. "Then go make her scream, *cuadro*."

"*Gracias, jefe.*" I finished my drink and set it on the table. I knew my own smile was cold, and more honest than I wanted to admit — because I really did like the way she screamed. Grabbing her bag, I pulled the strap over my shoulder as I stood and moved to leave.

"When are you going to stop being such a *pinche pendejo* and share the whore?" Diego swaggered in front of me before I could get out of the room, a bottle of liquor in his hand that could be a weapon in a flash.

I stared at him for a second, shrugging my free shoulder. "I tire her out, Diego, and I don't like to share."

"You fucking *maricón!* You're not fooling anyone here. That *puta* needs a real cock." Grabbing his crotch, Diego moved closer and I shifted my feet, ready for him to swing a fist or the bottle. "I can give her a real cock."

"Is that what you said when you tried to get in my room this morning while I was with *jefe?* Did you tell her you had a real cock, *pendejo?*" Dropping the duffel off my shoulder I took a step towards him. "What part of 'she's mine' did you not understand, Diego?"

"I went for her first!" Diego shouted and swung, but he was so drunk it was too easy to step in and grab his arm, bringing my elbow back into his face, and then my knee into his stomach. The spray of blood from his nose was satisfying, but as I twisted his arm and forced him forward, I loved the pathetic cry of pain more.

Pressing my forearm to his elbow, I kept him bent forward, and I knew with barely any weight at all I could snap his fucking arm in half. I wanted to do it, I wanted him to remember the pain the next time he even looked at Nicky. The next time he had to jack off left-handed.

"*Ella es mía, cabrón.*" I kept my voice low, speaking close to his ear, and he tried to move, but I increased the pressure and he shouted in pain. "Say it."

"*¡Vete a la verga culero!*" The fact that Diego had the nerve to call me an asshole, or say *fuck you*, with me about to break his arm confirmed that he was either a total idiot, or too proud to save his firing arm. Either way, it would be sweet to hear the bone snap.

"Wrong choice." I leaned into the joint, feeling his body shudder, hearing his groan.

"Stop." Paulo's voice was like a puppet master tugging my strings, and I hated it. Diego deserved this for daring to come after what was mine, but I leaned back just enough to keep him from breaking his own arm if he jerked.

"*Jefe*, he tried to break into my room to get to the girl this morning." I tightened my grip on his forearm, twisting it just enough for him to groan again. "And now he does this."

"I understand, *cuadro*." Paulo moved closer. "Diego, I recommend you say it before Andre breaks your arm."

"Fuck!" Diego growled, but finally dropped his head and mumbled, "The *puta* is yours."

Glancing up, I saw Paulo nod and growled because it meant I had to let him go. Leaning close again, I used my coldest tone. "Come near her again, and I'll put you in the fucking ground. *¿Entiendes?*"

Diego didn't speak, but he gave a single short nod and I let him go, shoving him away from me. He immediately grabbed onto his arm, muttering curses, and for a moment Paulo just stared at him with no expression on his face. Then he turned to me.

"Hit him, Andre. Just once, so he remembers the lesson." Paulo's eyes were coal-black and empty as he passed between us to return to his seat.

Diego straightened up, glaring at me, and I smirked.

Popping each of the knuckles on my right hand, I moved in front of him to ensure I landed the punch as hard as possible. There was no warning, no more words needed, I just pulled back and hit him. The impact jarred all the way up my arm, and Diego stumbled to the side where Nicolás caught him by the arm with one hand.

I waited for him to look at me, cursing through his bloody nose and mouth, and then I picked up Nicky's bag. "*Buenos noches.*"

"Don't you know not to fuck with Andre, *idiota?*" Samuel's voice and laughter followed me as I headed to the stairs and started climbing.

The smile was still on my face, my knuckles bleeding again as I got to my room and knocked. "Open the door, Nicky." When I didn't hear any movement, I sighed and knocked harder. "Nicky, unlock the door. Now."

Growling, I pounded my fist on the door once more.

Finally, I heard a crash inside the room and then the locks started moving. When the door opened she flinched against the light, hair a golden, tangled halo around her head, still in nothing but my shirt. Putting my hand on her chest I pushed her back into the room and kicked the door shut behind me, feeling the darkness humming in my veins.

She's mine, asshole.

SIXTEEN

Nicky

I was pulled from sleep by a hand between my thighs, fingers stroking through wet folds, and I squirmed because I was sore — but then Andre found my clit and I didn't care. Even the throbbing headache from the hangover faded as he woke me up with each sinful, swirling touch, each teasing dip inside me. In moments I was panting, moaning, not caring in the least that I was completely naked, fisting his sheets, and lifting my hips into the air.

I was close, so close.

"Fuck me," I whined, bucking my hips when he barely slipped his fingers inside again. *Pussy tease.* Trailing his wet fingers up my mound to my stomach, I felt his weight shift on the bed and finally opened my eyes to see his body stretched out beside me. Andre was hard all over, especially where it mattered most.

Before I could think through what I was doing, I sat up and wrapped my hand around his shaft. He hissed through his teeth, snapping back to the bed as I stroked up, rolling my thumb over the bead of precum leaking from the top of his cock. Hot, firm skin, and I wanted him inside me, but I wanted something else first.

"Nicky," he growled, reaching for me, but I took him into my mouth and he groaned.

Tracing my tongue along the underside of his shaft, I eased down, then back up, and down again. Steadily working him deeper, relaxing my gag reflex to take his girth into my throat. The first attempt made me choke, and I shifted onto my knees, bringing my other hand to his balls to caress and tease. Returning the favor. The garbled curses, half-English and half-Spanish, made me feel powerful, strong, in control for the first time since I was put in that fucking chair downstairs. Straddling his thigh, I eased down again and swallowed around his cock, finally feeling him slip into my throat.

"*Dios mío*, yesss…" Andre's hand moved to the back of my head, fist tightening in my hair, but it was just enough to send a thrill down my spine and make me hum a moan against his shaft. He tasted perfect. Warm, male skin, and as I spilled saliva down to his balls, I squeezed them softly and his hips bucked up, pushing him deep again.

Picking up the pace of my movements, I alternated teasing flicks of my tongue at his tip with deep throating him until my eyes watered and throat burned. It was a challenge I liked. Being momentarily in control of a dangerous killer. My jailer, my protector. He'd gone down on me the night before until I'd begged and pleaded for him to stop, and I had fantasized about *this*. Turning the tables, making him writhe and twist on the bed with a flick of my tongue and a swallow — and it was working.

He shouted some series of Spanish words at the ceiling and pressed my nose to his stomach, buried deep. No air, so I focused on making him come. Swallowing around his cock, tugging on his balls, stroking my thumb up the base of his shaft until I met my own wet lips. He groaned low, hips pulsing and I knew he was close.

"Fuck! Up, now." He pulled me off, and I growled, reaching for his cock again only to have him release my hair to grab my wrist. "Spread your legs, Nicky."

"I wasn't done." Staring at him, at the hard ridges of his abs, the ink stretching across his chest with each harsh breath, his dark eyes looking wild... I wanted to argue. I wanted to keep going until he came apart. I'd wanted to be the reason he lost control.

"What did I say?" he growled back, animalistic and raw, and then he lifted his thigh, rubbing between my legs as he flipped us. Immediately rocking against me, I felt the heat flood me as that perfect friction made me desperate again. "Spread. Your. Fucking. Legs." Each word was punctuated by a pulse against my cunt.

Meeting his eyes, I propped myself on my elbows to bring my mouth close enough to feel the heat of his exhale against my lips. Then I slowly moved my knees apart, his body shifting between them. The hunger in his expression would have had me soaking wet if I wasn't already, and when he traced his bottom lip with his tongue and looked between us I couldn't suppress the moan. It came out needy, eager, but in the haze of lust I wasn't capable of any shame.

Especially not when he looked at me like *that*.

As if I were something delicious, but valued. His big hand

stroked up my thigh, and I felt the scratch of the condom wrapper against my skin. That wicked smirk I'd seen only a handful of times spread over his lips, and I kissed him. Couldn't have stopped it if I'd tried, and as the heat of the kiss became an inferno, he nipped my lip and shoved me back to the bed. "I'm going to fuck you until it hurts."

"I'm already sore," I replied, grinning, and he muttered in Spanish as he ripped the wrapper open and slid the latex over his perfect dick.

"Then feel free to scream, *belleza*. You know how much I like it." Fisting my hair again he hauled me upright, and then lifted me as if I weighed nothing, positioning me over his cock. I reached between us to line him up, feeling the flare of his cock head as he pushed inside the first inch. My knees on either side of him, I was already breathing hard, the intensity of his gaze roving down until he was staring at the place we were joined.

In one hard jerk of his hands at my waist, he was buried deep and I gasped, arching, rolling my hips as the tender ache turned into a twisted kind of pleasure.

"Ride me."

I didn't need to hear it a second time, my body was already moving. Up, down, circling as his cock stroked every place I wanted it to, but with his fingers digging into my waist, his strength helping each of my movements along, I couldn't tell who was in control anymore. Him? Me?

Who the fuck cares?

Andre leaned forward, sucking a nipple into his mouth and I arched to make it easier, to soak up the pleasurable tug — but then he bit down and I screamed. Nails digging into his shoulders as the sharp pain spread, intensified, and then got confused as he slammed into me. Deep inside, and I spread my knees wider to let him do it again, harder. That strangely pleasurable ache as he hit my cervix overwhelmed the pain in my breast, and I was shivering, teetering, trying to push and pull against the blur of sensation. And then his teeth lifted, sucking the nipple in to soothe it with his tongue as he drove his cock in again, and I came apart. Ecstasy rushing in on the heels of the lingering pain, burning neon colored tracks through my veins, behind my eyes, scattering over my nerves to tighten every muscle as I cried out. Shouting *God*, and *Andre*, and a stream of expletives that would have made more sense if I'd been capable of thought.

I couldn't tell up from down, but I knew when Andre's weight settled over me, continuing to fuck me through the orgasm with every powerful inch of muscle in his body. He groaned against my ear, whispering shit I couldn't understand, and I dug my nails into his back to pull him closer. Dizzy when he kissed me and ripped the air from my lungs. It was as rough as he was, my lips felt swollen and bruised from all the bites and the brush of the scruff on his cheeks, but it was perfect. Just like the feel of his cock splitting me over and over.

"You're mine, *belleza*." The words came out against my throat as he kissed and licked, before the force of his thrusts made it impossible to maintain. I wanted to respond, to give some kind of answer, but even as my legs wrapped around his hips I wasn't sure if the answer would be positive or negative.

To be or not to be, isn't that always the fucking question?

Another orgasm forced the internal struggle to shut up,

and I reveled in the flush of heat up my chest as I moaned and gasped, holding on to his broad shoulders. For a moment everything fell away, in that bliss-filled escape where it was just us. No house, no Paulo, no debt, no threats — just Andre. The center of my fucked up universe for the space of a few breaths as lust and pleasure thundered through me with enough force to have me torqueing off the bed underneath him. Empty bliss. That's all I wanted, and it didn't seem like too much to ask.

"Again," I pleaded, and he laughed against my ear and bit down on the place where my neck met my shoulder. A painful thrill into the chaos of my nervous system, and I found myself moaning instead of screaming. Crossed wires, signals flooding down the wrong paths, but for once it was to *my* benefit.

Andre was everything wrong in my life. Violence, and drugs, and bad men doing worse shit. I should have been fighting him, should have fought him the entire fucking time… but I didn't. I was as weak as the next person, choosing the lesser of the evils instead of dying with my morals.

But, *fuck*, morality never felt this good, so why would anyone choose it?

"Please." I was barely aware of begging, but I wanted him to push me over the edge again before he came. Wanted to hold on to the haze of euphoria for just a little longer, and he could give it to me. He had every fucking time.

Then he pulled out, and I gasped, looking up at him as he turned and got off the bed, but he wasn't gone long. Big hands at my waist, he hauled me to the end of the bed with a sharp jerk, sliding his hands down my hips to the insides of my thighs. Gradually spreading me as he stared down between my legs. "Your pussy sore, *belleza?*"

"I like it," I whispered, swallowing when his fingers dug in.

"You like it when I make it hurt?" Andre slid his hands out, pressing my thighs wide as he went, until I felt that burning strain as he tested the limits of my flexibility. Still, I nodded, because admitting it couldn't make this situation any more fucked up than it already was. His tongue traced his bottom lip, one hand gripping his cock to run it over my entrance to my clit and back again. "Say it."

Looking up, I felt exposed, vulnerable, but not afraid, even though I had a million fucking reasons to be. Something about him made me want to trust him. I couldn't tell if that was insanity or lust or sheer stupidity — yet in the end none of my reasons mattered. I still wanted it. I wanted him to make it hurt. I wanted him to make me scream.

I wanted *him.*

"I like it when you make it hurt, Andre. I... need it." The last words came out on a whisper, but he stilled for a moment, and then slid deep. Slowly, until he could grind against me, teasing my clit with just enough pressure to make me pant, rocking against his firm grip in search of *more.*

"Again," he demanded as he slammed in a little harder, pushing my thighs wider until I whimpered from the strain.

"I need it to hurt!" As soon as the words left me he jerked my ass to the very edge of the bed, driving in until I felt the pinch of pain as he bottomed out, but I craved it, really needed it. That hadn't been a lie. When he repeated it, I moaned, arching off the bed hard enough to look at the wall behind me. The world narrowed down to the place where our bodies met. The steadily increasing impact of his hips, the ache as he pushed my thighs further, making me tighten around his cock as I struggled against his strength.

The moment his thumb rolled over my clit I tried to sit up. Too sensitive, too raw, but his other hand landed around my neck to pin me to the bed. He squeezed, and I couldn't get enough air. Not choking, not completely, but it meant I couldn't avoid the painful pleasure as he tormented that bundle of nerves that seemed to control my whole body. I twitched and tried to moan, to cry out, but it all came out as sputtered gasps and groans through his hold on my throat.

"Fuck… yes, *belleza*. Fight me." The twisted satisfaction in his voice made me want to struggle. Reaching for his hips with one hand, I pushed against him, and he laughed low as he slammed deep inside me again — but that hadn't been my plan. With his focus there, I hit his wrist with my other hand, and managed to knock his grip from my throat for a moment.

Deep breath, cool air into my lungs to soothe the raging inferno inside, even though I didn't want it to go out. I didn't even really want to win, I just wanted to make him work for it. His hand landed on my neck again, and I grabbed his thumb, wrenching it backward as I bucked my hips against his, tilting enough for his next thrust to be just a little deeper. Enough to make me gasp in delirious pain before he managed to break free and pin my wrist to the bed.

"You're such a brave girl, but you know you can't stop me, right?" His grip on my wrist tightened as his other hand returned between my thighs, finding my clit with way too much ease. I moaned, weakened by the steady pulse of his hips, the incessant drive of his cock that made my body jerk in response to the unmistakable pleasure. "I can make you take it for as long as I want you to…"

"Yes." I nodded, lifting my hips to meet his next thrust, and the clap of our bodies meeting made my inner muscles grip him tight. His deep groan was music to my ears, even pinned and tormented, it was a tilt of the control. "Make me take it," I urged, egging him on, practically purring as he bent over me and fucked me harder than before.

A stream of Spanish left him as he drove deep, pain and pleasure blending until I was nothing but a humming network of nerves, his fucking thumb tweaking my clit to drive me higher and higher. Precarious, hanging over empty space, I could barely breathe as I got closer and closer to my next climax.

"Hold it," he demanded. "Wait." But he didn't lift his touch from my clit, and suddenly my stomach was cramping, thighs painfully taut as I tried to hold it back.

"Please, Andre, pl—"

"No." The finality of it made me whine to the air above me. Closing my eyes against the unreal sight of his abs tightening and releasing as he drove his cock deep, he released my wrist to grab my thigh and bent me at just the right angle for him to hit that painful, but incredible depth again and again.

Over, and over, and over, and I knew I was babbling. Begging. Pleading. Fists clenched in the sheets just so I wouldn't stop it, because I didn't want to stop it. I just wanted him to come, to give me permission to come, to fall apart one more time so the world would disappear again. I wanted that emptiness, that perfect vacuum of post-orgasmic bliss.

"Hurt me!" I shouted, desperate, and his touch left my clit, one hand grabbing my jaw as the other pinched a nipple and viciously twisted, and I screamed. Loud enough to recognize my voice echoing off the ceiling.

Andre shouted, driving deep as his hand slid down to my throat and gripped tight. My scream choked off, and I felt his cock kick deep. The jerk of his body against mine pushing me over the edge, light exploding behind my eyelids like the flash of a camera but sustained for longer than possible. Everything hummed, from my hair to my toes, and I lost even the awareness of his touch for a moment.

Pure, absolute paradise… it was mine, and I held on desperately. Wanted to never let it go, because returning to my body was returning to all the fucked up shit that came with it, and so I let myself float. On a sea of ethereal after-shocks. Riding the tingling pulses of tender nerves. Pain and pleasure so inextricably intertwined that they held no real meaning anymore. I hurt, and I didn't. I was happy, and I wasn't.

It was perfect. And not.

Perfectly imperfect.

But, what more could I ask for? My life was a kaleidoscope of shit, and I deserved a few selfish moments of hedonistic pleasure. Something that was just for me. Fuck Andre, fuck *his* pleasure, I was surfing on a tidal wave of chemicals that let me rise above all of it.

I just wanted to exist for once. Not for someone else, not for any specific purpose. Just for me. *Was that so much to ask?*

When warmth wrapped around me, smelling like male skin and sex, I didn't flinch, I just let it happen. Let it soothe me. I let the sheets drape over me and breathed deep, because waking up was trouble and if this was a dream... I didn't want it to end.

SEVENTEEN

Andre

———————

The subtle, steady buzz of a phone vibrating roused me. Nose buried in the smell of summer, I didn't want to move. Nicky's warm body was pressed to my front, my all too sated cock nestled against her ass, and I had one arm around her, breast within a finger's twitch. I had no idea what time it was now, and I didn't care to check.

I'd been borderline drunk and high on adrenaline from the fight with Diego when I'd come up to my room, waking her up to unlock the door. And then all I'd wanted was her. She had been unsteady on her feet, easy to direct to the bed, easy to strip, easy to spread wide so that I could lick between her thighs until she was writhing and coming and grabbing for me. But I'd held back, made her come again, and again, until she was wild, desperate.

Then I'd fucked her. Grabbed a pillow to put under her hips and forced her face down over it so I could take her as rough as I'd needed to. Fist in her hair, hand in the small of her back. She'd screamed in pleasure, not pain. She'd said my name in that tortured moan that made my balls tingle just thinking about it.

I hadn't been gentle, it wasn't possible as far gone as I was, but I had made sure she came, made sure to put on a damn condom as clumsily as I'd done it. In the end, she came around my cock, gripped me tight as I'd joined her, and then I had pulled her against me to sleep.

When I'd woken up at a little after five to piss, Nicky hadn't even twitched. I'd come back from the bathroom and watched her sleep, tried to tell myself that she deserved the rest. But she was bare from the waist up, sheet tangled around her hips, wrapped around the pillow I'd been sleeping on. As soon as I'd sat down on my side of the bed she had rolled away. Onto her back, her breasts angled towards the ceiling. *Perfecto*. Just enough for a handful, with dusky rose-colored nipples that peaked in the cool of the air conditioning. At first I'd only drawn the sheet down the rest of the way so I could look at her.

Wasn't that always my excuse? Just wanting to look?

As if I could look at her and not touch. As if I could touch her without fucking her. I had no self-control with Nicky. For all the bullshit I handled with Paulo and the other *cabrónes* in this house, for all the shit I'd seen and done without losing my head… for some reason I couldn't do the same with her. *Mi belleza*.

I was still stunned that she was there at all. That I'd taken her for myself, acted on that dark impulse to possess her first, and when I ran my hand over her thigh I was once again amazed by the softness of her skin. But the most surprising thing of all had been her soaking wet pussy, and the way she'd moaned and rode my fingers, tilting her hips like she wanted me inside her — and then she'd told me to fuck her.

Demanded it.

Like I'd argue? But when I'd gone for the condom, she went for my cock, giving me the best fucking blow job I'd had in more years than I could count. Blowing my mind and almost causing me to blow my load before I got inside her again. And that was all I wanted. Her.

Nicky Harris was dangerous. A *weakness*. No, worse, a distraction.

I had planned to spend the morning asking her about the money, the stuff in her apartment, getting some real answers from the girl... and instead I'd fucked her harder than I thought she could handle. *Wrong again.* She hadn't just taken me, she'd begged for it. Told me she wanted it, needed it. Needed me, needed the pain. There wasn't a man on the fucking planet that could resist that.

Except, maybe a good man.

But how many of those were left anyway? This world chewed up and spat out weak men without any effort at all, and I couldn't afford to be weak. Not in this house, not even for Nicky.

The irritating buzz of my phone came back, pulling me from memory, and I cursed internally at having to let go of her warm body, her soft curves, but whoever was calling was obviously intent on speaking to me instead of leaving a fucking message. As gently as possible I moved away from her, trying to let her sleep, and then I dug my phone out of my pants on the floor and walked to the bathroom to answer.

I didn't recognize the number, but that didn't matter much. "*¿Aló?*"

"Andre?" Nathan's voice came through the line and all of Nicky's lingering warmth drained away.

"Yeah."

"Codes," he demanded, and I could hear the irritation in his voice.

What fucking time is it anyway? Glancing at the screen I saw that it was after nine in the morning and I shook my head, rubbing the heel of my palm against my eye where a headache was rapidly forming. "Blue. Zeta. Charlie. Quebec."

"Alone?"

"Yeah." I turned and leaned against the sink, keeping my voice quiet to keep from waking Nicky. She'd earned the rest, and I should be with her. Sleeping with her pressed to my front where I could breathe in summer and try to memorize what she felt like, smelled like, tasted like.

"You want to tell me why the fuck I didn't get a heads up that Nicolás and Samuel Martinez were in town? In the same fucking house that you're in?" Nathan was definitely pissed, but I just smirked as he continued to rant. "Do you know how many watch lists those assholes are on?"

"Two?" I asked, and he cursed on the other end of the line.

"Don't fuck with me, Andre. They were responsible for a bombing in León, and the *Federales* have a whole string of bodies tied to them in Guadalajara from 2015, and that's just the shit they've been able to find evidence on." Nathan growled, spitting just before I heard the click of a lighter and the deep inhale of a cigarette. "I'm guessing you have some kind of excuse for not reporting in on this?"

"Not a good one."

"Dammit, Andre…" Nathan puffed on the cigarette and it made me itch for one. "Look, forget the brothers, if Paulo has brought them in then something is going down. You need to keep your eyes and ears open for—"

"I'm already involved."

"In what?" he asked, and I sighed.

"*Un momento*." Opening the door, I leaned out into the bedroom to check on Nicky. She'd moved to my side of the bed again, face buried in my pillow, and the long curve from her neck to her ass distracted me until I heard Nathan take another drag. Moving back into the bathroom, I shut the door quietly. "There's a meeting, a big one. I'm along for protection."

"And the Martinez brothers?"

"Here to slit throats or blow shit up." I shrugged as I leaned against the sink again. "It's sort of their deal."

"What's the meeting for, Andre?" he asked, and in as few quiet words as I could, I explained what Paulo had said about the changes south of the border. Nathan's constant smoking wasn't helping my nerves, but I spelled it all out, feeling the hum of possibility once again. The chance that this could be over soon, that I could get out. Leave Hell like I'd finally done my penance.

"As soon as I know the location and the date, I'll reach out."

"You better, this could be it." Nathan was practically salivating on the other end of the line and I nodded, looking up at the ceiling feeling hope for the first time in… fuck, God only knew when.

Could this shit really almost be over?

All of the peace and warmth inside me suddenly stuttered. *Nicky.* What would happen to her? Would she go with me? Flinching, I rubbed my fingers into my eyes, trying to ease the headache. "Listen, Nathan, about the girl…"

"Don't, Andre. We're not risking this over some random girl, I don't care how hot she is."

"She's innocent, Nathan."

"So? If she's at Paulo García's house then she's probably not as innocent as you think. Stop thinking with your dick and focus on the goal. Taking him down and his contacts in South America. This is it, Andre. Everything we've worked for."

We. As if Nathan had been the one that had worked his way up through Paulo's ranks. As if he had been the one to torture men, to use his fists, to pull the trigger. Over, and over, and over. I growled, feeling the black rage eat away the momentary flash of hope I'd felt.

I wasn't going anywhere without Nicky. I wouldn't leave her to the wolves. Not even if it meant getting out.

"Either she's secure, or I don't make the move when the time comes."

"God dammit, Andre!" Nathan shouted, his own anger flashing across the line in a series of muttered curses interspersed with rough drags on the cigarette. "You have a fucking job to do. THIS is your fucking job, not some girl whoring around García's house—"

"Her fucking name is Nicky and she isn't a whore. He's got her imprisoned here because her brother made a deal that went south." I rubbed a hand over my face, feeling the scratch of my beard growth as I tried to contain the rage, to push down the black that wanted me to ruin everything just to spite him. "Either she is safe, or I don't play the game. That's the deal on the table."

"There's no fucking deal, Andre. You report to me, and if you want to keep your badge when this shit is over, and have the department's support when you're testifying to all the shit you've done undercover, then you're going to do whatever I tell you to." Nathan's voice was dangerously soft, and the black washed through me, turning me cold.

"That's how it is?"

Nathan laughed. "Yeah, Andre, that's how it fucking is. You knew going into this what it was, it's not my fault you got a hard on for some random bitch in his house."

"If something happens to her, I'm going to make sure everyone knows that I told you about this. About an innocent girl being imprisoned and hurt because you wouldn't act." As I spoke I tried not to think the word *killed*. Just the idea of finding her dead, of knowing I could have done something… I'd never come back from that. I'd kill everyone involved — Nathan included.

"Then figure out how to take Paulo and his connections

down before something happens to her. I expect a call soon with whatever details you're able to get. Understand?"

"Yeah, I got it." I wanted him to hear the rage in my voice, the threat. "I gotta go."

"Me too. I'll get a team ready to move and update my superiors. You just do your job." Nathan was already losing focus on the conversation, but my thoughts were completely centered on the innocent, naked girl in my bed.

"Sure. *Ciao.*" I hung up before I did something stupid like threaten him outright. I'd probably already crossed a line trying to give him an ultimatum, but I didn't give a shit. Thirty-one months of my life, and three days with Nicky, and none of it mattered to him.

He didn't care about the black marks on my soul. The stains that I could never wash clean.

I was probably damned, doomed, all so that we could stop Paulo García and whoever the fuck was taking over the supply chain from Columbia. Which felt so fucking pointless, because someone would just step in to fill the openings, to feed the needs of the US. Sure, they'd be weakened for a while, but it was a never-ending war. One I was tired of being on the front lines for… and Nicky didn't deserve to be here.

She'd just wanted to save her brother. To keep that idiot from getting killed, and now she was trapped here. Trapped with every fucking monster in this house… myself included.

If I were a good man I'd stop touching her, stop hurting her, stop fucking her.

But I wasn't a good man, and as I tightened my grip on the

phone in my hand all I could think about was crawling back into bed with her to soak up as much of her warmth as I could. To breathe in all of the summer I could from her hair, and hope that it would push the darkness back enough that when the time came I could get her out. Let her go.

EIGHTEEN

Nicky

Sitting on the floor with my plate in my lap, I felt like something less than human. All of the men were sitting at the table, most of them already done eating, as they talked and laughed and made jokes. A good portion of the jokes were about me, and what they would do to me if Andre allowed it.

I kept my head down, staring at my slice of the frittata the woman had made. A different woman this morning, but she still didn't look at me. Andre had been the one to give me my plate, my coffee, my fork, my napkin.

He had woken me up the second time today much more gently, not a word spoken about our early morning fuckfest, or the drunken insanity of the night before. I was sore between my thighs, aching all over like I'd had an intense workout, but he was just... him. The other men laughed and nudged him, and occasionally he would even smile, but it was never the smile I saw.

The wicked one. The one full of promise and life.

All of his smiles outside of his bedroom were hollow echoes of the real one. So what game was he playing? I swallowed and picked up the coffee cup, blowing on the surface before I took a sip of the hot, bitter, caffeine-fueled beverage. I needed it. I'd drank myself into oblivion the night before, barely managing to stumble to the door when I became aware of Andre's fist pounding on the door.

Everything else was a blur of hands and mouths and tongues and orgasms. Rough sex and oblivion. The morning hadn't been much different, except I'd been more in control, more aware, but the results had been the same. Me, unconscious in the bed, completely naked, soaking wet and incredibly sore.

My clit hadn't had this much attention since I'd binge-watched True Blood with Elise's login.

Stabbing my fork into the sausage, I took a bite, catching the grease with my napkin before I wiped my mouth. The food was sinfully delicious. Homemade and *not* healthy. I was amazed that none of them weighed a thousand pounds, because I sure as hell would if I stayed here. Doing nothing but reading in Andre's bed and occasionally being fucked into a liquid puddle.

God dammit. Trying to hide in my hair, I glanced at the men at the table. There were more of them now, ones I didn't know. Two of them were about the same age, but one was older. Stoic and cold, and he kept looking at me. It was unnerving, because he wasn't participating in the joking and boasting that the other men were. They talked about conquests, kills, fights they'd been in — and Paulo's absence was glaring.

I was relieved, but also concerned. Andre had influence

JENNIFER BENE

over the others, that was clear. Mostly because they were afraid of him, but there was only one final say in this house... and that was Paulo García. I cursed myself as I took another bite of food. From the moment I'd arrived at the address, I'd known that this asshole wasn't some run-of-the-mill dealer that Chris had messed with. To have a place this big, this beautiful, in Miami of all places, meant he had to have a lot of money. Money that came from a lot more drugs than my dumbass baby brother had ever hidden in the trunk of his piece of shit car.

Everything, *fucking everything*, was in that envelope I'd brought here. My hopes for a down payment on a house someday, mine and Chris' financial security — gone in a goddamn blink. The worst part of it was that, as I ate a cold bite of frittata, I didn't even know if my actions had made a difference. I didn't know if Chris was alive or dead. The last of my family, the only person I had left in the world that was physically connected to me... and I was failing him.

If I hadn't failed him already.

The thought of him dead in the hospital morgue turned the food in my mouth to ash and ruined the rest of my appetite. I poked and prodded at the rest of it on my plate, listening to the laughter and conversation at the table. A raucous clatter of male voices, each trying to one-up the other, but I hadn't heard Andre participate.

In a moment of weakness I looked over at him, finding his gaze already on me, and I saw my own feelings reflected in his expression for just a moment. A convoluted combination of regret and hunger. He wanted me, and I wanted him. We'd fucked too many times, and I couldn't even pretend I didn't want it. I'd begged for it, screamed

186

for it, demanded it. Hell, I wanted him even now. Even as I watched him among the other monsters in this house. There was something about him, something *more*, and I just couldn't figure out what it was.

He was gentle with me, speaking softly even when he was saying the most horrible, arousing things. Even when he was fucking me to the point of pain, making me scream, making me choke and cry and beg... he was still careful. All of those muscles, those bruised and bloodied knuckles, could do so much more damage than he'd inflicted upon me.

And while that definitely wasn't a love story, it was strangely nice.

Why hold back? Why tell me about Paulo? Why tell me didn't want to kill me... even though he never promised not to? This situation was so fucked. In a million different ways, in a hundred different directions. Completely and totally fucked. But when we were alone, it felt right and wrong at the same time. Like puzzle pieces almost fitting, just needing a hard tap to fall in place.

I just didn't know what it would take for that *click* to finally happen, or if that was even possible.

"You sure I can't have a little fun?" A man's voice caught my attention. Too close. I glanced up and saw one of the new men standing near me, looking down with a smirk on his lips. He had light brown hair and a dark tan, his thumbs hooked into the pockets of his jeans as he stared at me like I was on the fucking menu.

My eyes went to Andre, and I was relieved to see the aggression there. It meant I was safe for now. He wouldn't agree.

"I'll be real sweet to her, I promise," the man said, grinning wider when I looked up at him.

"She's mine, Samuel," Andre answered. Cold, clear, finite.

Samuel raised his hands up, laughing as he took a few steps backward. "Alright, alright. I just wanted to see. I don't need a lesson like Diego." The man laughed. "How is your face today, *cuadro?*"

Diego flipped him off, and I risked a look in his direction. Feeling way too much inner happiness at the swollen, discolored nature of his nose and mouth. José was next to him, and the two of them were talking, but their eyes were moving between me and Andre. *Not good.*

"I heard you bought her from Paulo... do you plan to sell her?" The older man finally spoke, and I felt a cold frisson of fear run over my skin. Panic made my mouth dry, my lungs tight, and I stared at Andre, willing him to protect me. To save me again.

His silence lasted longer than I was comfortable with, long enough for the side-conversations to stutter to a stop as everyone turned their eyes to him.

"I'll pay well," the man added, as if they were already negotiating. Over me.

Andre wasn't moving, alarmingly still as he stared down at his plate, and I wanted to speak up for myself but my mouth wouldn't work. Nothing was working, except for my heart that was trying to beat its way out of my chest. After what seemed like forever, he set his fork down and leaned back in the chair, crossing his arms over his broad chest. Biceps bulging under the sleeves as he stared across the table at the man. "Luis."

"I am only asking. I do not mean it as disrespect. If anything…" His eyes moved to me again, trailing over me in a way that made me nauseous. "If anything it is a compliment."

Finally, Andre turned and looked at me. Dark eyes boring holes through my skin, but I wanted him to look at me. I wanted him to see me and remember that I was a person. His jaw clenched tight, slipping his hand into his pocket to hold out the key, and then he tilted his head towards the doorway. "Go upstairs. Now."

With the weight of too many male stares on me from too many dangerous men, I didn't hesitate. Setting the plate down on the tile, I pushed myself up from the floor and took the key. Then I practically ran out of the kitchen, grabbing onto the banister of the stairs to haul myself up faster.

The second I was inside the room I locked every single one of his crazy paranoid locks. Although, it wasn't being crazy or paranoid to think that any man in the house could kill you. They *would* kill on Paulo's orders, they'd do anything on Paulo's orders.

Walking back to the bed, I toed my shoes off and climbed back in. It smelled like sex and Andre — as if those were two different scents — and I grabbed onto his pillow and pulled the blankets up over my head. Just like I had when I was a kid, hiding from the monsters under the bed.

Andre

The moment Nicky's footsteps faded up the stairs, I took my time to look around the room at each man. I could feel the rage moving inky black through my veins, that low hum in my ears as my blood pressure spiked and adrenaline dumped so that I could beat one of these motherfuckers to death.

Because apparently the lesson with Diego hadn't been enough.

I'd bit my tongue through most of breakfast, trying to ignore their jokes, their comments about taking turns with Nicky. Nicolás and Samuel and José had smoothed each fucked up suggestion with a loud round of laughs. Even Marco had cracked a few jokes, while Diego just talked about how good she'd looked crying with José's gun in her mouth. Describing it in detail for the brothers.

The twitch of my cock at that visual had only made me angrier, and then Samuel had actually approached her, and fucking Luis was talking about buying her off me like an old car?

No. This was going to stop now.

"I want to make something very clear. The girl is mine." I moved my stare from Marco to José and Diego, and then to Samuel and Nicolás. "I'm not sharing her, I like fucking her. Alone." Finally, I stared directly across the table at Luis, who I had thought was different, less cold than Paulo — but now their closeness made more sense. It wasn't just his loyalty, or his work ethic, it was because he was just like him. Just as hollow on the inside, as dark and tainted as every killer in the room. "And I'm not selling her. She is mine. Just mine."

"And *jefe* agreed to this?" Luis asked, not showing a hint of a reaction until one eyebrow lifted a bit. "You going to use that knife, Andre?"

Glancing down at my hand I saw that I'd picked up the knife I'd been using on the sausage, my thumb stroking across the sharp edge. For a flash I measured the weight of it in my hand, a little too back heavy to make for a good throw, but it's not like any of the bastards were far away. It wouldn't have to fly straight for long.

Be smart. Don't fuck this up. You're so close to getting out, and if you can get out, you can get Nicky out too.

"No. I just like knives." That wasn't a lie, I loved knives. Had an entire case of them in the floor of my closet, but I knew that had nothing to do with why I'd picked up the blade subconsciously. I wanted to hurt them. All of them. But… I couldn't. It wasn't even possible to take them all on, and I was sure the brothers were carrying guns anyway, so I pressed the knife back to the table.

Luis tilted his head, studying me like Paulo always did, but I was skilled in keeping up the mask, the empty expression that made his efforts useless. Luis leaned his elbows on the table. "I asked you what *jefe* said about your decision to keep her for yourself."

"I went to him first, Luis, and he agreed to it. She became mine when I handed over the money to cover her debt."

"After he kicked me out of the basement so he could fuck her first." Diego looked like shit. Bruised, swollen cheek, his nose was a wreck, and I had to fight the urge to smirk at him.

"I wanted her, *cuadro*. So I took her."

"I was going to fucking take her, you pulled me off her, *cabrón!* Fuck this!" Standing up, he flipped me off and stormed out of the kitchen, shouting a series of insults over his shoulder. I waited to see if I heard his feet on the stairs, but he'd moved towards the front and I refocused on the more immediate threat.

Luis sighed, clearly not entertained by Diego's antics, and his steady gaze returned to me, as if we didn't have an audience to whatever the fuck this was. I was aware though. José was smirking, Samuel and Nicolás were leaned back on the tall counter, whispering to each other, and Marco was sulking at the far end of the table. That bitter glare that he wore around me all the time now.

Diego wasn't the only one throwing a fit over me getting Nicky.

Grabbing his coffee cup, Luis leaned back, never one to rush his words, and I didn't want to be having this bullshit discussion anyway so I let the silence stretch. Watching the others in the room, studying José's amused expression which had all of my instincts pointing to danger.

It ruined my fucking appetite. Pushing the plate away, I was barely aware when Laura came to take the plate to continue cleaning up. She was purposefully deaf and blind to everything happening, as all of Paulo's *staff* were. If I hadn't been here they could have run a train on Nicky on the tile floor, left her broken and bleeding, and Laura would have just stepped around her to keep picking up. I knew it, because I'd seen it fucking happen.

This whole goddamn place needs to burn.

With the itching rage moving under my skin, I wanted to go cold, to separate and operate like I always did — as if none of this bothered me — but I was finding it harder to do that when it came to Nicky.

Luis finally spoke again, soft and steady. "You keep saying that Nicky is yours, but, tell me… is that completely true, Andre?"

Shit.

He knew. He fucking knew. I could tell in that sly tone to his question, which meant Paulo had talked to him about our arrangement. I couldn't even begin to contemplate the why, because I had to deal with this shit right fucking now before my claim on her grew shaky. "We all work for *jefe*, Luis. If he wanted Nicky, he would have her."

"So, if *jefe* took her from you?"

Something was wrong in my chest. Breathing uneven, and a growing pain under my sternum as I used every trick I knew to keep myself stoic, steady enough to talk with him. I swallowed past the spreading ache in my ribs, and answered. "Then he would take her. I have to admit I don't know where you're going with this."

Lie. I knew exactly what he was doing, and the momentary smirk that passed over Luis' mouth told me he was all too aware.

"It's a question of loyalty, Andre. Either you are a good soldier, or you are cannon fodder." Luis shrugged a shoulder at the casual death threat. "She is a pretty girl, gets a lot of attention. If you don't think that Paulo will expect to benefit from the woman sleeping and eating in his house… you're wrong, *cuadro.*"

"*Jefe* and I discussed it already." The worst part of that sentence was that it was true. I had agreed that if he wanted her I would hand her over. But I had never been sure what I would do if he actually did it. It's not like Paulo didn't have options, girls that came home with him just to be close to the power and the money and the danger. It didn't have to be Nicky, but it would be. I knew it. At some point he would want her. I just had to keep her safe until the meeting, and make sure Nathan was ready to move. But if he took her from me before that?

I could barely stomach the idea of Paulo touching her. The idea of him keeping her was worse by far. Would it be for a night? A week? Forever? What the fuck did it look like if Paulo told me to hand her over and I told him to go fuck himself?

A body bag, and Nicky with him anyway, or dead in front of me as some kind of lesson.

It was a no win situation, and any act that even looked like disloyalty would ruin everything. I'd be cut out of the meet with the new Columbian leadership. I'd get shut out of Paulo's inner circle of trust. Nathan would want my balls on a plate. Swallowing the heartburn creeping up my throat I lifted a shoulder in a slight shrug. "If this is your way of telling me that Paulo wants her, then just spit it out. I'll bring her to him myself."

Was that a lie? I couldn't tell.

Luis waved a hand. "No, no, that is not necessary. I just wanted to have a better understanding of the situation with the girl."

"And?"

"And it seems you have the situation well in hand. I just wanted to remind you of where your loyalties lie." He stood up from the table, his chair squeaking over the tile as he turned on the vaguely friendly persona I'd always encountered.

"My loyalties are never in question," I countered, more of a growl to my tone than I meant, because even though I planned on betraying Paulo and all of these evil fucks, I still didn't like being called a traitor to my face, even if he hadn't used the word.

A flash of Francisco's bloody body slumping to the floor came into my mind. The sight of him curling around the bullet wound, burning a hole through his gut, permanently imprinted on my brain. That could be me if I refused Paulo. Or he might hand her over to every other man in the house and make me watch, just to remind me who was in charge. So many horrible possibilities, so much danger.

Why the fuck did you come here, belleza?

"Trust is earned, or lost, with every action, Andre. Remember that." Luis nodded at everyone as he walked out of the room and I felt the doom settling over me. Not my own, but Nicky's.

Paulo was coming for her, and I knew that I wouldn't be able to stop him. Not without risking her life… and the thought killed me.

NINETEEN

Nicky

The house was buzzing with activity, and Andre was distracted and anxious. For two days he'd dragged me around the house for meals, never letting me out of the room unless he had to, and it was his behavior that had me more worried than anything.

He was twitchy, tense, and had snapped at me more than once... but the sex was still amazing. It was the only time I felt normal, as fucked up as that was, because with him I forgot everything else. I forgot about the threats of the other men, the fact that I was still a prisoner. And last night he'd whispered against my hair, *'It's almost over, belleza. Just hold on.'* He had probably thought I was asleep, hazy and relaxed in post-orgasmic bliss, but I had heard him. I'd clung to the words, awake long after his soft snores rumbled behind me.

I wasn't crazy, I knew it deep down. Andre was actually trying to help me, to save me from this nightmare. I just wished he would be straight with me, but he never was. His wild swings from hot to cold, from violent to gentle, made it fucking impossible to read him.

When I'd dug through my duffel bag and found my blue slippers from the house, I had hugged him. They had been my mother's, and when I felt the tears sting my eyes I'd held on tighter so he wouldn't see them. Then, with a quiet voice, I'd explained what they were, and even though he hadn't hugged me back, I'd felt his big, warm hand on the small of my back.

It was a perfect moment in this fucked up place.

When he tried, Andre could be so thoughtful, so damn *sweet* when he kissed me in the night, when he wrapped his arms around me and pulled me against all of that hard muscle. When he did that, I felt safe, protected... almost happy, as wrong as that was. But he could also be terrifying, violent, and unpredictable. He could hurt me, and I knew he enjoyed it. Hell, he'd even admitted that he liked to hear me scream, but even at his worst I kind of enjoyed it too. Not like I'd ever admit it when I wasn't approaching an orgasm and desperate for anything to push me over the edge.

The real problem was that I never knew which version of him I was going to get.

Lying back on his bed, I blew out a breath, wishing he'd snagged a bottle of liquor last night before he'd dragged me upstairs and told me to lock the doors. Or he could have at *least* brought one when he showed up buzzed and aggressive and fucked me into oblivion. At least then I'd have something to drink in my boredom. I'd read almost every book he had, and was now a quarter of the way into the Louis L'Amour book, somewhat irritated at myself for even enjoying the ancient western.

But what else was there to do?

If Andre wasn't fucking me, or sitting in the room with me in awkward silence, then all I could do was read. I'd managed to pry a few conversations out of him, but hadn't learned a single fucking thing about him. All I knew was that he wanted to keep me for himself, to protect me from everyone else. It was almost like Andre hated the other men in the house. I caught little hints of irritation, or disgust, whenever the others spoke during meals, although he mostly kept that empty, scary expression on his face that I'd seen the first day. But it didn't make sense why he was *here* then. Why work for Paulo? Why surround himself with people he didn't like? Or, was it possible that he'd liked them until I arrived, and now they were just competition?

I shook my head and sat up, burying my face in my hands. I was losing it, spending too much time in my head and spinning up ideas about something more than just sex between us. Yes, he protected me, but it was just because he didn't want to share me. Something that I agreed with, but how long could I live like this? I still had trouble believing it had only been five days. It felt like more, a lot more, but he'd told me the date and he had no reason to lie about it.

Just hold on.

His words echoed in my head, and I wanted to ask him about it. Wanted to ask what I was holding on for, because if it was more of this tense and terrifying existence, I wasn't sure I wanted to. More than once I'd thought about running out the front door. When the house sounded quiet with my ear pressed against his door, knowing all I had to do was undo all of those locks and creep down the stairs and then outside. I'd even opened his bedroom door a few times, but panic had always gripped me and made me shut it.

I didn't feel safe without Andre beside me. Not in this house. And there were too many men here now, too many guns, to risk it. They'd kill me if they caught me trying to run, just to keep my mouth shut. No, the only time I felt safe leaving the room was when Andre walked with me. All that muscle, all that dark ink on his tan skin, all that potential violence coiled tight. His knuckles were still scabbed and bruised from the day he'd killed someone. The same day he'd hit Diego for threatening me.

Andre was confusing, a constant contradiction, and I was stuck with him — which really should have bothered me more than it did. I should hate him, I should hate the things he did to me, but for some insane reason I didn't. Instead, I was hopelessly convinced he was protecting me. In some twisted way doing whatever he could to keep me safe, even when he was the one to hurt me. And I still looked forward to that moment just before sleep took me, when I felt his strong arm around my ribs pulling me tight to his chest. That moment when the world melted away and I sank into sleep beside him.

But this place wasn't safe, and things seemed to only be getting more dangerous.

There was no way in hell he'd tell me what was going on, no matter what I said. I'd overheard talk of a big meeting, something that Andre would be attending to help Paulo, but he wouldn't answer me when I asked about it. Still, whatever it was had every asshole in the house on edge.

Even the new guys, who were apparently a pair of brothers, had calmed down their joking at breakfast this morning.

Tomorrow.

Whatever the fuck it was, it was tomorrow. I just didn't know if that was what Andre was asking me to hold on for, or if I was just kidding myself. I could be completely wrong about all of it. Wrong about Andre's intentions, wrong about my future, wrong for hoping for anything less than a swift, painless death… because if I was wrong, if Andre wasn't trying to help me, wasn't trying to protect me, then death was all I had waiting for me at the end of this.

Andre

Planning was in full swing. Luis had told me, José, Samuel, and Nicolás about the location as we'd sat around the poker table, pouring rum into glasses of coke before ten o'clock in the morning. I had to admit that I was glad that Diego wasn't included in this little circle of trust, and I felt that urge to smile when I imagined Diego's bruised ego as he was sent on yet another errand for Paulo.

Fetch, cabrón.

"Anything could happen, and that is why you must be prepared to respond. If this is some attempt to replace Paulo here in Florida, then we will kill them, because if Paulo goes down we all go down with him." Luis was intense, focused, like a general directing his troops, and I found myself nodding with the others. *Shit*, even Nicolás and Samuel seemed serious. "Are there any questions?"

"I'll need to look into some routes if we need to get out fast, I haven't been to that area of the city in a while," José answered, and I nodded.

"I agree. If we're going to a location they chose, it's more likely that it could be a setup. We just need to be prepared." *Bullshit.*

I'd been spewing bullshit for days, playing my part as the concerned muscle for the bastard who paid me, but all I'd been able to actually focus on was Nicky. I'd been waiting for Paulo to make his move, keeping Nicky shut in the room as much as possible to limit their contact, but I wasn't stupid. Paulo had wanted her since the first time she'd shouted at him in this fucking room. He wanted to hurt her, wanted to break all of that fiery spirit that I liked so much. It wasn't just the way she responded to me, or the inherent light and strength in her, it was her stupid fucking bravery. The way she'd come barging in on her brother's behalf to demand Paulo settle a debt he would never have cleared once he saw her. Who could walk away from a woman like Nicky?

Brash, beautiful, brazen, and so fucking strong. It was like a challenge, and every time she gave in with me felt like another win. A sensation I was getting addicted to.

"Do we know who they're bringing with? There should be some kind of agreement so that we don't show up and be so out-gunned that pulling our weapons is fucking stupid." Nicolás was toying with his glass as he spoke, tilting it back and forth, and then he clapped it down on the table. "I don't even know this Márquez family, and Sam and I have spent more than enough time in South America to know the players."

"That's what I have questions about. How sure are we that these guys have even taken out *jefe*'s current suppliers?" Samuel asked.

"Paulo has confirmed the Santiago's deaths, and the fact that there was a coup of their properties. Both their coca fields and their processing facilities." Luis glanced at the doorway, and then took a drink. "Look, I do believe that they just want to maintain a relationship with Paulo for distribution purposes here in the US, but there is always a risk that they want to put their own man in position."

"And that's why he called us in," Nicolás finished.

"Yes," Luis answered, and I glanced at José to see a serious look on his face. This was deep shit, and if it went sideways the whole goddamn situation could explode. Nathan knew the date and the time, and now I had the address. As soon as this little meeting concluded, I'd give him the information and then whatever the fuck the Columbians had planned wouldn't matter because the assault team would show up — and I'd be out. Finally fucking free.

Still, Nathan had been reticent to even put Nicky's name on the list of people to protect, but he'd promised her name was there. Someone had filed a missing persons report with her name, and for now Nathan had been able to shut down a full investigation into her disappearance, but at least he finally believed me. Nicky was innocent in all of this, a beautiful blonde warrior caught among devils because of one love-fueled, stupid decision. And as dumb as walking into Paulo García's house had been, she didn't deserve to die for it.

I'd die before I let someone kill her.

"How heavy can we carry? I've got an AK-47 if we want to make an impression—"

"No." Luis cut José off, raising a hand as he shook his head. "Handguns only, but be ready if things go south. I don't want to appear like a threat, this could be good for all of us, but I don't want us to be unprepared."

"I understand," José answered, always the good little soldier.

"And the explosives?" Samuel asked, and my ears perked up, all thoughts of my golden Valkyrie vanishing.

"Paulo already explained what he wanted done with those. They may be watching the location right now, so we can't do it ahead of time, but I want you to make sure to place them once we're there. Use the excuse of checking the perimeter, alright?" Luis waited for Nicolás and Samuel to nod, and I catalogued the information because this was something Nathan definitely *wanted* to know for once.

"We won't make a mistake, Luis. You know us better than that," Nicolás answered with a smile, and his brother nudged him, laughing as he grinned broad.

"That's why you are coming with us." Luis turned to me, expression unreadable even though he was sporting a smile. "Any questions, Andre?"

"No." I stared at him after I answered, irritated that he'd called me out.

"*Bueno*. Then I want you all to get a good night's sleep. We will not have drinks tonight, Paulo wants everyone sharp tomorrow morning." He shrugged. "What you do for the rest of today, I don't care."

"Sounds good to me! José, you still want to show us where to find some girls?" Samuel asked, grinning broadly.

"*Claro*, I know where to get some good pussy," José answered and as the others stood up I did as well, but Luis waved at me to stay behind.

When they walked out, I continued standing for a moment until Luis tilted his head toward my chair and I sat back down. My skin was fucking itching with the urge to get Nathan the new information. I needed to know they were ready, prepared. I just had to be in this hellhole one more day. Just one more, and then it would be over.

"Is there a problem?" Luis asked, and I felt my muscles tense.

"What do you mean?"

"When we were going over the meeting you seemed… concerned." Leaning forward, Luis put the cap back on the rum. "So, is there a problem?"

Fuck. I'd been focused on Nicky, thinking of her and everything I needed to tell Nathan. Had I really slipped so much? Upending my glass, I finished my drink, searching for something to say that would make sense, wouldn't make Luis question my loyalty, and wouldn't make me look like I'd been obsessively thinking about Nicky. *Think, motherfucker, think.* "I… look, Luis, I don't like these others choosing the location. It's in an area we're not familiar with, and there only seems to be one reason they'd insist on choosing it."

"Because it's a setup," Luis finished the thought, and I nodded. "*Jefe* and I have discussed it and we have the same concerns, but it is why we have planned. Prepared."

"And my job is to kill any threats to *jefe*."

"Yes." For a moment it seemed like Luis was going to say something else, but then he leaned back in the chair, expression flattening out once more. "You are a good soldier, Andre. Serve *jefe* and all will be fine."

"*Claro*, Luis. That is what I've always done."

"I know, *cuadro*. It's why you were at this table."

"*Gracias*." I nodded, taking a deep breath where the tension eased. They weren't questioning me, not now. I was still in the circle, which meant this information should be good. *Had* to be good or I was dead… and Nicky would be dead if she was lucky.

"Go enjoy your day, and your girl, Andre. We leave early."

"I know, I'll be ready." Standing up, I waited to see if Luis would stop me again, but he stood as well.

"See you at dinner, *cuadro*." Luis picked up his glass, and I grabbed the rum. I needed to take the edge off, I needed to fuck Nicky, and I needed to figure out what the hell to do… because tomorrow was it, and most of all? I needed her to be alive at the end of it.

Nicky

The sharp rap of Andre's knuckles on the door pulled me out of the western, and I quickly tossed it aside to get to the door. As soon as it was open, he moved through and I shut and locked it, smiling when I saw the rum in his hand. "Thank fuck, all I've wanted all morning is a drink."

He didn't say anything at first, setting the rum on his desk, and then taking the gun out of his pants to lay it down. His silence stretched, and while I was used to it, it didn't make it any less irritating.

"Andre." I said his name with the exasperation I felt, and he turned to face me. *Fuck.* He was gorgeous. The day before he'd finally shaved the scruff off his face, and now I could easily see the hard line of his jaw through the stubble. He still looked like death embodied, dangerous and full of potential violence, but I wasn't scared of him anymore.

Which could be Stockholm Syndrome, pure lust, or a mixture of the two.

Finally meeting my eyes, I saw something there. Something in the dark brown of his that was no longer empty, hadn't been empty for days, I just wish I fucking knew what it meant. I wished I knew *anything* about what the hell was going on. He held out the bottle of rum, and I came close enough to take it, fingers brushing his as I grabbed it to unscrew the top and tilt it up.

"Have you taken a shower yet, *belleza?*" he asked, gesturing for me to take another drink when I offered the bottle.

"Not yet." The sweet burn of the rum was welcome, and I didn't even care how early it was. Time didn't mean anything when I spent my entire day in his room, or sitting on the floor of the dining room hoping and praying that I didn't attract the attention of the bastards sitting around the table. Drinking and reading were my only sources of entertainment.

"Go ahead and grab a shower. I promise there will be plenty left to drink."

Something was off, something that I couldn't figure out, but it didn't feel good. Handing him the bottle, I pulled my shirt off and watched his face as he looked over my body. I hadn't bothered with a bra, and it wasn't difficult to push the shorts and underwear down, leaving me naked in front of him — yet another thing I shouldn't be so comfortable with. Stepping close, I traced my hands over his ribs, dragging my fingers over his hard muscle beneath the shirt to distract him. "What's going on, Andre?"

"Nicky…" he groaned, the bottle slamming onto the desk before he grabbed onto my hips to pull me against him.

"Just tell me? I'm sick of being in the dark." I leaned in, peppering kisses to his chest as I pressed closer, snagging the bottom of his shirt to lift it — but he grabbed my wrist.

"Go shower, Nicky. Now." With a fist in my hair he bent me back, kissing me roughly, hard enough to make my lips feel bruised as he opened my mouth. Tongue clashing, demanding, hungry… and then he pushed me back. Left me dizzy and confused, even more confused than before, with no more information than I'd had. "Do it."

Heat spiraled through me, plumes of smoke clouding my mind and I wanted to ask why he couldn't fuck me first and *then* have me take a shower, but I could tell from the look on his face that arguing wouldn't go well at all. And what I really needed wasn't sex, it was answers, and I wouldn't get those if I pissed him off. "Okay, I'll shower. Leave me some rum though, please?"

"*Claro.* I will."

Andre turned away to pull out the desk chair, settling into it as I kicked my clothes out of the way and marched to the bathroom to shower like I'd been told to. *God dammit.* Not only was I excited to see him, lusting after him, and not afraid of a man who'd admitted to killing with ease... but I was obeying him like a dog. As I shut the door and turned the water on, I couldn't help but turn everything over in my head. The man protected me, but liked to hurt me. He was feared by other killers, trusted by a man like Paulo García, and obviously not a good guy. Definitely not a good guy, but couldn't bad men still do good things? Could I convince him to save me?

Just hold on.

Hold on, survive, be smart... all things he'd told me. But what was I holding on for? That had never been explained, never answered, and it was going to be what we talked about before anything else. Before I fell into bed with him yet again... before I completely lost my mind.

TWENTY

Andre

Staring down at my phone, I had the smallest spark of hope. It was tiny, and weak, but still there and I couldn't decide if that was foolish or just... human. How would I know either way? I hadn't felt human in so long, it had been years of nothing but cold and violence and all of that darkness inside me that I'd fed and fed as I worked my way into Paulo García's trust.

So much fucking blood, so much death, so much violence and so many times I'd stood aside and let terrible things happen. There was no salvation for me, no redemption, but there *was* Nicky.

The only halfway decent thing I'd done in almost three years was stop Diego from raping her. Even though I'd taken her myself, and then continued fucking her every chance I got. Still, none of the other monsters in the house had touched her. Just me.

A fucking imperfect monster that couldn't decide to be

good or evil. I was somewhere in the middle, and it was miserable.

Maybe that was why God had finally given me a way out of hell, maybe saving Nicky would ultimately be the thing that let me bring them all down. It wouldn't erase the blood from my hands, or the things I'd done to her — nothing could do that — but maybe it was enough to get me out. That shred of hope grew, and I remembered when I'd decided to be a cop instead of a thug. The day I'd had to come home and tell my mother that Hernan was dead. My younger brother, shot while we were selling stolen car stereos. Those assholes had run as soon as Benito and I had pulled our guns, taking the money and the shit with them, but Hernan hadn't stood a chance. Two shots to the chest, he was choking on blood before I'd even had the chance to beg him to stay with me.

He'd died with Benito and I shouting at him on the hot, filthy concrete. Benito had run off, intent on finding them and killing them, but I'd stayed and stared at my seventeen-year-old brother, with his brown eyes open to the sunny skies but seeing nothing. I'd wanted to go back in time and not show up to the deal, go back and refuse to let Hernan come with us, but at the time it had seemed like the only answer. The only way to make rent that month, to have money for food, gas, and everything else we needed. Still, my mother had damned me, told me I was just like my father, the bastard who had died bleeding on a different stretch of concrete in Miami, forcing me and my brothers to step up to make the money. To keep us all afloat. But with Hernan dead, the *whys* didn't matter.

I was supposed to protect him, I was supposed to do the

right things, I was supposed to be better. I *could* have done better if I'd only tried. All things she yelled at me through her tears, through the slaps and the screams as she'd told me to leave. Leave and not come back, because God knew what I'd done and only he could forgive me. I had wanted to stay, to say goodbye to my younger siblings, but I had let her five-foot-two frame shove me out the door and slam it in my face.

Those two memories were burned brightly into my brain. The sightless eyes of my brother, and the agonizing fury of my mother mourning one son while she kicked out another for getting him killed — which was exactly what I'd done. I had been sure there were no other answers, no other ways to get money, but there were. They just weren't as easy, weren't as thrilling.

Weeks later I'd learned that one of the men who'd killed Hernan was dead, probably at Benito's hand, and the other had been arrested. I'd never wanted to be a killer, never wanted to be a thug, a monster. I wanted to be the man my mother thought I could be. I used to be the one who helped my mother carry groceries, who talked to her while she cooked, who took care of my siblings and changed diapers and did everything in my power to make our lives better. The next week I'd applied for the police academy.

Only possible because of my GED, grateful my mother had insisted on it, covered in tattoos and already more dangerous than every other man in my class. I'd had dreams of doing good, of being someone my mother would be proud of — but before I'd even finished the academy I was approached to be exactly who I was trying to escape. Go undercover, take out the bad guys from the inside. They'd looked at me and seen the monster, and I'd agreed because I'd never known anything else.

Rubbing a hand over my face, I cursed under my breath. My mother wouldn't be proud of who I was, worse than I'd been when she'd slammed a door in my face. More blood on my hands, more death on my soul, but I could do one good thing. I could get Nicky out as I took Paulo's empire down from the inside. Nathan didn't care about her, I could tell, but he'd insisted she was on the list — I still didn't trust him though. I didn't trust any of those fucks that were supposed to be my backup. They just saw the thug, the cold violence, and I knew they didn't trust me either.

Which meant I had to get Nicky out before the meeting. Tonight. The idea formed in my head and I knew it was the answer. After everyone was asleep, I'd sneak her downstairs with her bright purple duffel bag, get her purse and keys, and make her leave the car behind. Open the gate and watch her go, ensure she was safe before tomorrow happened.

Because I could die tomorrow, we all could die tomorrow, and then Nicky would be lost in the chaos... but if I was going to die, I wanted one good thing when I stood for judgment. One act that I could point to. Then, even if I was damned to Hell, I'd go with a soul that wasn't completely black. I'd go knowing Nicky was safe with the brother she'd given herself to protect.

Nicky

Squeezing out my hair with the towel, I rubbed until it wasn't dripping anymore and then wrapped it around me to step out into the room. Andre was leaned forward in his office chair, elbows braced on his knees as he stared down at his phone. Tension was etched into every line of him, his bruised knuckles bulging with how hard he gripped the little device.

I leaned against the wall and watched him for a minute, wishing he'd just fucking talk to me. Tell me whatever his plan was so that I could help, or at least understand what was happening so I could feel better. When he didn't budge, I walked over and sat on the edge of the bed closest to him, his dark eyes lifting to me.

"We need to talk," I said, trying to sound confident.

"We do," he agreed and I huffed out a surprised laugh.

"Shit, that was easy. I should have done that two days ago! I just want to—"

"Listen to me, Nicky." He cut me off, shaking his head as he reached over and unscrewed the rum, which didn't seem to have been touched at all. Andre took a drink first, and then handed it over. "Tomorrow is dangerous, really fucking dangerous, and there's a good chance I won't be back."

My blood ran cold, panic surging through me as I tried to speak. "Bu— but, you have to! You *have* to come back, Andre. You can't leave me here!"

"I know." Again, he stunned me by agreeing, but the panic

wasn't going anywhere. "I need you to trust me, and I know I haven't fucking earned it, but when I tell you to move, I need you to just do it. Okay?"

"Are— are you getting me out?" I pointed at the phone in his hands. "Is someone coming?"

He shook his head. "No one is coming for you, *belleza*. I just… I want you to know that all I've tried to do is keep you safe."

Something warm fluttered in my chest, and I had to swallow more of the rum before I spoke. "I know that."

"And — *fuck* — I'm sorry for everything. Everything that's happened, everything I did, I just…" Andre leaned forward and plucked the rum from my fingers to take a few large mouthfuls, but I couldn't even react. This was good, or possibly really bad.

"Are you going to die?" I asked, and I knew even as I said it that I didn't want that. I didn't want him dead. I didn't know what the fuck I wanted otherwise, but that was absolutely clear. Andre needed to live, even if I had no idea what that would mean for me, for us if there was an 'us' at all.

"I don't know, but I can't have you trapped here if things go south." He rested his forehead in one hand, the bottle of rum hanging between his knees, and I gambled.

"Is… is this what you meant when you asked me to hold on?"

His head snapped up, eyes intense. "You heard that?"

"I wasn't asleep yet, Andre."

The series of curses, a mix of English and Spanish, were full of anger and frustration, but they weren't directed at me. He was furious with himself, and I didn't care.

"Andre, I don't know what's going on. I wish you'd fucking tell me. I wish you'd tell me why you're here with these men you clearly despise, I wish you'd tell me why you're trying to help me at all — but if you're not going to do that, for God's sake just tell me how you're going to try and get me out." I slid off the bed, moving to my knees in front of him so I could catch his eyes as he stared towards the floor. "I want to help. I can help however you need me to, because I don't want to die either."

"*Belleza…*" His large hand brushed my cheek before he held the side of my face, and stared into my eyes. So much turmoil in his gaze, those dark eyes completely alive and desperate. "I'm not going to put you in danger, and in this house knowledge is dangerous. You're better off not knowing anything until you have to. But I swear, I swear to God, I swear on my mother's life, that I will get you out of here if it's the last thing I do."

Tears stung my eyes, and I tried to blink them away as I leaned up to grab his face in return, still wishing he would open up and fucking talk to me. "I believe you, okay? I believe you, but I'm not going to be any help if I don't know what's happening."

"What's happening is that I want to drink, and then I want to get into bed with you and fuck you until you pass out." His hand drifted into my hair, fisting it at the base of my scalp hard enough to make me hiss between my teeth as I grew warm and wet below. "No more questions, Nicky. Drop the towel and get in bed."

Obeying, again, I tugged the fabric free and let it fall. Enjoying the way he groaned and his tongue ran over his bottom lip. He released me and I stood, walking backwards slowly to the bed, as he followed me, prowling like a wild animal.

When I sat down on the bed, he shook his head. "Lay out, knees wide, I want to watch you touch yourself."

A blush crept into my cheeks, but I did it. There wasn't an inch of me he hadn't seen or touched, and I could only hope that if I did this he would fuck me into oblivion like he promised… and then let me go.

Andre sat down on the edge of the bed, eyes intent between my thighs as I reached my fingers down, spreading my lips to find my clit. Starting to rub in slow circles as he took another drink. "Faster," he demanded, and I felt the heat building as I found my rhythm.

Closing my eyes to relax into the bed and do what my body wanted. Dipping my fingers into my pussy, feeling the way I was still tender and reveling in it, wanting his cock inside me again. I moaned. "Andre…"

"Yes, *belleza?*"

"Touch me?" I begged, not even caring as I moved my fingers back to my clit and spread my legs wider. Then his fingers slid inside me, much larger than my own, and I gasped, bucking my hips to the rhythm we were creating as I focused on the bundle of nerves under my control. He stroked and thrust, teasing my g-spot with taps and rubs until I was squirming and trying to make it last. It was so intimate, being spread out in front of him like this.

"Open your mouth," he demanded and he held up the back of my head as he poured rum in. I almost choked, but managed to swallow, and when I opened my eyes he was smirking. "More?" he asked.

"Yes," I moaned, hips twitching as I fought the orgasm that was edging closer. Spicy and sweet, more rum flooded my mouth and I swallowed but some escaped and Andre leaned forward to lick me from neck to cheek to lips, capturing me in a kiss. Heat exploded, and my veins caught fire as I came, pure ecstasy erasing everything else from my mind except for his touch and his mouth on mine.

He nipped and groaned against my mouth. "I don't deserve you, *belleza*, but I don't want to give you up either."

"Just fuck me." It was all I wanted, because I didn't want to stay here, I didn't want to be a prisoner, I didn't want to die — but I also didn't want to leave Andre to this hell either. I could tell he wanted out, he wanted to escape, but there was no way out for him and all I could give was this. Exactly what he gave me, a few moments of forgetting, a few moments where the rest of the world fell away.

Andre didn't waste time, setting the rum down on the table to rip open the drawer with the box of condoms. He tossed one on the bed and then stood to tear his shirt over his head, and I let myself enjoy the view. He really was beautiful, the ink and the hard muscle, the intense expression on his face, and the tease of dark hair that wound from his belly button down to the edge of his jeans. Soon, those were gone too and there was just his cock, hard in his fist, as he tore the condom wrapper and rolled it on.

I started to turn over so he could fuck me while standing, one of his favorite positions, but he stopped me. "No, I want to see you."

Damn that warm little flutter in my chest, I needed to crush it before I lost myself to this monster. But then he moved onto the bed, settling between my thighs, his chest pinning my hips as he kissed across my ribs. Taking one nipple, and then the other, to gently suck and tease, leaving me to writhe against him, seeking friction that I couldn't find. "Andre, please!"

"Hush," he demanded, and I whined as he kissed and licked his way down, leading his mouth lower until he ran his tongue between my pussy lips and growled.

In an instant all the sweet touches shifted, and he devoured me. Fingers slid deep, holding my twisting body to the bed so he could do what he wanted. Another orgasm and I was pleading for him to fuck me, wanting him on top of me, inside me, but after the next I was screaming for it. Desperate, needy, craving the feel of him filling me, the power of his thrusts, the weight of him holding me down. "Jesus Christ, Andre, *please!* Please fuck me, please."

A low growl rumbled against my tender cunt just before he nipped my thigh and then shifted over me. Propping himself up on one arm he bent my knees and looked down to slide slowly inside. I couldn't help but watch as well, staring down between us as he eased himself in, not rushing, even though we both wanted it, and I managed to keep my hips still, to wait.

When he was finally balls deep, skin to skin, he dropped to his elbow, dragging me into another deep kiss as he barely shifted his hips. "You are perfect," he whispered just before he pulled back for the first hard thrust.

I cried out, in pleasure and sweet pain, reveling in how sore I was, enjoying the strength he could put behind each thrust. But he never did more, this was slow and intimate as he alternated between world-blurring kisses, and soft licks and nips across my neck and shoulders. I was dizzy from pleasure already, constantly whispering moans as I dug my fingers into his back to pull him closer, wrapping my legs around his hips to get him as deep as he could possibly go in this position. His purposeful strokes brought me to another orgasm and I was lost in a haze, a golden swirl of warmth and heat. I was barely aware when he hooked one of my legs over his arm and managed to thrust deeper, a little harder, but his lips were on mine again. Whispering in Spanish with words I sometimes caught, and sometimes didn't. Words like *pretty, perfect, sweet,* and *mine.*

I'd never wished more that I had studied Spanish harder, but I hadn't been a serious student, never had, and so the harsh whispers were mostly lost. Just an odd collection of broken vocabulary that made that warm fluttering intensify in my chest as his thrusts increased in pace, growing rougher as he leaned his forehead against mine. "Nicky," he groaned just before he came, cock kicking deep, but instead of pulling out of me he kissed me. Let his weight drop over me to press me to the bed, still linked, connected, and I poured everything I couldn't manage to find words for into the kiss.

All I wanted was for everything to work out, for us all to be safe. Me, Chris… and Andre. But even as I wrapped my arms around his neck and kissed him again, refusing to let go, I knew I was being stupid. If I managed to live through this, I'd be lucky, asking for anything more was ridiculous. No matter how intense the pain in my chest became as I imagined Andre dead. Dead for trying to protect me, to save me from my stupidity.

If he died, it would be all my fault. All mine.

TWENTY-ONE

Andre

I was going to get Nicky out tonight. Just a few more hours and she'd be safe, and then I could finally focus on the meeting without the distraction of her life in my hands. I knew for sure that earlier in the day would be the last time I fucked her. I couldn't risk the distraction, or falling asleep, the closer we came to nightfall, and I was trying my best to engage in the discussion.

Dinner was tense, everyone a little more somber and serious with the weight of tomorrow hanging over all of us. Paulo was absent, but I wasn't surprised. He tended to seclude himself before anything important, likely going over his plans, and back-up plans, and emergency plans. Tomorrow could be death for all of us, but as long as Nicky was safe I wouldn't care.

Maybe this was how it was supposed to be. My fate. And for some reason that thought brought me an odd peace instead of fear.

"Sam and I need to finish the work before the morning, so

we're heading upstairs." Nicolás pushed his chair back, and Samuel did the same beside him.

"See you *cabrónes* in the morning, eh?" He laughed a little, and then slapped his brother on the back to get him walking. Everyone made quiet comments of good night, but nothing more. I was prodding at the enchiladas Laura had left us for dinner, knowing they were probably delicious, even though I couldn't taste anything. It all felt automatic. Take a drink, cut a bite of food, chew and swallow. Repeat. We were all having water, no booze, and that explained some of the quiet, but it was still a little eerie. I appreciated it though, because no one was looking at Nicky sitting against the wall, and no one was forcing me to talk.

Marco stood and scraped his plate clean before leaving it in the sink. Then he came back to do the same for Samuel and Nicolás' plates. Normally, someone would have given him shit for it, but José just did the same with his own plate.

"Watch your backs tomorrow, okay?" Marco said, and José grabbed his shoulder, and nodded.

"*Gracias, cuadro*, we will be fine. *Jefe* knows what he is doing."

Smiling, Marco stepped away from José, moving to the door as he called back, "Night."

"I'm heading to bed as well, we have to be downstairs and ready to go by nine," Luis spoke as he stood, cleaning his plate as well so that Anna Maria would be able to handle them quickly in the morning.

"*Claro*," José answered, looking at me and then Nicky

before he settled his eyes on mine. "Do not let yourself get distracted by pussy, *cuadro*. Tomorrow is important."

"I know. It's not a problem." I managed to keep my voice steady, even as tense as I was with Diego still squatting at the end of the table.

José nudged the man's shoulder. "Diego?"

"I'm not going tomorrow, remember? Watching the house with Marco." Diego sounded bitter, and looked worse with the greenish tint some of his bruises had taken. "I can drink all I want."

"No, you can't. *Jefe* expects you to be ready if things go south and a call comes in. It's your responsibility to clear the house and get the others informed so we can respond." Luis snapped his fingers and pointed at the doorway. "That means you don't get shitfaced, you act like a soldier and do what *jefe* told you."

Diego's knuckles went white, but José squeezed his shoulder hard. "You heard Luis, *cuadro*. Get up, and be sure you're ready in the morning when we leave."

"Fine." Diego shoved his chair back hard enough to knock it over, and left his plate on the table as he stormed out.

José sighed and he and Luis looked at each other for a moment until Luis tilted his head toward the door. "Go make sure he doesn't do something stupid and piss off *jefe* even more."

"*Si. Buenos noches.*" With a sigh José followed after Diego and I couldn't believe my luck as the house was already settling down, barely after nine o'clock at night.

"I'll get it," I spoke up as Luis bent down to pick up the

chair, but he'd already set it upright before I'd managed to stand. "Or I'll handle the plates."

"*Gracias*, Andre. Everyone is just tense, but *jefe* is sure that the meeting will go smoothly. They don't have another man in Florida with the kind of reach and connections Paulo has. It would be foolish for them to do anything." Luis looked over at Nicky behind me and I fought the urge to tense. *It's almost over.* He walked around the table and stopped close to me, his voice low and serious. "Just remember what *jefe* expects of you, *cuadro*, and all will be fine."

"*Claro*, I know. I will be ready in the morning."

Luis nodded and left the room without another word, and I almost sagged in relief as I turned to see Nicky's wide blue eyes on me. I could see the hope in her, and it was almost painful how much I felt it too. This was going to work. She would be free, and I would take down Paulo García, the new Columbian supplier, and this entire corrupt fucking house would collapse.

"Bring your plate," I ordered, keeping my voice tight just in case anyone was lingering to listen. Thankfully, Nicky just did it. No smart-ass comments, no attitude, and in a few minutes we had the plates and glasses stacked in the sink, and the table cleared.

"Are we—"

She started to talk, but I shook my head and pointed to the doorway. "Upstairs, now."

I had to control myself for once. I couldn't fuck her when we got back to the room, I needed her packed and ready to go. I needed to be ready to get her out, and then in the morning I could just tell them all I left her in the room so we could get going. Everyone would be too distracted to question it, and then we'd be gone and everything would go down before anyone had a reason to check my room and find it empty.

But when I lifted my eyes to see her hips swaying, her thighs shifting as she climbed the stairs in front of me, I worried I wouldn't be able to do what I had to.

Nicky

"What are we doing, Andre?" I asked, tense with excitement as he shoved my dirty clothes into the duffel bag, pulling out the darkest items to lay them over the back of his desk chair. A pair of black yoga pants, a dark gray shirt from work that had the logo of the bar on it.

He didn't answer me, he just dragged the long black duffel from under his side of the bed and dug through it, pulling out a messy stack of hundreds. I had no idea how much he counted out, but he shoved it into my bag as well, and I didn't know what to say. Didn't know if I *should* speak, because this was it. After more than five days of chaos, Andre was finally proving I had been right. He was a good man, somewhere underneath all of the shit he'd had to do in life, he was good.

When he stood upright again, one fist moving into his hair to grip it as he thought things through, I ran forward and hugged him. Wrapping my arms tight around his ribs, squeezing until he finally put his arms around me too.

Cheek pressed to the top of my head, he crushed me to his chest, and I felt tears again.

"Please don't die," I whispered, and he leaned down enough to lift me, forcing my legs to wrap around his hips so he could kiss me. But it was soft, no raw, feral hunger, even as his tongue danced with mine and his strong arms held me close. I'd never felt so safe, not since I was a kid with my parents. Maybe not even then, because this was a man who had fought for me. "Please," I breathed the word against his mouth, seeking his eyes until his gaze locked onto mine. "Please don't die."

"I'll try not to, *belleza*." He kissed me again, and then let me down to the floor. "You need to get out of that apartment, use the cash to rent a new one. It would be better if you could have a roommate, have their name on the lease. Make it hard to find you."

"What about you?" I asked, wanting to know how to find him again, as stupid as that was.

"I—" Andre started to answer when a soft series of knocks came at the door, and he went rigid.

"Who is it?" I moved towards the door, but he grabbed me and dragged me to the wall beside the bed.

"Stay here." His voice was harsh, and he pointed at the duffel on the bed. "Hide that, and don't make a sound. Got it?"

I nodded, grabbing my bag and shoving it under the bed before returning to my hiding place as I listened to Andre undo the locks on his door. The voice that came through as soon as it was open made my heart stop.

"*Cuadro*, I'm not... interrupting anything, am I?" Paulo

asked, that terrifying calm to his voice, and I started shaking, digging my nails into my palms.

No.

"Of course not, *jefe*. What do you need?" Andre sounded like he always did around Paulo. Empty, dark, terrifying.

"Need? Nothing, *cuadro*. I do want the girl though. Just for tonight." There was a pause, and then he continued in that smooth, accented voice. "You will have her back tomorrow, I just need to take the edge off. *¿Entiendes?*"

The world shifted under me, like it was splitting and in a moment the earth would crack open and swallow me whole — which would probably be better than Paulo García taking me out of this room.

"I understand, *jefe*, give me a moment to get her for you." Andre's words felt like a knife being buried between my ribs. A sharp, surprising pain, and even as I heard the door fall shut and saw him come around the corner, it didn't stop. It just got worse, the intense expression on his face making the tears flow faster as fear took over.

"No, no, Andre, don't do this. Please, God, don't—"

He moved forward fast, wrapping me in his arms again and hugging me tight even as I tried to push him back, tried to pull free of his grip. I couldn't breathe, I couldn't think straight as terror took over me. "Stop, *stop*, Nicky. You have to listen to me, you have to fucking listen to me."

"Don't do this, please Andre, please…" I stared up at him when he pulled back, and he grabbed my face, his warm hands on my damp cheeks, and I saw the pain in him.

"You have to go with Paulo—"

The words barely left his lips when I felt my knees give out, but he held me up, pinning me to the wall with his body, refusing to let go of my face, forcing me to look at him as he spoke. His jaw was clenched tight, and I wondered if I saw the beginnings of tears making his eyes shine in the dim light.

"Listen to me, Nicky. We do not have time for this, if I refuse he will kill you, or me. This is a test, Nicky, are you listening to me? This is a fucking test. There is no refusing him, do you understand?"

"Please," I begged, not wanting to admit that I understood, that I was hearing every damn word he was saying even as I fought it.

"Nicky — *fuck* — if I try to refuse he will take you anyway. I know him. Then he will either kill me for refusing, or kill you in front of me to teach me some kind of lesson in loyalty… or he might just take you, and then give you to everyone else and make me watch." Andre's voice was deadly quiet, and stone cold, even though I could see the pain on his face, but my ears were buzzing. I felt light-headed, and all I could do was try to shake my head against the grip he had on my face. "Tell me you fucking understand, Nicky. Swear to me you won't do anything stupid, swear to me you won't get yourself killed."

"Andre…" Words wouldn't come, I was terrified. I was supposed to be free, Andre was supposed to be taking me out right now. Right fucking now.

He kissed me roughly, and I couldn't find it in me to kiss him back. When he gave up and leaned his forehead on mine, I heard his voice break, low and tortured. "Just survive, Nicky. I'm so sorry, I'm so fucking sorry, but… just please survive so I can come for you. Make it through this so I can get you back."

There was a knock at the door and Andre cursed, looking towards it. His eyes pleaded with me, and I hated that *this* was when he finally showed me the man I'd known was in there, the one worried for me, the one protecting me, the one trying to get me free.

Not like it mattered now.

"Will he kill me?" I whispered, and Andre cursed and pulled me tight to him again, wrapping his arms around me.

"Just do what he wants, don't fight him, *belleza*. Please, just survive. I will come for you. I swear it, I swear I will get you out." The door opened and he pulled me away from him sharply, once again the serious, dangerous man I'd first met. "Throw a fit," he hissed.

It took me a second to process what he'd said, but then I threw myself back against the wall, slamming into the standing lamp he had in the corner. "No, no, please!" I shouted, just as Paulo appeared behind him.

"I'm not fucking asking, *puta*," he growled at me in a voice so full of cold rage I almost didn't recognize the man standing in front of me. He was terrifying, and I didn't have to fake the fear of him. When he lunged to grab me I kicked at him, and he grabbed my arm and I found myself face down on the bed, arm bent painfully behind me as I shouted in pain. "You know what happens when you act like this. You want me to hurt you before *jefe* even gets to touch you?"

"No! No, please!" I begged, voice breaking when he intensified the pain in my arm.

This is how he could have been all along. It could have hurt this much.

"She looks like she'll be fun, *cuadro*. There is no need to subdue her, I'll handle that myself."

I heard Paulo's voice growing closer, and I fought harder, ignoring the pain in my arm, and then Andre released me completely. I flipped over trying to get some space from both of them, but Paulo caught me by my shirt, and then he was there. Leaning over me, that empty smirk on his face as coal black eyes watched me. The *snck* of a knife opening made me tense and whimper, and I couldn't pull my eyes from it when he held it up.

"I look forward to you fighting, *belleza*, but not until you're in my bed. So, will you behave on the way there, or do I need to have Andre and the others help me." The blade trailed over my cheek and I stilled completely as he stroked the tip down my neck. "Of course, if I ask them to help, they will want a reward."

The others. Not just Paulo, but Diego, José, all of them.

"I'll go," I whispered.

"*Bueno.*" Paulo stood, tucking the knife away, and then he offered me his hand like a fucking gentleman. I glanced at Andre, who was all the way on the other side of the room, back against his dresser, so tense that I was sure if I fought again he'd pull one of the guns I knew were hidden in those drawers and kill him. And then we'd both be dead, or maybe I'd be worse than dead. There was no choice. None.

Taking his hand, I let him pull me off the bed, and lead me toward the door. "I will see you in the morning, Andre," Paulo said, and Andre nodded.

"Yes, *jefe*. Enjoy your night." The fact that he'd got those words out in such a cold, steady tone, made me cringe. I tried to remember the way he'd held me, kissed me, whispered against my ear. I tried to remember that he wanted to save me — but as we left the room and Paulo let the door close behind us, I couldn't feel anything but fear.

TWENTY-TWO

Andre

I heard the door shut and instantly hit the floor, my knees slamming into it with enough force to send shocks of pain up, but I barely felt it. Cold, black rage was swarming inside me, and somewhere in the mix was actual fear. Something I hadn't felt in so long, but it was there. Desperate and terrible.

I slammed my fist into the floor. Two, three, four times, until I knew my knuckles were bloody again but it wasn't enough. It didn't hurt enough, it wasn't getting through all of the shit crowding my head.

Paulo has Nicky. He has her right now, in his room, and he's going to hurt her, fuck her.

He might kill her.

My ribs hurt, there was pain in my chest, and I'd never felt so fucking helpless. Not since I'd knelt over Hernan and tried to convince him to stay alive — and I couldn't do that again. I couldn't do that with Nicky.

Standing up, I ripped the top drawer of my dresser open and grabbed a gun and a clip, loading the weapon and going for the door, but I stopped with my hand on the doorknob. Resting my forehead on the door I cursed, and collapsed again. Back against the wood, I tapped the gun against my head, harder and harder.

There wasn't an out. I couldn't fix this. I couldn't fix it without ruining everything, without getting us killed. I hadn't lied to Nicky, I knew this was a test. I knew exactly what it was, and Paulo had planned it perfectly. He'd backed me into a corner just so that I'd have to do this, just so that I would have to be the one to hand her over.

Futile rage burned me up from the inside, and I couldn't stop the sting in my eyes because I had a horrible feeling that me hurting her, making her cry out in pain, would be the last time I ever touched her. That me handing her over to Paulo would be the last thing I did to her, and the worst. I'd failed to protect her, and even if she survived, even if she did whatever she had to in order to survive this — I wasn't sure she'd ever let me hold her again, and with a groan I realized that's all I wanted at the end of this nightmare.

I just wanted to be able to hold Nicky again and promise her that she was safe and mean it.

As I stared at the gun in my hands, the edges blurry through the angry tears that I refused to let fall, I knew without a doubt that if Nicky died I'd be right behind her. As soon as I put a bullet in every bastard involved in this, with Paulo first on the list.

But if she survived, if she did what I'd begged her to do, then as long as she was free I'd never darken her door. I'd disappear from her life forever, and just be the bad memory I should have been already.

Nicky

Paulo led me to his room at the end of the second floor, on the opposite side of the stairs from Andre's room, and I felt myself trying to fade. To not be present for whatever was about to happen. I had no doubt this man wanted to hurt me, that he would fuck me whether I fought or not, but he was a perfect gentleman as he opened the door and gestured for me to go inside.

It was a huge room with a pair of French doors that led to a balcony. Through the gauzy curtains over the windows, I could see the grounds outside, dark and sprawling, with lights in the distance. A reminder of just how fucked I was. In the middle of Miami, but I may as well be on the moon for all the help it gave me. There was a large sitting area in front of the balcony on the left side, including a television on the wall, and the right side held a massive bed, and the entrance to a giant bathroom. Everything was done in light colors, except for the dark brown leather of the chairs and couch, and the dark wood of the headboard and posts on the bed. It was like a suite at some luxury beach resort, but as the door clicked and locked behind me I didn't feel relaxed at all.

I stopped walking forward, and *felt* Paulo approach me from behind, long before he laid his hands over my waist. "Tell me, *belleza*… have you showered since Andre fucked you last?"

His touch made my skin crawl, and the feel of his breath on my shoulder made me nauseous, but I managed to shake my head.

"Then go clean up. Quickly. There is no need for clothes after." He let go of me, stepping past me to move to a small bar set up near the sitting area, and I hurried to the bathroom to escape him. Anything to delay what was coming.

My hands were shaking so badly that I had trouble undoing the button to my shorts. Eventually I managed to strip and step into the frosted glass of the standing shower. Paulo had a collection of soaps and things, but I barely skimmed the labels as I found one to wash me. I let myself cry in the shower, because I needed to get it out. I didn't want to cry in front of Paulo, I wanted to be as detached as I could when he… did whatever he planned.

It was worse when I thought about it, so I tried not to. I tried to be a robot, as cold and empty as Andre, but I hadn't had near enough practice and by the time there was nothing left to do I had no choice except to turn off the shower and step out onto the plush rug. The towels in here were softer, larger, and I dried my body quickly so I could wrap one around me, and use another on my hair.

"*Belleza*, come." Paulo's voice came from the bedroom, and I took another minute to squeeze water out of my hair, before I managed to drop the towels. The huge mirror above his double sinks reflected my fear, and the pale bruises across my body. Most were healing, Andre hadn't been as rough in the last few days, but I was sure that I would look very different in the morning. When Paulo was done with me.

If you're still alive.

I flinched, and forced myself to walk to the doorway, letting Andre's urgent voice echo in my head. His pleas for me to *just survive*. That was all I had to do, I just had to live until the morning, and then he would come for me. He would get me out. I knew it, I knew it with everything in me… but it didn't help.

When I stepped into the room, I'd expected Paulo to be near the bed, ready to get this over with, but he was in one of the chairs. Worse, he wasn't alone.

I recognized Luis from the pepper in his hair, unable to make myself move forward until Paulo beckoned. "Come here, arms at your sides. I want to see what has Andre so enamored."

It took every bit of self-control I had to make myself walk towards them, fists clenched tight at my sides, and I found a bit of space on the wall and focused on it. It wasn't until I was standing near the couch that faced the television that Luis finally turned to look at me. They both had drinks in their hands, and Paulo gestured to a third drink on a coaster in the center of the coffee table in between them.

"Kneel there." He pointed at the space between the couch and coffee table. "And have a drink, *belleza.*"

My nerves were shot as I did what he said, confused that he wasn't violent, that he was almost being… polite? Yet, I knew how quickly that could turn. He'd drawn a knife on me twice, and ordered me into the basement in the same tone. Still, I finished the tequila in one go, and he chuckled.

"Give her some more, Luis." Paulo watched me, even

though I strained to keep my eyes on a neutral patch of wall, his gaze was so insistent that I had to look. There was something wrong with him, something *off* in the way he smiled like the world was wonderful as he gave me drinks and had me naked in his bedroom. *With Luis.*

Just to spite him, I finished the second glass just as quickly, begging to be drunk enough not to care what they did.

Unfortunately, Paulo just seemed amused. "Why do you think Andre wanted you?" he asked, and I twitched as I set my glass back on the coaster, hoping Luis would refill it.

"I don't know."

"Why do you *think* he did?" Paulo clarified, refusing to drop it, and I sighed.

"Because he wanted me, he didn't want to share me. He's said as much more than once." I twitched when he shifted on the couch, muscles shaking with the urge to run, even when I knew it was pointless.

"The others wanted you as well. I've had several discussions about my decision to allow Andre to keep you." Paulo made a thoughtful sound as he took a small sip of his drink. "Of course, he was always aware that I could have you if I wanted you."

"I know."

"How does that make you feel?" he asked, and I wanted to scream at him. I felt my anger spike, momentarily overwhelming my fear before I pushed it back.

"I just want to go home," I answered, reaching for my empty glass just on the off-chance it had magically refilled — it hadn't.

"Yes, I know. Your brother was released from the hospital, by the way. I believe he is back at his home recovering." Paulo's spontaneous offering of the information made my mouth drop open. "And his debt to me is resolved... I do hope he is grateful for your sacrifice."

Sacrifice?

I swallowed, my mouth going dry, and I wanted to ask for more tequila, but I knew it was pointless. "Is he safe?" I whispered.

"From me and my men? Yes."

"Thank you." Nodding, I tried to sit up straighter, to look stronger than I felt. "Then this was worth it."

Paulo laughed softly, a low and sinister sound that made chills rush over my skin. "Do you think so, *belleza?*"

I didn't answer, I just looked at him, trying to gauge how dangerous he really was.

He snapped his fingers and pointed at the floor in front of him. "Come here. Crawl."

With a sickening twist of my stomach I obeyed, crawling on hands and knees around the edge of the coffee table to situate myself on the floor between his feet. He cupped my chin and forced me to look up at him, into those coal-black, unfeeling eyes.

"I want to see what José did with you. Open your mouth." Just as he finished speaking he lifted a gun from beside him in the chair, and I leaned back. His expression flickered, and he slapped me across the face. Just hard enough to make me catch myself on the floor, the bright spark of pain bringing the tears back to my eyes as I knelt upright again.

Paulo didn't repeat himself, I just opened my mouth and for the second time in my life I felt the metal of a gun barrel between my lips, the metallic taste of blood and oil on my tongue. I almost instantly gagged from the memories of Diego and José doing this as Paulo started to move it back and forth. Then he pushed it farther back and I choked, gagging, but he forced my head to stay still. "Luis, come help her."

The man approached from behind and fisted my hair, just like Diego had, and I whimpered around the metal as drool pooled in my mouth.

"This is a nice sight, don't you think?" Paulo asked, and I heard a grunt of agreement from behind me. "I have a better idea. Put her on the table, Luis."

Luis surprised me with his strength, jerking me upright with a stinging rip of hair and shoving me down onto the coffee table as I yelped and whined. On my back, I immediately snapped my knees together, but Paulo only laughed softly.

"Tsk, tsk, *belleza*. Open your legs." He tilted the gun back and forth in the air, and then drew back the top of it with a dangerous *snap* of metal. "Now," he ordered, and I knew I was crying as I let my knees part. "Wider."

Survive, just survive.

I spread them wide, keeping my eyes clenched tight, and then I felt the gun at my entrance, the pressure as the hard metal forced its way inside where I wasn't wet at all. I cried out when he shoved it in harder, my hands reaching for him, but Luis caught my arms and pulled them back.

"That's better," Paulo said quietly, and then he started to fuck me with the gun. Rough thrusts of metal that felt like it was scratching inside me, and I tried to struggle, whining through clenched teeth, but Paulo had shifted his legs inside mine, his other hand holding my hip still with a painful grip.

"Please stop, please!" I was terrified that he would accidentally pull the trigger on one of those hard shoves inside me. It stung, and ached, but then I just tried to stay quiet. Tears leaked out of my eyes and into my hair as I pulled at Luis' grip on my arms, just wanting it to be over already, even though I knew they were just starting.

"This looks good," he mused. "What do you think, Luis?"

"Very nice, *jefe*."

"Yes..." In and out, cold, hard metal being warmed by my body as he violated me with it. I was too afraid to scream, imagining the sound of the gun firing, the pain.

"Let her up," he suddenly commanded, and he pulled the gun out of me at the same time. I almost choked in relief. Covering my eyes with one arm, wanting to be anywhere else, wanting to ignore my own steady tears, but Paulo wouldn't let me escape even into my own head. "Sit up, *belleza*."

I obeyed slowly, sitting on the edge of the table, almost eye-to-eye with him. Luis returned to the chair behind me, and I tried to stop the shaking, the tears, because Paulo was looking me over and noticing all of it.

He reached forward to brush his thumb across my lips,

catching my chin when I tried to pull back. "Normally, I would make this last, but as you know we have to be up early. So, we're going to go ahead and start the real fun."

"Please don't do this," I begged, and he laughed.

"Oh, you do have a sweet voice when you're scared. I'm sure you sound as good as Andre described when you scream…" He smirked, releasing my face. "I've only had the chance to hear you scream from downstairs, it will be nice to have it in person."

"Mr. García, I—" My plan to bargain, to plea, was cut short with a hard slap that burst in a bright white flash of pain across my cheek. I gasped, but barely had the time to process it as he grabbed me by the hair and dragged me up from the table and out of the sitting area. Throwing me to the open floor, I caught myself and tried to push up, but he kicked me in the ribs before I managed it. Collapsing back to the floor I choked on my first cry, trying to curl up when he pushed my hip with his shoe to put me on my back.

"I thought you fought, *belleza*. This is rather… pathetic. Is it because I'm not trying to fuck you?" His smile was dangerous when he looked down at me, unbuttoning his shirt slowly. "I find the fight to be entertaining, and, trust me, you don't want to bore me."

Looking over at the door, I wondered if I made it to the door if Paulo would let me keep running. Let me run to Andre's door and beg him to save me. Just as I tried to move toward it, he kicked me again, on the other side, making my ribs a matched set of pain.

After a moment, he leaned down, grabbing my face hard. "Well?"

"Go to hell," I hissed, and then spit into his face. Paulo barely flinched, he just wiped his hand over it, and then flipped me to my stomach, knees between my thighs to spread me open. I tried to drag myself forward, but he grabbed onto my hips and dragged me back. I kicked and screamed, reaching back to scratch at his hands, and he laughed.

"That's it. *There* is the fight I wanted. Luis come over." Paulo smacked my hands away, landing a punch to my already sore ribs that had me collapsing back to the floor, the pain sharp and radiating.

"Don't, please, don't!" I choked out, desperate, but a moment later Luis had my wrists in his iron grip, pinned to the floor in front of me by his weight, crushing them.

"See, you have to understand that letting Andre keep you from the others is just interesting to watch. To see him act so possessive over some *puta* when he has never even touched a woman in my house?" His hands ran over my hips, and then I heard him opening his pants and I whined, trying to gain some leverage, but there was none. "That was fascinating… but to have him declare he won't share you? That you are *his*, and his alone? Well, you understand why I can't have that."

"I *am* his," I growled, and I meant it. I remembered the warmth of his body against mine, the desperate plea in my ear as he begged me to survive — and I planned to survive this, but I wasn't going to let Paulo twist this into anything but what it was. No matter how much it hurt.

"You belong to me, cunt." He ripped my head up by my hair, the strain all the worse from Luis' hold on my arms. "And I'm going to hurt you, make you scream, *puta*, so you'll remember it when I *let* you limp back to Andre tomorrow."

"AH!" The pain as he forced his dry cock into my ass was impossible. A horrible burn, a sharp agony as he shoved himself inside me, and I was barely aware of the guttural scream until I had to breathe.

"That's right," he growled, pushing deeper, forcing me to take him as I tried to fight. My toes slid on the tile, nails digging furrows into my palms, and then he thrust in harder and I screamed as my back muscles tensed with the pain. Harsh and unforgiving, making me choke on the next sob that tried to escape my throat.

"God! Stop!" I begged, mindless from the torture as he started to thrust. And it only got worse as I found myself pressed into the floor, his hand between my shoulders, trying to clench my teeth through it, just to survive.

Please survive so I can come for you…

The pain was becoming a high-pitched hum in my head, a constant note that I couldn't sustain. I couldn't even scream anymore as he slid back and slammed inside me again and again. When I finally went limp, in too much agony to fight, he pulled out.

No. I managed a quiet sob because I hadn't felt him come. He wasn't done. He wasn't done?

"Get her on the bed and clean her up. It's fine if you get blood on the sheets." Paulo walked past me to the bathroom, and I was useless as Luis tried to haul me upright.

Blood, he'd said blood. Had he made me bleed?

Finally, Luis just knelt beside me and picked me up in his arms, standing up and wavering for a second before he walked over and dropped me onto the sheets. "Spread your legs, knees to your chest." With that command he walked away to the bathroom, and I heard the sound of water running, them talking, but I couldn't focus. It had already hurt so much, what else did he want from me? Was this how I was going to die?

TWENTY-THREE

Andre

———————

I wasn't sure when I'd finally fallen asleep with my face buried in Nicky's pillow, but the alarm on my phone woke me up like a gunshot. I sat up straight, unconsciously searching the bed with one hand before I remembered why it was empty.

Nicky is with Paulo.

Cursing, I felt the rage and the fear again, and shoved myself out of bed to get dressed and load my guns and extra clips. If I went downstairs early, there was a chance I could check on Nicky, and get her secure in my room before we left. I could let her know who I really was, what was happening today. Hell, I could leave her my phone so she could call Nathan and have them come get her out.

I don't think I'd ever been dressed so fast in my life, and I was still tucking one of the guns into the holster when I starting unlocking my door. Out in the hall my eyes went to Paulo's door at the far end, and I contemplated knocking — but that would cross a line. The best chance I had of getting her back, getting her safe, was to pretend I didn't give a fuck what he'd done to her.

Anna Maria was still cooking when I walked into the empty kitchen, and she turned to apologize. "*Lo siento, Señor* Andre. Breakfast is almost ready."

"*Gracias*," I growled out, taking a seat where I would be able to watch the doorway. She served the food on the table about ten minutes later, and I made a plate just as Marco walked in. His eyes moved to the place on the wall where Nicky *should* have been, and then he gave me a confused look. Just as he opened his mouth to ask, I shook my head, and he sat down in silence.

Next were Nicolás and Samuel, laughing, with two black backpacks that they sat against the wall. "Where's your girl this morning, *cuadro?*" Sam asked, and I forced myself to sound okay with all of it, as cold and empty as I should be.

"She spent the night with *jefe*." I summoned a cold smile. "I think he wanted a little stress relief before the meeting today."

They both laughed, while Marco just stared at me. Nicolás snagged a seat first, immediately dumping food onto his plate. "Well, I can understand that. José took us out to find some girls yesterday to take the edge off. Although nothing beats a girl that has to do whatever you want."

"Got that right," Sam laughed, nudging his brother with his elbow as he dove into his own food.

"Right," I agreed, but my eyes wouldn't leave the doorway. José was next, then Luis who only nodded at me before he took a seat at the other end of the table. Finally, Diego joined at about 8:30, and my panic was through the roof.

Where the fuck was Paulo? What had he done to Nicky?

I closed my eyes and looked down at my plate, praying for the first time in years. Really praying, to a God that probably didn't want to listen to me anymore, but I wasn't praying for me. I just wanted Nicky to be alive. That was it, I just wanted Nicky to survive. Even if she never wanted me to touch her again, or speak to her, or even see her. I just needed to know she was alive.

At ten to nine, Paulo appeared, alone, and I wanted to throw up everything I'd eaten that morning. He smiled at me, that cold shark's smile, and took the seat across from me. "*Buenos días*, are we ready to leave soon?" he asked in a light tone, and I had to swallow both my rage and my breakfast back down.

"Yes, *jefe*," I answered along with the others.

"Good. I have a feeling today will go well." He beckoned Anna Maria over so she could bring him coffee, and then he put some food on his plate to quickly eat. I thought through a hundred ways to ask about Nicky, but all of them sounded demanding. Finally, as if he could read my fucking mind, Paulo looked at me, his dead eyes glittering. "Go on, ask."

"Where is the girl?" I kept my voice soft, and his false smile widened.

"In my room. I'll return her to you when we get back from the meeting." He took a bite of sausage, savoring it for a second, and then he laughed quietly. "She does scream so nicely, *cuadro*, you were right. I will have to enjoy her again sometime."

"Whenever you want, *jefe*." I said the words on automatic

because he'd implied she was alive, that he *could* have her again in the future. She was alive, she'd survived. I said a quiet thanks to God for giving my black soul one good thing, but the relief I felt was short-lived, because I still had no idea what he'd done to her. No idea if he had snuffed out that light, damaged her beyond repair, broken everything in her that I loved.

Fuck. Loved?

That was too complicated a word to process right now, when every man in the room was carrying multiple weapons and prepared to kill. The only comfort I had was that Nathan and the assault team would have every one of these motherfuckers in handcuffs or a body bag by noon.

And I would be damn sure they got Nicky out of here.

An hour later, we were pulling up in two separate SUVs at the meeting. It was near the harbor, an actual warehouse, and there was someone at the gate to open it for us. Early Saturday morning the place was a ghost town, perfect for slaughter if that was what the Columbians had planned for Paulo and the rest of us.

I had to focus, had to get my head on straight and be sure I'd told Nathan the right warehouse number. Fortunately, it seemed Luis hadn't lied to us. It was the right warehouse, and there were two other SUVs outside of it, and one man at the door.

Paulo looked over at me and smiled. "Do you have my back, *cuadro?*"

I kept myself calm, trying to look a little confused. "*Claro.* Why ask, *jefe?*"

"Want to make sure last night didn't make you feel any different."

"No different at all," I said without a bit of a lie.

"*Bueno.* Let us go make some money."

We walked inside, and Paulo nodded to Sam and Nicolás who separated in different directions to walk the perimeter. When the man with us tried to speak up, Paulo cut him off. "If you think I will not have my men check the building, you are wrong. Now, take us in."

The Columbian looked between all of us, completely outnumbered, and finally led us on a winding path into the center of the warehouse. Past giant boxes, plastic wrapped pallets, and huge containers, until we stepped into a cleared area where a group of armed soldiers stood around two men wearing button-down shirts and an older woman in a black skirt suit.

"Ah, Paulo García, it is good to finally meet in person." The woman walked forward alone, extending her hand as Paulo did the same to shake.

"*Señora* Márquez, I am glad we were able to arrange this." He sounded as smooth and calm as he always did, but Jose, Luis, and I still spread out behind him.

"Yes, and here are my sons. Daniel and Tomás." She leaned back to wave them forward, and they did, taking up flank on either side of their mother. One looked to be almost thirty, the other a little younger.

"*Bueno.* It is good to meet all of you, but let us discuss what we came for. You know I have had a business relationship with the Santiago family for many years... I understand that your family had a disagreement with them and it was handled."

"It was handled, and while that was messy, we want this transition to be simple. And I wanted to meet you myself to understand what kind of man you are, beyond what I have been told." *Señora* Márquez had a smile as cold and practiced as Paulo, and it made me tense even as I forced myself to forget about Nicky, forget about what the bastard had done to her.

Paulo smiled, opening his arms wide. "I am an open book, *señora*. Ask me what you want, and then we will come down to the details of this new arrangement."

The fake polite shit was getting old, and I didn't have the patience to listen as they talked. Two of her men brought over boxes for them to sit on, one of the men removing his jacket so she could sit down on the fabric instead. His guns were not a surprise, but it still made me glance to José to make sure we both had access to ours.

Samuel and Nicolás joined us again a few minutes later, and walked to Luis. "All clear," Sam said, loud enough for the others to hear, but the smile on his face told me the opposite. They'd set up explosives around the building, and I had to hope that Nathan's team would take them out before they could set them off.

And where the fuck was Nathan anyway?

They had been talking for at least ten minutes about the area of Columbia they each grew up in. She talked about her sons, the death of their father, which seemed to be rather recent, and more drivel about how beautiful it was and how Paulo would like to visit the facilities to see them in person. *Señora* Márquez agreed easily, and then they finally got down to business. Reviewing the numbers from the previous arrangement, bargaining in polite tones, but no one in the damn warehouse believed it.

To take over another operation in Columbia the Márquez family had to be cold and vicious.

Shit. As I tuned back into their conversation, I could tell that they were already close to a new agreement. What would happen if they wanted to leave before Nathan's team was in position? I was tempted to go for my phone in my pocket, to see if he'd sent me a coded message of some kind, but then I heard the door bang open, and I reacted with everyone else. Gun out, I moved with José to grab Paulo. The woman's sons immediately drew weapons, pointing them at us, and I shielded Paulo just in case this shit went sideways and I was still in.

I heard boots, men shouting, and Luis yelled across the room, "Is this you?"

"NO!" One of the Márquez men shouted back, and I cursed.

"We have to get Paulo out," I told José, playing my part to the last, and Samuel walked up at the same time.

"Do I blow them?" he asked.

"No! We could block ourselves in. *Fuck!*" José was panicking, looking around, and then the first shots went off and the whole room exploded.

"Kill them and get us out of here," Paulo commanded, and I was tempted to put a bullet in him myself. Somewhere that would make him fucking suffer.

Shouts of "Police!" and "Drop your weapons!" rang out as the assault team poured into the narrow space, wearing tactical gear as the Márquez team tried to flee the other way, firing shots back at the cops. I couldn't see faces through their masks, but I hoped Nathan—

POP. POP.

Pain exploded in my chest and I stumbled and then hit the ground, hearing José and Paulo shouting as others yelled. Someone cried out in pain, and gunfire rang out across the warehouse, but none of it mattered because I was hit. I couldn't breathe, and I looked down at my chest to see it wet. Swiping my hand over it, I saw blood and I knew I had to be in shock. It had to be shock, because as I pushed at the wounds on my chest to stop the bleeding, they didn't hurt as much as they should.

A masked face hovered over me and I tried to grab on to them, to explain who I was, why I was here, but then the man pulled the mask up and I saw Nathan. "Shot. They fucking shot me." I spoke fast, trying to grab onto him as he looked around the room, and then leaned over me again. "Nicky, get Nicky. She's in Paulo's room."

"It's okay, Andre. You did it." He was looking around, another member of the assault team guarding his back, and then I felt a sharp pain in my neck. The world dipped, swam, and I tried to grab onto him again.

"Nicky." My tongue wasn't working right, the lights funny as they dimmed, and then I realized she was alone in the house. With Diego. No, *no.* "Nicky, get…"

I tried to focus, tried to explain, but Nathan wasn't even looking at me, he was looking away and I cursed him just before the dark swallowed me whole.

TWENTY-FOUR

Andre

———————

I woke up disoriented with a vicious fucking headache. It felt like the worst hangover I'd ever had, and as I tried to sit up, the muscles across my chest argued and I fell back onto whatever I was laying on. *What the fuck—* The meeting. The assault team. I'd been shot by one of those idiots!

Forcing my eyes open against the bright lights I scrambled for my shirt, and finally felt someone grab my hand. "Whoa, whoa, Andre! Chill out, man. We got them, we got'em."

It took a minute for the glaring lights to let me focus and see Nathan's face. I growled. "Who the fuck shot me?"

"I did." He laughed as I tried to reach for him, and then poked a finger hard into my chest and I groaned. "Well, not really. They were rubber bullets, have these blood caps on the end so they explode on you, makes it look like you've been shot. Pretty cool, actually, but I've been told they hurt like a bitch."

"Fuck you," I growled, but I had to admit I was relieved I hadn't actually been shot. Still, my head was foggy, confused. "Why did I pass out then?"

"I drugged you. Just a simple sedative, but we needed everyone there to think you'd died. Carried you out in a body bag and everything." Nathan looked proud, and I wanted to punch him in the face. "Now, no one is going to look for you while we take these bastards to court. Smart shit, right? We had someone from DEA on the team and it was their idea, and although they're cocky bastards, it worked great."

"Would you shut up for five minutes? Christ..." I grumbled, rubbing my face, and then I flinched. "How's Nicky?"

"We'll talk about that later, I need you to wake up and give us a report-out." I heard an edge to Nathan's voice and I forced myself up, realizing I was on a couch of some kind. There were people all over the house we were in, people talking and making calls, but I didn't see Nicky.

"Where the fuck is Nicky?" I met his eyes and saw the flicker in them.

"Give us your report-out, and we'll talk about—"

I grabbed Nathan by the shirt and hauled him towards me, ignoring the ache of the bruised muscles in my chest. They were just bruises, I'd survive, Nicky might not. "No. Right fucking now. Where is she?"

He shoved my hand away, straightening his shirt as he leaned back in the chair he'd pulled over. "We sent a team to Paulo's house, but it was empty. We've got the missing persons report out across the city, and have sent up alerts to be on the look out for—"

"You son of a bitch!" I forced myself to my feet, swaying for a moment, and I cursed him again for drugging me. "I told you, I fucking *told* you to get her out of there."

Stumbling forward, I caught myself on the door frame and Nathan grabbed my arm. "You need to sit your ass back down and let the other cops do their job. *You* have to do yours."

"I'm not doing shit until Nicky is safe."

"Fine, then it's a fucking order. Understand? You will sit down, you will complete the report-out, and you will meet with—"

I decked him before I could even think through how stupid it was, and Nathan went down hard. If I'd knocked him out, it would just be returning the favor. Walking through the next room, I ignored the stares I got and wandered into a kitchen. There was a set of keys on the counter and I snagged them and stumbled to the front door to get it open.

Nicky. I had to get to Nicky.

Walking outside was painful, the sun too bright, but I just squinted through it, pressing the lock button on the keychain over and over until I heard a horn honk and moved towards it. It was a plain sedan, probably one of the cop's unmarked cars, but I didn't give a shit. Climbing in, I dug in my pocket, relieved to still have my cell phone on me. As soon as the GPS figured out where the fuck I was, I floored it to Paulo's house.

If there were any clues, that would be where I'd find them.

It took almost forty minutes to get to Paulo's, and I was grateful to see that they'd left the gate wide open after the assault team had hit it. There was police tape across the front door, and I parked right in front of the entrance.

She's not here. You already know she's not here.

Still, I couldn't help but rush inside. Ripping the tape down and breaking the seal on the door to get inside. I took the stairs two at a time, only tripping once with the lingering effects of the damn sedative, but when I got to Paulo's room the door was wide open. I'd never been in his bedroom, and was surprised by how large it was. At least three times the size of my own, which wasn't a small room. Then my heart stopped.

There were dark, crimson smears on the pale sheets on the bed. Not a lot of blood, but enough to know the bastard had hurt her. I fought down the rage, pushing it down, and tried to focus so I could think. I needed to be cold. There was a length of chain extending into the bathroom from one of the posts on the bed and I followed it, but it abruptly cut off. Broken links on the floor that gave me more questions than answers.

Shit. Nicky couldn't have broken that without help, which meant... I ripped my phone out of my jeans and called Diego. I'd skin him alive if he had her. I'd rip him to shreds and make him suffer long before I let him die. It rang to voicemail the first time, and I stomped down to my room, fumbling for the key tucked in my front pocket.

My room was untouched, and I dug out Nicky's duffel bag and mine, filling mine with weapons, my laptop, my books, the notes from my closet, and other shit I didn't want the idiots who'd search this place going through. The bag weighed a ton when I started back down the stairs, ignoring the pain in my chest as I called Diego again.

"Who is this?" Diego answered this time, sounding like the asshole he always did.

"Did you fucking take Nicky from the house?"

"Andre? How the hell are you out? I heard you all got snapped up by the cops—"

"Dammit, Diego! If you took Nicky I'm going to put you in the ground, *pinche pendejo*. You better not have touched—"

Diego laughed, actually fucking laughed, and I let the black surge inside me. "Are you fucking kidding me? Paulo was *arrested*. We're all fucked! You think I'm going to drag some angry *puta* with me when I'm trying to get out of town before I get locked up?" He laughed some more and I hung up on him.

If not, Diego… then… I called Marco as I walked out of the house, throwing the bags in the trunk before I got in the car.

He finally answered just as I shut the door. "*¿Aló?*"

"Marco," I growled as I pulled out of Paulo's long drive, grateful that I hadn't run into anyone else yet. "Nicky is gone, do you—"

"She's safe. I've got her with me at the safe house on Jardín." Marco's voice had never sounded so good, and I braked hard to pull to the curb before I lost it. It was like I'd been trying to breathe underwater for an hour and I'd finally broken the surface. Lungs finally filling, heart beating again, all of the black inside me sinking away.

Alive. Safe. Nicky is alive.

"I heard the cops got everyone, how did you get out?"

"That doesn't matter. I'm on my way. You keep her safe, understand?"

"Yeah, man. She's sleeping right now, she... shit, Andre... Paulo and Luis hurt her. Bad."

"Luis?" I asked, feeling the rage surging again, confused as to why Luis would be involved at all, but for the moment I didn't care. I just needed to see Nicky. "Fuck it, I'm on my way."

"Okay, *cuadro.*"

My head spun as I drove, pushing the speed limit as much as I was willing to while hauling weapons and cash in a stolen car with dried blood on my fucking shirt, but the closer I got to Nicky the less I could think about anything else.

What did they do to you, belleza?

TWENTY-FIVE

Nicky

Someone touched my face and I jerked back, out of sleep, and immediately winced. *Fuck.* I hurt everywhere, and it took me a minute to realize I wasn't in Paulo's room anymore, or Andre's. I wasn't even in the house.

Marco had taken me out, broke the fucking chain Paulo had put on me with bolt cutters, and now he was sitting on the edge of the bed in this weird little house he'd brought us to looking concerned. "Hey, how are you feeling?"

"Like shit," I snapped. Defensive. I was sick of him talking to me, sick of him touching me, even if he hadn't made a move yet.

"Right… well, I've got good news."

"You're letting me go?" I asked, too bitter to believe it. Marco wanted me, I could see it in him, and I was pretty sure the only reason he hadn't tried to fuck me was because I was bruised all over, and could barely walk without wincing.

"You can go if you want, Nicole. I… I wasn't going to keep you." He looked down at his hands for a moment, and then blew out a breath. "Andre is on his way. He called while you were asleep."

I sat up fast and immediately regretted it, sore muscles screaming at me. "I thought you said they all got arrested? Some kind of raid?"

Marco shrugged. "I don't know, maybe he got out? Our contact that was watching the meet was the one that made the call. Cops showed up in a swarm, guns and everything, and he immediately called us to get the word out. When I got another call later it was to report body bags and arrests, but we didn't get names."

"That's good." I nodded, surprised and a little impressed that Andre had made it out of that kind of situation, but if anyone was capable of it… it would be him. "He's alive," I whispered, unable to explain the relief I felt in my chest.

"Yeah, he is. Thought you'd want to know." Marco stood up, walking out of the bedroom to the living room. He was angry, even though I'd thanked him for getting me out of the house, but when he'd asked me what had happened I'd refused to talk to him about it. I'd shut down completely, not wanting to remember the night before. All I had wanted was a shower and to possibly soak in bleach for twelve hours, but since the latter would probably kill me I'd settled for the longest shower I'd ever taken.

Paulo and Luis were sick fucking monsters. I'd been terrified of Diego and José, and they probably would have hurt me just as bad, if not worse, but for some insane reason I had been less scared of Paulo. Luis had creeped me out with his looks and his questions, but neither of them had been at the top of my list in that nightmare of a house — but they should have been. To be the uncontested leader of an empire like that meant Paulo had to be a fucking psychopath, and since Luis was apparently his best friend I should have known better.

Not like it would have mattered.

Andre had been right. If he had refused, Paulo would have taken me anyway just to prove a point. Possibly killed Andre because he wouldn't have trusted him anymore, and then when they'd had their fun he probably would have killed me too. He'd said as much when he'd hurt me, over and over, constantly reminding me who I *really* belonged to.

I hope he's fucking dead. Both of them. All of them.

I just wanted Andre back. I wanted to feel safe again for five minutes. I wanted to forget about everything that had happened last night. I wanted to stop feeling the pain between my thighs, the aches in my ribs every time I breathed. I didn't want to look at the bruises, or the bite marks. I wanted the world to disappear again. Curling into a ball I felt myself dozing, not quite asleep, but floating in that gray haze that made the world fade just enough to not be so painfully miserable.

Then I heard it.

"NICKY!" Andre's shout echoed through the house and I sat up again, ignoring the pain as he appeared in the door frame and then he rushed me. Pulling me off the bed, he hugged me tight, and I squeaked in pain but hugged him back anyway. "God, I thought — *fuck*, I thought so many horrible things." He leaned me back enough to meet my eyes, fierce, dark brown that promised violence, and vengeance with his next growled words. "But I swear, *belleza*, I will make Paulo and Luis pay for touching you, even if I have to call in every favor owed to me. If they're not already dead, they *will* die. Even if I have to get to them in prison."

"Yes." I nodded, emotion choking me as I dug my fingers into his arms. Everything was shaking, falling apart inside me, but I knew if I just held on to him that he would keep my upright. Keep me afloat, keep me from drowning. "I want them dead."

"Done." He spoke with the confidence of a killer, a man who had pulled the trigger enough to know what that promise meant, and I loved him for it. Loved him for the rage that I could feel almost singeing my hands. "I swear I will kill anyone that even tries to hurt you again. No one will *ever* hurt you."

The vicious hiss to his voice made his accent stronger, and I pulled him against me to feel that he was real. "I thought you were gone," I whispered, tears falling half from pain and half from the insane joy I felt at having his arms around me again. Safe again for the first time in almost a day.

"No, *belleza*. Never. Didn't I tell you I would come for you?" He leaned back and kissed me softly, and then he stopped and leaned back again, brushing his thumbs over my cheeks. "What the fuck did they do to you?" There was a dark edge to his tone again, dangerous, but it made me want to lean into him again to feel his strength wrap around me.

"Just one more minute of this. Please?" I asked, and he blew out a breath and wrapped his arms around me again squeezing, and I yelped.

"Shit. I hurt you. Sit down." Guiding me back to the edge of the bed, he pulled me more gently against him. Folded into warmth and safety with the least likely candidate on the planet. "I want to know what they did to you so I can make sure they suffer the same."

I smiled, feeling evil and a little crazy as I took comfort in the promise. "I'd like that."

He sighed, kissing my hair before he leaned his cheek against my head. "I've got a lot to tell you, Nicky."

"I think we've all got some things to talk about," Marco spoke up from the doorframe, and Andre twitched.

"Marco…" Andre ran a hand down my back before he stood and stepped forward to shake his hand. "Thank you for saving Nicky, I thought Diego had her and— well, I don't know what would have happened."

"I think we both have a good idea what would have happened to her," Marco answered and a chill went down my spine as the two men stared at each other. "Fortunately, Diego cared more about loading his car with drugs, liquor, and other shit from the house."

"I owe you, *cuadro*," Andre spoke low, his eyes drifting back to me. "For getting her out, and keeping her safe."

"Well, we've got to decide what we're going to do. Where are we going to run? We can't stay in Miami right now, not when they're looking for all of us." He shrugged. "I've got some family in Mexico, but getting there and across the border could be a mess if they have our names."

"About that… I don't need to run, *cuadro*, and neither does Nicky."

"What do you mean?"

Blowing out a breath, Andre pushed a hand through his hair and looked at me. "I said I had a lot to tell you, right?"

"Yeah…" I watched as he shifted his weight, finally moving closer to reach down and grab one of my hands in both of his.

"I— I've been… *shit.*" Andre stared into my eyes and sighed, releasing my hand as he stood up straight to face Marco. "I've been working with the police."

"What the fuck, *cabrón?*" Marco shouted, moving closer, and Andre shifted in front of me as he held up a hand.

"Listen, Marco. There's no more bullshit. I know you didn't agree with the fucked up things Paulo did, but you were in already and couldn't defy him or José, or any of us without risking your fucking life. I get that. And if I'm wrong, if you wanted to be in that house, if you wanted to be involved in all of that shit… then I just painted a fucking target on my back telling you that." Andre growled, wiping a hand over his face. "But I'm hoping I'm right, that all those pissed off looks you've been giving me were because you hated what was happening in that house, hated me for what I did, and you wanted out of it. Here's your chance, *cuadro.* Probably the only one you'll ever get. Just go. Get out. Disappear."

"No one can just disappear," Marco muttered, pacing across the room.

"Yes, you can. As far as anyone knows, I'm dead. I died in front of Paulo and José and all those fucks." He pulled at his shirt, and I saw the dark stains on it. They looked like blood.

Marco seemed to notice too, because he stopped pacing, facing Andre with a dark, unreadable look on his face.

"Everyone thinks I'm dead, *cuadro*. Well, Diego will think I'm alive, but I think after a while even he will be confused about that call." Andre sighed. "You can empty your accounts, and just leave. Go to another part of the country, go North. And as a thank you for saving Nicky I won't ever mention your name. I won't put you in a single fucking report. As far as anyone knows, I don't know you exist."

"And… you're dead," Marco finished.

"Right." Andre turned to me as I shifted on the edge of the bed, only peripherally aware of the aches and pains as all his words sunk in. "Nicky, talk to me."

"All this time?" I asked, somewhat dazed, thinking back to that first night in the basement when he'd faked his way through fucking me, at least at first, to keep me from Diego.

"Yes. The whole time I've been in Paulo's organization."

"But you killed someone. You said you killed someone, right? Did that happen?" I looked up at him, and he nodded.

"I didn't have a choice."

"This is fucked up, Andre," Marco spoke up from behind him, and I definitely agreed. *How was this possible?*

"You should go soon, Marco. They're busy processing the others, but they'll widen the net soon. You should take a page from Diego's book and get out of town now." Andre stood up, and I just stared at him. He looked the same. Still tattooed and big and scary, but he had actually been the good guy. Not just the criminal with a good side, but an actual fucking good guy. Well, the really fucked up good guy. And he had always meant to get me out, even tried to get me out, had tried to keep me from Paulo and the others.

"I know. I'll leave soon, but..." Marco stepped closer, waiting until I raised my eyes to look at him. "Nicky, you should know you don't have to stay with him. No matter what he says, you should find someone worthy of you."

Andre stiffened, jaw tense as he looked away from me.

"You deserve better," he said, his own anger surfacing as he looked at Andre, but Marco didn't know the whole story. Didn't know any of it really. Didn't know the times in Andre's bedroom, didn't know the pain in him, the fear I'd seen in his eyes when Paulo was at the door. Marco didn't know how all of the violence in Andre was balanced out with a warmth that I wasn't even sure Andre was aware of.

I had to stretch, which hurt like a bitch, but I reached over to wind my fingers into Andre's and squeezed. "I'm good, Marco. I promise. And... thank you again for getting me out of there."

"Yeah, *de nada*." He sighed, stepping back as Andre moved closer to me. "I couldn't leave you there for the cops to find. They'd ask all kinds of questions you wouldn't want to answer." Marco gave a little smile and then turned to the doorway. "I'm leaving, going to try and get out of Miami. Out of Florida if I can before I have to stop and sleep."

"I've got some stuff that can help you in the car, I'll walk out with you." Andre turned back around and held my face for a moment, just looking at me, and then he kissed my forehead and stood up. "I'll be right back, *belleza*."

"You better be, we have more to talk about." I smiled when he gave me a look that seemed surprised by my tone.

It was weird to know I could just get up and walk out. Go home. Call Elise and tell her a version of what had happened, have her come over so we could drink rum and watch Netflix until we passed out. It sounded good, all of it did, but I couldn't imagine leaving Andre. Not when I could so easily remember the pain in his face when he'd promised to get me out. Swore that he would do whatever it took. And I remembered the way he would hold me in the dark, the things he whispered against my ear, the raw protective rage in him when he'd done exactly what he'd promised and come back for me.

When would I ever find another man willing to risk everything for me? Willing to kill for me? To die for me? To come back to life and potentially blow his cover just to get to me?

All I'd wanted was for us all to get out. For Chris, and me, *and Andre*, to make it out of all of this shit alive — and we had. We'd survived, and I didn't want to run from him now, not when I still wasn't sure what it could be like with Andre outside of the danger of Paulo García's house.

Not when that warm flutter was alive and burning in my chest, insisting that I find out.

Andre

Shifting my personal shit out of the black duffel bag, I kept a grand for myself and left the rest of the cash in the bag. Along with all of the guns, the bullets, and a few of my knives. The others had been mine before Paulo, and I wasn't giving them up. I really *did* like knives.

"You sure about this?" Marco asked.

"It would all just end up rotting in an evidence lock-up. You need it, and I hope it helps you get out. Start over, maybe in something that won't put you in prison." I shrugged. "Just a suggestion."

"*Gracias.*" Marco took the bag and dumped it into his own trunk, shutting it hard as he moved to the driver's side. "Look, maybe I was wrong about you, but that doesn't make the shit you did to Nicole okay. Even if you didn't hurt her like they did... you still hurt her."

"I know." Looking at the door to the house, I felt the guilt and the rage in equal measure. "I'm going to handle it, make sure she's safe, and then walk away if that's what she wants."

"I don't think that's going to work, *cuadro.*" Marco chuckled as he got in the car. "You were the first person she asked for when I woke her up, and she says your name in her fucking sleep. I'm not sure she's going to let you walk away."

I turned to look back at the house, not sure I could believe that. Not after everything I'd done to her, not after I'd handed her over to Paulo. Clearing my throat, I faced Marco again, nodding to him. "Good luck, *cuadro.*" It was all I could think to say, because everything else was too complicated.

"You too." Marco waved, and I watched as he drove off down the street. Then I shoved everything into her duffel, carrying the bulging bag back into the house.

When I got inside I saw Nicky standing by the window, clearly favoring one side, an arm wrapped protectively around her ribs. She turned to give me a small smile. "Marco is a good guy."

"Yeah, he is," I admitted, even though that was tough when I knew he'd seen her naked, had her here alone. "I still would have killed him if he'd touched you."

She laughed a little. "Not sure you can kill people anymore if you work with the police. Or for the police? I mean, are you a cop? An informant? What?"

"Undercover." I swallowed, wanting to hold her again, just to feel her against me. "Are you angry?"

"That you kept it from me? Even though I asked you over and over who you called? Even though I begged you to give me just a little bit of hope in that place?" There was pain in her voice, and I cursed under my breath.

"I'm sorry." That was the only answer, the only thing I had. "Nicky…" I dropped the bag on the floor and moved closer to her, relieved when she let me touch her, even though I didn't deserve it. "I don't think I can ever earn your forgiveness, but—"

"Stop. You protected me, I know it. I know that's what it was, I know that's what you did."

"I'm still a bastard, a monster." I cringed, gently tracing

her arms where I saw fingerprint shaped bruises that had the black swirling deep.

"You are a bastard for keeping that shit from me… but you're not a monster, Andre." She sighed, and I saw that light in her eyes, and I was hungry for it. Wanted to kiss her to taste it again, to taste her sweetness, and drive back the dark and the bitter for just a little while longer before she pushed me away.

"I am a monster and I know it. I accept it. I fucking *hurt* you, Nicky." I hated myself when I thought of everything I'd done to her, just because I could. Just because she was mine in that hellhole, and I wanted something good, wanted to feel something good, and so I'd taken it. Taken her. *No better than them.* "All of this shit, this life, it's ruined me. I think I could have been good once, but not anymore. I'm tainted, I'm just as fucked up as *jefe* — Paulo."

"You were trying to get me out, though. All that time. You kept me from Diego."

"Not like it fucking mattered, Paulo… he and Luis — FUCK!" I pulled my hands away from her. I didn't have the fucking right to touch her. I needed to turn away and walk out right now. Leave her to get on with her life, just be the bad memory I'd sworn to myself I would be as soon as she was safe.

But then Nicky sat down carefully on the couch and patted the seat beside her, and I couldn't resist the pull. I wanted to be near her more than I wanted to be alive, and leaving her would be like death. When I moved toward her, I found myself kneeling in front of her. Knees hitting the floor hard like they had when Paulo had taken her out of the room. Resting my forehead against her knee, I stroked my thumbs over the strong muscle of her calf.

"I'm sorry. I'm so fucking *sorry*." The pain was back in my chest, the one that had felt like my ribs were collapsing as I thought I'd lost her. "I failed you, *belleza*. I tried to keep you safe, to keep you out of it all, and in the end I handed you over to the head fucking monster. I should have just killed him."

"And then?" she asked, and her soft hands moved into my hair to lift my head. "What would have happened after you killed him?"

"I would have had to kill them all."

"And the meeting?"

"It would have been fucked." I felt a bitter laugh surface as I realized a whole other layer of *fucked up* that I hadn't even thought of in the house. "Nathan would have probably tossed me in prison. Hell, he might still do it since I decked him earlier today."

"Who is Nathan?" she asked, and I shrugged, stunned by the ability to actually talk about this shit with someone.

"My handler, the contact I had within the department. He tried to keep me from leaving to find you when I woke up."

"So, you hit him?" Nicky was smiling, and I found myself smiling too.

"Yes, *belleza*. I told you, nothing was going to keep me from getting you out." I sighed, sitting up to move my hands up to her waist. "Marco was right, you don't have to stay with me. You can leave, do anything."

"What if I want to stay with you?" she asked, and I didn't

want to admit just how much I wanted that. Didn't want to admit that just the idea of her wanting to be with me felt like the difference between being human, or eating a bullet in the next five years.

"You don't want that, Nicky." I tried to argue, to do the right thing, even though part of me was telling me to shut the fuck up. "My life is going to be really fucking complicated. I'm supposed to be dead, and the case against Paulo and the others could go on for a while. Years."

"And?" She leaned down and kissed me, her hands on either side of my face. "I'm not going to leave you behind either, Andre."

I felt that shred of hope in the black and reached for her, taking control to open her mouth so I could taste her again. Feeding that glimmer of light with all of her goodness, the sweet taste of her, the insane decisions she was making no matter how stupid. The soft sounds she made were making my cock twitch, but I could wait. She was hurt, in pain, but she was alive, so I could wait.

I would do anything for her.

Shifting onto the couch beside her, I kissed her again, grinning like an idiot when she nipped my lip, and moaned against my mouth. *Feisty.* Everything about her was perfect. Brave, stupidly brave, and clever, and beautiful. She was fearless, and if I had even one more day with her I would be more blessed than I deserved. Nipping her lip back, I kissed her soft lips once more, mumbling, "I love you."

The words had tumbled out, and I shook my head. "I didn't—"

"Shut up." She laughed, pressing her thumb over my mouth. "I think I love you too, Andre."

"What the fuck did I ever do to deserve you, *belleza?*" I asked, kissing her again, and she broke the kiss with another laugh.

"You bought me for five grand and saved my life." She shrugged. "And my brother's life too."

"Speaking of your brother, I think he and I need to have a talk about the kinds of things men involve their sisters in…"

"Don't talk about my brother when you're kissing me," Nicky growled, and our lips met again, all of the black rage falling away as I wrapped my arms around her. She was everything I never knew I could want, never dreamed I could have, but she was there in my arms. Feisty, and mouthy, and absolutely fucking *mine.*

Epilogue

NICKY

One Year Later

Somewhere in Missouri

Parking the car, I smiled, watching Andre on the front porch of our little house. He was anxious, I could tell just from the way he was sitting. Bent forward, elbows on his knees, but he lifted his head to smile at me when I opened the car door.

I hurried up the steps, leaning down to kiss him, but he grabbed me and pulled me over the arm of the chair and into his lap, leaving me laughing as he kissed his way down my throat to the neckline of my shirt.

"*Hola, belleza,*" he growled, sinfully soft, and I felt heat purring down low.

"*Hola, mi amado,*" I answered, and he chuckled against my skin.

"Your accent is terrible."

Huffing, I stood up, but he caught my hand with that grin that promised so many things. Things that we could *not* do right now. "Think your mother is going to be mad you're with some *gringa?*"

The tension was instantly back in his muscles, tightening his shoulders beneath his t-shirt. "I think you'll be the least of her concerns…"

"Andre… your mother agreed to meet you. Do you really think she'd do that, go through all the shit they're making her do, just to show up and tell you off?" I leaned down until his eyes met mine again. "It's going to be okay. I promise."

"How do you know?" he asked quietly.

"Because if things start to go south, I'll just start yelling at her in terrible Spanish and she'll be so confused and irritated by my accent, that she'll forget she was ever mad at you." Winking, I turned toward the front door and laughed when he spanked my ass.

"*Mi loca gringa.*"

I could hear him laughing as I walked inside our little house, proud of how much it felt like home now after ten months of living here. In middle-of-nowhere Missouri. Still, it was a two-bedroom house surrounded by forest, absolutely beautiful in such a different way than the sun-drenched beaches of Miami.

The day shift at the restaurant I worked at had not been fun. I'd take the bar shift any day of the week over smelling like French fries and ribs, but I had to be here this evening when Andre's mom arrived. He'd told me about his brother, about their split, and swapping with Diane had been worth it. Even though I needed a damn shower.

Stripping off my clothes, I rushed through it so that I didn't miss her arrival. I needed to be there, beside him, holding his hand even though he'd never admit he needed it. I'd just pretend I was nervous to meet her — which, if I was honest with myself, I was. Andre talked about his mother like religious people talked about saints. She was a source of awestruck fear and unending devotion, and to know that it had been almost a decade since they'd seen each other last was heartbreaking. I didn't have my parents anymore, and since we'd first approached the U.S. Marshals about reaching out to her, I'd known that it was what Andre needed more than anything.

Even more than he needed me.

As I was blow-drying my hair, I saw him appear in the mirror, leaning against the doorframe to look me up and down with that slight grin on his face that he seemed to wear all the time now. For another minute, I finger combed my hair, shaking it out to try and get it dry, even though the humidity was going to frizz it no matter what I did. As soon as I turned off the blow-dryer, Andre stepped forward to slip his arms around me.

"You're beautiful, Nicky…" The words were whispered against my neck as he buried his face in my hair, and I reached back to run my hand through his.

"I know you want to be outside watching for the car. You should go, I'll be right out." Even as I said the words, I immediately didn't mean them, because his hand moved over my hip and between my thighs. "Andre…" I warned, breathy, trying to remember why I needed to get dressed, and put makeup on, and look presentable and not *just fucked*.

"You're wet," he purred, and I sagged against him as he teased my clit. Dipping his fingers between my folds to ease the torturous circles he made around that bundle of nerves.

"Your mother is on her way!" With more self-control than I thought I had, I shoved Andre's hand from between my thighs and turned around. "I will be outside in a minute. Why don't you make us a drink?"

Tracing his tongue over his bottom lip, he grinned like the devil and I felt a warm flush inch up into my cheeks.

"Go on," I insisted, pushing him playfully out the door of the bathroom and to the doorway of our bedroom. "*Por favor,*" I added when he looked over his shoulder at me, a playful mischief in his eyes.

"I lied before. I fucking love it when you speak Spanish." Grabbing me, he kissed me hard, and I swooned against him for a moment, enjoying the play of his tongue on mine, but then I snapped out of it and pulled away.

"Outside!" I shouted and laughed, pointing past him, and he raised his inked arms, winking at me before he walked away. Breathless, and way too turned on to be meeting his fucking *mother*, I dug out the jeans and nice shirt I'd planned to wear this evening. I put just enough makeup on to look like I at least tried to look pretty, even though my normal wear was either *nothing*, which Andre preferred, or yoga pants and a tank top with no bra. Complete with my face washed and my hair in a knot at the top of my head. He still looked at me like I was a gift from God, but I knew it would take a bit more to impress his mom.

With one last glance in the mirror, still trying desperately to even out my eyeliner, I gave up and walked back out to the porch. Andre had a glass of rum waiting for me, and I snagged it as I dropped into the chair beside him. "Has Greg called yet?"

"Not yet." Andre looked at the phone sitting face-up on the table between us, and I sighed.

"You know they're on their way, it's a long drive."

"And there's *so* much traffic," he replied, dripping with bitter sarcasm as he took another drink.

"Patience, *mi amado*. She'll be here soon." I looked over at him to see his deadpan stare and it took clenching my teeth to keep from smiling. "Don't you think he would have called if she hadn't been at the airport?"

"Yes," he reluctantly agreed, finishing his glass and reaching for the bottle he'd brought outside to pour some more.

"Going to be drunk for your mom?" I asked, and he scoffed.

"I hadn't had anything to drink before you got here."

"Just sat here staring at your phone after work?"

"Yeah, I did." He sighed and I smiled, reaching over to brush my fingers over his strong arms. Working construction for the state highway department had actually managed to make him *more* muscular, which balanced out well with the weight I'd gained working at Benny's Inn, the local home-style BBQ restaurant and bar. Andre loved my curves though, and he could still pick me up like I was light as a feather and toss me onto the bed, and then— *nope*. I was definitely not thinking about that stuff while I waited for his mom.

Staring out at the long dirt drive, surrounded on all sides by trees, I took a moment to enjoy the pinks and oranges of the setting sun. It would be dark soon, but it was okay. We had dinner. *Shit.* I stood up and set my drink down. "I left the food in the car, I'll bring it in and—"

"I brought it in while you were showering." Andre caught my hand, smirking, and I rolled my eyes as I sat down.

"You distracted me."

"Thinking about fucking me?" he asked, and the blush burned in my cheeks even as I glared at him.

"Mostly thinking about *you* fucking *me*, but yes." I sighed heavily, snagging the rum to refill my glass. "Could you at least try to help me stay calm? I'm about to meet my *mother-in-law.*"

Andre chuckled, reaching across the table to stroke my arm. When I looked at him, he was still smiling. "You know I'm going to make that ring real someday."

I tilted my left hand, looking at the simple gold band that let us pretend we were married. All a part of the agreement we'd made with the authorities — either we went into WITSEC together, or not at all. They valued Andre's testimony more than keeping me from him, and now I was testifying too, so it all worked out. Still, I shrugged. "It doesn't matter."

"Why?" he asked, and I heard the slight concern in his voice. He still doubted himself, even now, and it made me smile.

"Because I'm yours no matter what." Those words brought a big grin to his face, and then a flash of headlights in my peripheral vision drew my attention and I pointed. "Look!"

"She's here!" Andre jumped out of his seat, and I almost laughed but managed to keep it in as I set my drink down and took his hand, squeezing as we walked down the steps together.

The dark sedan pulled to a stop on the patchy grass that served as a driveway, and Greg jumped out to open the back door. I didn't even see anyone get out until a small, dark haired woman walked around the front of the car. Andre let go of me and walked towards her, but the tiny woman broke into a run and they collided in the middle.

Andre

My mother only came to my chest, and I'd forgotten how small she was, but I didn't care as I felt her hug me and heard her crying. "*Mi corazón, mi hijo…*"

I leaned down to hug her tighter as the words rang in my head, *my heart, my son.* Better than anything I'd imagined as she pulled me close. "*Mamá*, I've missed you so much." I whispered it, I couldn't do anything more, and I was grateful that both Greg and Nicky stayed back.

She pulled out of my arms, grabbing my face on either side as she looked at me and then let go, looking me over. "You're grown up, all grown up."

"*Sí,*" I whispered, nodding, and she grabbed onto my hands to grip them tight.

"You must tell me everything. All of it." Tugging my arm like she had when I was a child, I felt her stop as she saw Nicky, but the look she gave me was comforting. "And who is this, *hijo?*"

Leading her to the porch I looked up at the woman who had changed my entire life, the woman who had taken me out of Hell, brought me back from the brink of death like a true Valkyrie, and I smiled. "*Ese es Nicky, mi alma.*"

We were close enough for Nicky to hear me, and she glanced at me in confusion, but recovered enough to step forward with her bright smile. "*Hola, Señora Morales,*" she said, and her accent was terrible as always, but I watched my mother smile.

"*Hola,* Nicky. I understand my son cares for you very much."

Nicky grinned, looking at me as their hands separated. "He means a lot to me too."

"That is what I like to hear." My mother smiled up at me, patting my arm as if to comfort me, and I turned to beckon Greg inside.

"Come eat with us," I called.

He waved, bringing up a small suitcase. "Nah. I'll be back the day after tomorrow, enjoy the family time."

"Okay," I answered, secretly glad to not have him staying.

"*Gracias,* for bringing me to my son," my mother said, smiling, and he nodded at her as he walked back to the car.

We all stood on the porch, watching as he drove off into the dusk, but I knew I owed him a bottle of whiskey for helping me make this happen. All of the flights, the confusing schedules, just to get my mother here from Miami without alerting anyone. We were still *pretty* sure that no one knew I was alive, especially since Diego had been shot when police had tried to take him into custody, and Marco was still a ghost — but precautions were always necessary.

"Dinner?" Nicky asked, and my mother let go of me to reach for her hand, patting it as she walked inside with the love of my life. The two most important women in the world to me finally in the same room, and I couldn't even try to suppress my grin as I grabbed her suitcase and followed them inside. "I'm sorry," Nicky apologized with a frown. "It might be a bit cold. I brought the food home from work."

"No, no, it will be good. This is what I came for," my mother said, reaching back to pull me forward as Nicky started to unpack the containers she'd brought. "I just wanted to see my son again."

"I really have missed you, *Mamá,*" I whispered, hugging her again, and she sniffled against my chest before she stepped away to pull out a chair at our small table.

"Come, come, let's sit and catch up."

Holding her chair, I pushed it in when she sat down, and then tilted my head to encourage Nicky to sit too, doing the same. She gave me a look, but I just winked when I grabbed the last container of food to set in the center of the table, because I'd laid out the plates hours before.

As soon as I took my seat and reached for the food, my mother swatted my hand. "Prayers, *hijo.*"

Nicky gave me a surprised look, but she bowed her head

and I smiled as I did as well. It had been as many years since I'd seen her that I'd prayed before a meal. *Mi Mamá* said the same prayer she'd said when it had been my siblings and I eating, and I almost choked on the lump in my throat as memories surged, before she raised her head and I whispered, "*Amén.*"

We passed the dishes around, filling our plates with the simple barbecued chicken and sides that Nicky had brought home, and it still smelled amazing. Just as I popped the first bite into my mouth, hungry from the long day, I heard my mother clear her throat.

"You have been sending me money, *hijo.*" It wasn't an accusation, more a statement, and I nodded as I chewed.

Swallowing hard, I shrugged a shoulder. "I didn't want you to struggle when I could help."

"And you joined the police?" she asked, clarifying what I was sure she already knew.

"I did." With the salty sweet sauce on my tongue, I wish I had the rum we'd left outside, but I had to settle for the water in front of me.

She nodded, poking with her fork at the beans on her plate. "Because of Hernan?"

Pain surged behind my ribs, an actual heart ache, and I nodded again, staring down at my plate because I couldn't face her. Not when I could so easily remember the emotional rage she'd had the last time I'd said his name.

"Did you know that Benito died four years ago?" she asked, and the pain increased.

"*No, Mamá,*" I answered, and she leaned over to grab my arm, squeezing tight.

"He was killed in some foolish drug house. Dealing, just like your *padre.*" She shook her head, leaning back in her seat, and I could tell Nicky was frozen. "Just like you would have been had you continued on that road, but you did not. *Gracias a Dios.*"

I flinched, sad to know that my older brother had died in such a lonely way. I had hoped he would have cleaned up his act, stuck around to keep the family going while I stepped away. Taking the brunt of my mother's anger over Hernan's death. To know he'd acted just like my father, and died for it, hurt on a different level.

"Andre saved my life," Nicky said, breaking the spell as I jerked to look at her, and my mother turned as well. "He got me out of a very bad situation when he was undercover, kept me as safe as he could."

"*Belleza...*" I groaned at the lie, but my mother raised her hand to silence me.

"My son saved you?"

"Yes." Nicky smiled, looking up at me with her perfect blue eyes, the slight blush highlighting her cheeks easier since her tan had faded. "I would have died, or worse, if he had not protected me. He risked everything, his whole assignment, to keep me safe."

"That's not true," I tried to argue but both of them spoke over me.

"Yes, it is."

"*Shh, hijo.* I want to hear this!" My mother patted my arm

as if I were a child interrupting adults, and I sat back in the chair grinning as Nicky leaned closer, describing me in kinder language than I deserved. Calling me her *hero* as if I'd never made her scream in pain. Never terrified her, or made her cry.

I'd learned over the last year how to temper that aggression, to take her in a way that made her cry out in pleasure, even with a little pain mixed in. Still, *not* the right thing to be thinking of as my mother grinned broadly at Nicky, glancing at me occasionally with pride in her eyes.

More than I could have ever hoped.

"Did you know Andre had siblings?" my mother asked, her accent thick, but Nicky just leaned her chin on her hand as *mi Mamá* dug her phone out of the little purse she had. "Andre was the second oldest," she said softly, swiping through her phone. "But this is Rosa, his younger sister. She is twenty-six now."

My heart stuttered seeing Rosa as a full-grown woman with a toddler on her hip. "She has a kid?"

"Yes, his name is Michael. Almost two." My mother was a proud grandmother as she swiped through more photos. "And here is Miguel."

"He's tall," I said softly, staring at the five o'clock shadow on my baby brother's face, but he was clearly a man now. "That makes him twenty-five?"

"Next week," she answered, and of course she remembered his birthday and I didn't. I couldn't even send him anything, which felt worse. Touching her phone again she finally smiled even broader. "Look at Josefina! She is graduating community college. The first of us, although Miguel has been taking classes."

Staring at the phone I felt like she was talking about different people, like the photos were of strangers, not the kids, the teenagers, I'd left behind in that small apartment when she'd kicked me out.

Benito was dead. Hernan was dead. But I had survived, and so had the others.

As if my mother knew what I was thinking, she reached over to grasp my hand, squeezing as hard as she could. "We have missed you, *hijo*."

"I couldn't put you at risk, *Mamá*. I wanted to reach out, I wanted to talk to you, but... this was where they needed me." I swallowed down the lump in my throat. "And I wasn't sure you'd want to see me again anyway."

"Andre..." she stood and moved to wrap her arms around me, and for a moment I felt ten years old again. Young, untainted, and innocent, with my mother making everything fade away. "I was wrong, so wrong to send you away. I knew that too late. I could not find you. Benito could not find you... and then you sent the money. Every bit I got was like a sign from God that you were okay, and I only prayed that you were somewhere safe."

As soon as she started crying, I stood up and hugged her, in disbelief that she'd thought about me as much as I had her. It was better than I'd ever dreamed, and I looked up to see Nicky with her hands pressed over her mouth, tears in her eyes. She had pushed me to ask for this, for the Marshals to reach out to my mother, and it had taken months of arguing — but Nicky had never backed down. Even when

I had told her to drop it, sure that my mother didn't want to see me, she had insisted.

And now *Mamá* was here.

Maybe I had finally done something good enough for God to forgive me. To let me have Nicky, to let me see my mother again… it was an answered prayer I'd never even had the balls to whisper aloud.

"*Lo siento, hijo*. I am ruining dinner with tears!" She pulled back, wiping her eyes as she squeezed my hand and took her seat again, finally taking a bite. "This is good."

"Not homemade. I'm sorry about that, but I'm really not a great cook." Nicky laughed, unashamed, and my mother laughed too.

"Andre knows how to cook. Don't you, *hijo?*" Grinning, she launched into talking again. "He used to stay in the kitchen and help me, it was my favorite time of day. Making dinner with my boys as their little brothers and sisters ran around." Her expression grew softer, a little sad, and I knew she was remembering Benito and Hernan. "Those were good days."

"They were, *Mamá.*"

My mother took a deep breath and turned toward Nicky. "Where are you parents?"

She stopped with her fork almost to her mouth. "Oh, um, they died in a car accident. Almost six years ago, I was twenty-two." Smiling sadly, Nicky lifted a shoulder in a slight shrug. "My mom didn't cook either, but she always had friends over. She loved to have a full house of people enjoying themselves. It's probably why I ended up as a bartender."

"I didn't know that," I said, surprised by the snippet of her childhood.

"You never asked." Smiling, she winked at me to let me know she wasn't upset, and then she turned her full attention back to my mother. "My father was a mechanic. He could fix *anything*, and cars were his life. He would trade work for parts all the time, always working on a few old pieces of junk, convinced he could bring them back to life." Nicky laughed, bright and airy. "I did *not* inherit those talents."

I felt bad for not asking more about her parents, for not bothering to get to know her better. It used to be a painful topic for both of us. "I could teach you a few things about cars. I'm no mechanic, but I can do some stuff."

"Sounds fun," she answered, smiling.

"Do you have any siblings?" My mother prodded, always the talkative one, the one too curious about others to bother with things like tact. Fortunately, Nicky didn't seem bothered at all.

"Just a brother. He joined the military when we moved out here, with a little... help."

"Help?" *Mamá* asked, and I laughed as she looked at me.

"He'd been in some trouble when he was younger, but the department helped us clear a few of those indiscretions off his record so he could enlist."

"And *who* encouraged him to do that?" Nicky prompted, eyebrows lifting.

"I had a *talk* with him about the situation he'd put Nicky in with his decisions, and *suggested* he join the military in exchange for his record getting tidied up." I grinned. "He needed the help, *belleza*."

"Right." She laughed a little, popping another bite in her mouth, and my mother laughed too.

"You two are so good together! I am so happy my Andre found such a good woman. When do you plan to give me a grandbaby?" Her question hung in the air as I choked on water and Nicky turned bright red, before we both started laughing.

Nicky

A whole day with Andre's mom had been even more of an adventure than dinner had. She was insistent that we *actually* get married after I admitted to her the rings were just for show, and I got to witness a first-hand Catholic-mother lecture — as Andre called it — when she confronted him about it.

The words *living in sin* were spoken amidst a lot of rapid Spanish, with hands waving, and I couldn't help but smile as Andre cowered before his mother that was a full foot shorter than him. In the end, he'd said it wasn't up to him, it was up to me, and I'd received a barrage of questions on why I didn't want to marry *her son*.

Even the memory made me laugh, because that wasn't the issue. I loved being with Andre, I loved *him*, but right now we weren't even real people. We were fictional identities created by the cops so we could testify against Paulo García, Luis Ramirez, José Rodriguez, and Samuel Martinez. Samuel's brother Nicolás had died in the raid on the warehouse, but otherwise everyone there was in custody, dead, or extradited back to Columbia to be tried there.

Andre didn't think that would even happen, but it wasn't our concern. The Columbians didn't know Andre, and they'd never met me. Still, all I really wanted was to be myself before I even thought about marriage. Missouri was pretty, but it wasn't Florida. It wasn't Miami with the beach, and the sun, and the afternoon rain that made the whole area smell fresh for a few minutes. I missed the bustling city, and the intense nightlife that made me a fuck of a lot more in tips than this small town. I wanted *my life* back — but being with Andre was worth it. I'd never felt more loved, more safe, than when we were in bed together with his arms around me.

Although for two nights in a row that had been *all* we'd done in bed.

"Nicky, *Mamá* wants to tell you goodbye." Andre poked his head into the bathroom, and I nodded, grabbing my shirt to pull it on.

"Is Greg here already?"

"Yeah, he showed up early." He was sad about his mother leaving, I could tell, but I also knew that this visit had done more for him than anything else. He'd needed to know that his mother forgave him, still loved him, and wanted him back.

Someday I hoped we could even move back to Miami so he could see the rest of his family, so I could *meet* the rest of his family, but the courts moved slow, especially on something this involved. *Someday*, I repeated in my head as

I took his hand and walked out to see his mother by the door, already crying.

"Oh, *hijastra*, I will miss you." The tiny woman hugged me, and I smiled as I hugged her back, more relieved than I cared to admit that she liked me.

"I'm going to miss you too, *Señora*—"

"No. You will call me *Mamá*, because I know you will marry my son." She leaned back, patting my hand as she squeezed it tight. "Please? I have not seen him in so long, but you have made him happy. I see it in his eyes, *su corazón*. His heart." Laying one of her hands over her own heart, I saw the tears slip down her cheeks once more as she hugged me again, pressing a kiss to my cheek.

"I love him, and one day… maybe." I smiled, but she huffed and threw up her hands.

"You will! And it is *Mamá*, yes?" She gave me a look, and I sighed.

"Yes, *Mamá*," I answered, and she cheered and clapped her hands together before she beckoned Andre closer to hold him tight.

"Do not let this one go, *mi hijo*. Bring her home to us." His mother spoke quietly, but I knew she used English so I'd know what she said.

It made my heart flutter to think of joining such a big, loving family, but there was anxiety too. I really needed to get better at Spanish. I needed to not be such a mess all the time, and I needed to be sure that we'd survive the court case before I even imagined a future beyond tomorrow.

A knock at the door made us sigh. We could see Greg's shape through the frosted glass panes of the front door, and his mother's tears just flowed faster as she hugged Andre tighter. I went and let Greg in, tilting my head toward them as he stepped inside. He flinched, and looked at me apologetically. "I'm sorry, this was all we could do. Any more time away and people are going to ask questions."

"I know," I answered, but I still felt terrible that they were already being ripped apart again. "Maybe she can come back?"

"I can ask," he said, giving me a tight smile as the two finally separated.

"We do need to go so she can make her flight, Andre. I'm sorry."

"It is okay," his mother said, holding Andre's face as she stared up at him. "I have seen him, held him, told him I loved him. That is more than I thought I would get in this life."

"*Mamá...*" Andre hugged her again, and I appreciated Greg staying quiet as they embraced, but he did pick up her suitcase and open the door again to signal that it was time.

"Why don't you walk out with us, Andre? See her off." Greg gestured outside, and they followed him as I stepped out onto the porch to watch. It was bittersweet, watching as he put his mom in the car and stepped back to talk to Greg. After a few minutes, he laid his hand against her window, and then waved as they pulled away.

I waited, not saying anything as he watched the car pull

down the long drive to the main road, but eventually he turned and came up the steps, pulling me into his arms.

"How are you?" I asked, keeping my arms wrapped loosely around his waist.

"Grateful… I really never thought I'd see her again." He hugged me tighter, leaning down to press his cheek to my hair as he whispered, "Thank you, *belleza*. For making it happen."

"You deserved something good, Andre."

"I already had you, and that is more than I deserve." Pulling back just enough to look into my eyes, he leaned down and captured my mouth. Tongue teasing my lips until I opened and tasted him. I moaned into the kiss, desperate for his touch, wanting nothing more than to take advantage of our solitude, but he stopped me as I went for his jeans. "Wait, I have something to tell you. Greg…"

"What?" I asked as he trailed off, a somber expression on his face that made my stomach clench tight.

"There's a new judge on the case, and he's challenged some of the evidence that the prosecutor has on Paulo and the others." Andre sighed, fingers digging into my hips as he fought the anger I could sense swelling in him. "Greg isn't sure what it means, not really, but he wanted to warn me that there's a chance they may rule a mistrial."

My head spun, chest tightening as I found it hard to breathe. "But… if they do that, he'd go free, right? He'd be out there?"

"Greg says the locals are fighting it, reminding the judge that there are witnesses, like us, that are still meant to testify— but there's a chance that, yeah, he could get out."

"And the others?" I asked on a whisper, my mind filling with memories of Paulo and Luis and José. Pure fear skittering down my spine. Fear of what they'd do to me if they found me, fear of them killing Andre if they learned he was alive. Miami wasn't free of corruption, and there were enough people that could be bought off with the kind of money Paulo had that Andre's undercover role could be revealed. And if they learned about him, they might learn about his mom, his family...

"I don't know, *belleza*. If they ruled it a mistrial, I think it would be for all of them, but I'm not sure. I'm not a lawyer."

"No! They can't do this!" I shouted, and he pulled me with him to the chair on the porch, tucking me into his lap. But not even his warmth was enough to push back the chill in my bones.

"You know I'll never let anything happen to you. Ever again. Right?" Andre tilted my chin toward him so I could see his eyes. Warm brown in the sunlight of the morning, but the forest around us suddenly didn't seem peaceful — it felt treacherous. As if it could be hiding men with guns, men sent by Paulo.

"We have to testify. We have to call Greg back and get him to take us back to Miami so the judge can't do this." I knew I was panicking, but it had taken weeks for the bruises Paulo and Luis had left on me to fade completely. The mental shit had taken longer to deal with, and if I were honest with myself there were times, like right now, that I still couldn't handle it. They were nightmares, bogeymen, and to think of them outside of a jail cell was too horrible.

"There are... other options, *belleza*." His tone was empty, cold, dark, but it drew me closer. An unfulfilled promise that we rarely spoke of, but it was always there. Waiting.

I swallowed and sat up in his lap to look at him, my shadow casting half his face into light and half into dark. Andre was my hero, I hadn't lied to his mother, but I knew that what had made him capable of being my hero was his darkness. It was what made him dangerous, what made him so easily able to slip into Paulo's world and stand on his own two feet.

"You're serious?" I asked softly.

Reaching up, Andre brushed my hair back from my face, tucking a strand over my ear. "I swore to you that I would kill them for what they did to you. You stopped me once before, you said you wanted them convicted, to spend their lives rotting in prison, but…"

"They might get out," I finished.

"I won't let that happen, *belleza*. Just the possibility of them being a threat to you, of them seeking you out… it's too much. I would never be able to sleep, I would never be able to watch you drive off to work. I'd always wonder if you would come home. I'd always wonder if you'd still be safe when I got home."

"Andre…"

"I will *never* let them hurt you again." It was a statement, said in that tone that still brought a frisson of what I would describe as fear if I didn't know that Andre would never really hurt me. But he would kill for me, if I said the word.

It was a heady power, knowing that the man that held me and kissed me would orchestrate the deaths of each of the men who had hurt me, and all I had to do was say it. Agree. Take back my pleas to let the courts handle it.

But the courts aren't handling it.

Rage sparked somewhere in all of the anxiety and fear, and it flared up like a wildfire, burning and singeing as it rampaged inside me. A single flash of that horrible night, of screaming as Paulo laughed, and I knew I'd made my decision. "Kill them."

Andre jerked in the chair, reaching up to gently cup my face so that he could look into my eyes, his gaze flicking between them as he studied me. "Are you sure?"

"I'd do it myself if that was possible, but I can't get to them. Neither can you, not directly, but... I know you have connections. People who can."

"I need you to say it, *belleza*. Look me in the eyes so I know you mean it."

Shifting to look directly into his face, I let the anger burn, let my hate of those bastards off the leash. Not just for what they'd done to me, but for everything they'd made Andre do, for everything they'd done to him, and to so many others. To Chris. "I want them to die, *mi amado*. I want them to die painfully, bleeding and afraid of the end."

"Thank you," he whispered just before he kissed me. Raw and hungry, devouring me as he nipped my lips and lifted me.

We had to break the kiss so I could lean down to open the door, but then he kicked it wide and sat me down on the first available surface. Our kitchen table. Standing between my thighs he started to kiss me again, rough, but in control

— but all I wanted was for him to lose control and give me that escape from all the memories and rage swirling inside me.

"How did I get so lucky to find you?" Andre growled, grabbing my shirt to rip it over my head and toss it somewhere, his hands returning to my breasts, molding them through the bra until I reached back to unsnap it. Gone in a second, his fingers caught my nipples, twisting until I hissed air through my teeth and whimpered, feeling the hot spikes of pain spreading over my nerves. Nails digging into his arms I arched my back, leaning closer, hungry for more. Needing to lose myself in this, in him.

"You saved me," I whispered and he shoved something out of the way before he pinned me back to the table by my throat. Wild darkness in his eyes, a flash of the Andre I'd first met. Dangerous, sexy, and absolutely deadly.

I was soaking through my panties in a second.

"I didn't save you, *belleza*, I took you. There's a difference." His words were low, rumbling, making his accent thicker as he skimmed my ribs with his mouth, biting down occasionally just to make me yelp.

"I wanted you."

"You were terrified of me," he corrected, looking up at me before he released my throat and grabbed onto my jeans. Pulling the button free and the zipper down, he grabbed onto the waist and hauled them down with my underwear. Shoes knocked free, jeans yanked off, he pushed my knees wide. "All I wanted was to see you, to taste you."

"To protect me." I tried to argue, to remind him of how he'd pulled Diego off me, but then he was between my thighs, licking and sucking at my clit until I was crying out, one hand fisted in his hair — which I would have never dared to do in that godforsaken basement.

"I wanted you for myself." Sliding two fingers inside me, and then three, he propped one hand on the table so he could watch me writhe. He thrust them inside me, teasing, angling his touch until he found my g-spot with impossibly perfect precision, and suddenly I was panting and moaning and begging.

Close, *so fucking close*, and I was about to come when he pulled his fingers free.

"FUCK!" I growled, grabbing for his shirt to pull him on top of me, kissing him hard, tasting myself as I rolled my hips against him, moaning into the kiss. "Don't tease me, not now."

"You know this isn't your choice, *belleza*." Grinning, he stood up, breaking my hold on his shirt like it was nothing, and then he flipped me to my stomach, pressing me into the table. "You're mine, remember?" He nipped my waist as he caught my hand and pinned it to the middle of my back. "Bought and paid for."

Those words still turned me on. It made no sense, a lot of shit with Andre and I didn't make sense, but all that mattered was that it worked. *We* worked, and we never had to pretend to be someone else. Not with each other.

We were a little fucked up, far from perfect, but I loved him, his dark side, and he loved me.

"Tell me you're going to kill them." I spoke with my cheek against the smooth, pale wood of the table, and I grinned when I heard his groan.

"I'm going to reach out to my contacts"—he hauled me to the edge of the table, my breasts aching as my body dragged over the wood—"and I'm going to find someone with connections inside the county jail."

"Yeah?" I encouraged him to continue, aroused beyond explanation as he spoke of death and unzipped his jeans.

"And then each and every fucking one of them is going to die. Slowly…" Andre teased his cock at my entrance, and I lifted my hips, wordlessly begging him to fuck me. "Painfully…"

"Yes…" I purred, knowing just how wrong it was for me to want this so badly. Knowing that I was getting even more wet just imagining him doing it with a handful of phone calls, a swap of favors, a stack of cash from the stash he'd hidden from the authorities. "Tell me, please."

Andre slammed inside me, not bothering with condoms anymore now that I had the birth control implant, and we were everything to each other. It was as sinfully perfect as it always was, but even more so as his grip tightened painfully on my wrist, making me whine as he slammed into me again. Hips bruising against the edge of the table, I didn't give a fuck. I wanted more, I wanted him to tell me everything, all of it, while he was inside me. While it hurt in all the right ways.

"Please!" I shouted as he pulled almost all of the way out to drive in hard again, making me ache just a little as he bottomed out — my favorite.

"It will probably be a shiv. A razorblade at the end of a toothbrush. They won't even see it coming." He started to fuck me in steady, hard thrusts, and I rolled my hips as much as I could, tilting to get him deeper, whining when he pushed my wrist up my back just to hear me cry out in pain.

"All of them?" I asked, breathless, moaning, half-delirious in that golden space between pleasure and pain.

"Tell me what you want, *belleza*. It's yours." Andre nipped at my ribs, thumb stroking my tender wrist, but he didn't let me move. He held me in place, driving his thick cock into me over and over until I was murmuring with the promise of release, trying to focus enough to answer.

"Both of them have to die slow. Violated and in pain."

"I'll tell them," he answered. Gifting me violence and death like others brought home flowers, but this was what I wanted. Needed. Growling behind me, he slammed in hard, and I almost came, that glittering edge of bliss so fucking close I could taste it — but then he held still. "And the others? José? Samuel?"

"Dead. That's all I want." I licked my lips, panting. "Except I want you to fuck me, Andre. Please?"

"I love you, Nicky," he groaned and released my wrist to slip his touch between my thighs. Deftly teasing my clit as he started to move again, fucking me in deep strokes that sent me higher and higher, until I couldn't do anything but say his name. Over, and over, and over, until the tension finally snapped and I screamed in pleasure and pain as he joined me a second later and bit down on my shoulder.

Dizzying waves crashed inside me, the orgasm so destructive to my thoughts that for a solid minute the world faded to white noise and I floated. Unaware of the hard table underneath me, or Andre's heavy body against my back. It was glorious freedom, from all the shit, from every dark spot in our lives.

As he kissed my skin, stroking me with his large hands, I stayed as still as I could. Not wanting to feel him slip from me yet. I wanted the connection, wanted the world to say blurred for just a little while longer.

"I love you, Andre," I whispered, and he hummed against my back as he kissed along my spine. Finally, he slid from me, but he immediately pulled me up from the table to hold me close. We half-stumbled to the couch, lying down in a tangle of limbs, with me half on top of him, but I didn't complain. I had his body against mine, his heart beating under my cheek, and his promise to get the revenge we both craved.

"Once they're gone, I think they'll let us move home," he mumbled, running his fingers up and down my side.

"Think they'll suspect anything?" I asked, snuggling closer to my not-so-good guy, who treated me like something precious, who made me *feel* loved instead of just saying it.

"How could I be involved, *belleza?* I live in Missouri with my wife and work construction. What could I possibly do to a man like Paulo García from a thousand miles away?" There was a cold edge to his tone still, even with the sated rumble after we'd both come hard, and I couldn't help but smile.

"It will be such a tragedy, not to see them brought to justice."

Andre wrapped his arms around me, squeezing me closer as his body shook with a soft chuckle. "Oh, *sí, belleza*, such a tragedy. We will be so disappointed that they didn't live to see life in prison for their crimes."

"Disappointed, yes," I repeated, hiding my grin against his ribs as I felt the rage purr inside. Andre always described his as a black ocean inside him, a bottomless well of anger and violence, but I'd managed to find my own. That had been Paulo and Luis' gift to me. To be capable of being a monster when I needed it. To go cold when I needed it. It was a source of strength, something to push back the fear when I remembered the other side of life that I had only caught a glimpse of, but it was something Andre knew too well. The darkness would never leave him, and I didn't want it to. I liked him dangerous. I liked him tattooed and violent and insanely protective.

It turned me on.

Leaning up I kissed him, and when he grinned at me, wild and free, I felt so damn lucky to have walked into that house and into his arms. It had been scary, and horrible at times, but sometimes we had to walk through Hell to find our salvation, and I was his, and he was mine. Forever.

As he shifted to lean over me, kissing down my throat, his fingers dipping between my thighs to find the soaking wet mix of the two of us, I moaned and whispered his name. When he said my name back, his breath moving over my skin, I loved him all the more. For protecting me, for doing whatever it took to keep us both alive, for refusing to let me go even when it would have been easier, for fucking *fighting* for me — and I knew he always would.

Today, tomorrow, forever.

And he'd do the same if we ever started a family. As his lips found mine again, making me smile into the kiss, I promised myself I'd remember to tell him we could get married. For real. Because I wanted him, I wanted a life with him. I wanted all of it.

I just needed to nap first, and then I could think about the future, because we had one. We had whatever we wanted in life. Andre would kill to ensure that, to pave the way for us to have the life we wanted. A life with his family, a life in Miami, a life together. And maybe, *someday*, a family of our own. It would surely make *Mamá* happy, and I couldn't resist imagining what a little boy would look like with my eyes, and Andre's dark hair and mischievous smile.

We'd be a mess, every one of us, but I would be with Andre, and there would be love, and family, and it would be perfectly imperfect. What else could I want from this life, but that?

THE END

End Notes & Acknowledgements

I had no idea just how much I'd fall in love with Andre and Nicky when I first wrote the novella of this story for a boxset that has since come down, but by the end of the novella I knew I needed to tell their whole story. Not just because they *wouldn't stop talking to me*, but also because of all of the wonderful readers and bloggers out there who took the time to give 'Monster' a shout out in reviews, and to message me when that boxset came down to tell me they needed to know the end. Truthfully, how could I deny you? Or myself?

So, first, I have to thank every one of you that supported Andre and Nicky when they first showed up. You made this book a priority for 2018, and look at that. It came out in January!

Next, obviously, I have to thank my incredible PA, Michelle Brown, who is always there to support me and give me a boost of confidence and tell me to get my ass off social media and fucking WRITE. Yeah, yeah, lady. I'm taking time away from putting together the final draft of this book *just to thank you*, and you can't do anything about it! Niki Roge has to get a shout out too, because she helps Michelle and I do everything we do, without her I would have been all alone at my first major signing, so… it's love. You gotta admit. These two ladies make all the gears turn behind the scenes, and I love them both! Circle of Trust 4 Ever.

Laura Hidalgo, girrrrlllll… you know how hard I love you by now. We were meant to meet, and the way that you pulled this cover out of the ether to somehow create exactly what I dreamed of (only a thousand times better) is exactly why you're one of the best damn cover designers on the planet, and I am just lucky to know you.

Ohhhhh, Myra Danvers and Addison Cain. Did you think I'd leave you two out of this? Hell no. Without your eye for story tweaks, your love of the dark and twisty, and helping me trim down when I get super into a scene, this book would have been a mess. Not sure what I'd do without my chaos demon and my dark soul sister. I love you both!

Measha Stone gets a warm, fuzzy, anxiety filled shout-out for reading through this mess when it was completely unedited, and still telling me the sweetest things to help me crawl out of my fear-filled hole and make deadline. Love you, lady.

I'm sneaking in a thank you for my Dom for always supporting my writing, loving my anti-heroes, and encouraging me to keep going. He's pretty fantastic, and provides some excellent inspiration.

To my ARC team, I hope you're ready for a wild year, because we're just getting started, and I've got lots more dark and devious and sexy stuff to put on your kindles. So, hang in there through all of my crazy, okay?

Finally, all of the lovely individuals on the *Dirty Subs* street team, those in the Dark Haven, and those in the Dark and Dirty Romance Book Club thank you guys for helping me to spread the word, helping new readers find me, and for supporting me!

You lovelies make this adventure worth every minute.

About the Author

Jennifer Bene is a *USA Today* bestselling author of dangerously sexy and deviously dark romance. From BDSM, to Suspense, Dark Romance, and Thrillers—she writes it all. Always delivering a twisty, spine-tingling journey with the promise of a happily-ever-after.

Don't miss a release! Sign up for the newsletter to get new book alerts (and a free welcome book) at: http://jenniferbene.com/newsletter

---

You can find her online throughout social media with username @jbeneauthor and on her website: www.jenniferbene.com

Also by Jennifer Bene

The Thalia Series (Dark Romance)

Security Binds Her *(Thalia Book 1)*

Striking a Balance *(Thalia Book 2)*

Salvaged by Love *(Thalia Book 3)*

Tying the Knot *(Thalia Book 4)*

The Thalia Series: The Complete Collection

Dangerous Games Series (Dark Mafia Romance)

Early Sins *(A Dangerous Games Prequel)*

Lethal Sin *(Dangerous Games Book 1)*

Damaged Goods *(Dangerous Games Book 2)*

Fragile Ties Series (Dark Romance)

Destruction *(Fragile Ties Book 1)*

Inheritance *(Fragile Ties Book 2)*

Daughters of Eltera Series (Dark Fantasy Romance)

Fae *(Daughters of Eltera Book 1)*

Tara *(Daughters of Eltera Book 2)*

Standalone Dark Romance

Taken by the Enemy

Imperfect Monster

Corrupt Desires

The Rite

Deviant Attraction: A Dark and Dirty Collection

Appearances in the Black Light Series (BDSM Romance)

Black Light: Exposed *(Black Light Series Book 2)*

Black Light: Valentine Roulette *(Black Light Series Book 3)*

Black Light: Roulette Redux *(Black Light Series Book 7)*

Standalone BDSM Ménage Romance

The Invitation

Reunited

Made in the USA
San Bernardino, CA
29 December 2019

62484872R00195